EMILY

EMILY

JACK WEYLAND

Deseret Book Company
Salt Lake City, Utah

Library of Congress Cataloging-in-Publication Data

Weyland, Jack, 1940–
    Emily / Jack Weyland.
       p.   cm.
    Summary: After being badly burned and disfigured in an accident, college freshman Emily finds help in the power of Christ and true love in Austin, who has himself been spiritually transformed by a difficult Mormon mission.
    ISBN 1-57345-576-8
    [1. Burns and scalds—Fiction.   2. Mormons—Fiction.   3. Christian life—Fiction.]   I. Title.
    PZ7.W538Em   1999
    [Fic]—dc21   99-35841
                                                    CIP

Printed in the United States of America   54459-6518

10 9 8 7 6 5 4 3

This book is based on a true story. My thanks to the real Emily for being willing to share with me her experience as a burn survivor. I also express my appreciation to the nurses and child-life specialists at the Intermountain Burn Center of the University of Utah Medical Center for their assistance. One cannot spend time with them without gaining a profound appreciation for their dedication, expertise, and compassion.

1

Blonde, blue-eyed, and beautiful in her wedding dress, Emily waited anxiously at the entrance of the Ogden Temple for her true love to show up so they could be married for time and all eternity.

There was just one problem, though. She couldn't remember his name.

Every few minutes a young man would approach the place she was standing. She looked hopefully at each one. Some smiled, some even said hello, but none of them took her by the hand, and all of them entered the temple without her.

"So, what's keeping him?" her older brother, Jeremy, finally asked.

"He'll be here."

"Why don't you call and see if he's left yet?"

Emily had gone her whole life being made fun of by Jeremy, so she didn't want him to know she couldn't remember her fiancé's name. "I don't know his phone number," she said.

"So? Look it up."

"Yes, I could do that if . . ." her voice trailed off.

"You do remember his name, don't you?"

"Well, not actually, but I'm sure it will come to me."

"Oh, man, I can't believe this." Jeremy banged his forehead with his hand. "Look, if you can't remember his name, you're probably not ready to marry him."

"Stop talking down to me, Jeremy."

"Why should I?"

"Because I'm a woman now."

"Yeah, right," he scoffed. "You're no woman. A woman would at least know the name of the man she was about to marry."

"Oh, look, maybe this is him." A boy she recognized from school approached her, smiled, then continued on his way.

"So what are you going to do? Marry the first guy who stops to talk to you?"

"I know who he is. I just can't remember his name, that's all. Look, this could happen to anybody."

"I don't think so."

A car pulled into the parking lot of the temple. "That's Austin," Jeremy said. "We're going to do some baptisms. He's right on time."

Austin walked up the steps of the temple to where they were standing.

"Hey, man, what's happening?" Jeremy said.

Austin nodded vaguely at Jeremy, then approached Emily and, taking her hand, asked, "Are you ready for this?"

"You know I am," she said, kissing him on the cheek. *So this is who I'm going to marry!* she thought.

"Let's go then."

"Hey, wait a minute. What about me?" Jeremy asked. "I'm your best friend."

"I know, but I can't marry you. Sorry," Austin said with a smile, then gazed into Emily's eyes and kissed her on the lips.

Oh, yes! Emily thought. *This is the kiss of the century!*

2

Jeremy broke them up and pulled Emily aside. "You can't marry Austin, okay?"

"Why not?"

"Well, for one thing, you're way too young for him."

"Not anymore."

"What do you mean, not anymore?"

"I'm a year ahead of him in college."

"Since when? How could that be?"

"You and Austin have already served your missions."

Jeremy looked puzzled. "We have? How come I can't remember?"

"Only you can answer that question, Jeremy," she said mysteriously. She then took Austin's hand and, together, they entered the temple.

And then, unfortunately, Emily woke up.

It had been the most wonderful dream she'd ever had. And it had seemed so real, especially when Austin had looked into her eyes and tenderly kissed her. More than anything, she wanted to return to her dream. Not only because it was so romantic but also because she wanted to get some ideas for when she actually did get married. She wanted to see what the reception would be like. She pictured herself standing next to Austin, greeting friends and neighbors.

She wanted to get to the part where the bride and groom share the wedding cake. That had always been her favorite part. She smiled as she thought of shoving the cake into his mouth and smearing it all over his face and of how their friends and family would laugh at their antics.

She wanted to see what it would be like sharing the first dance together with all their friends looking on. She would be elegant in her gown, and he would be handsome in his tux. For that one night they would be royalty, the lovely princess and the handsome prince, together at last.

3

She wanted to see what the cake and the table decorations looked like. She wanted to get every little detail right.

She and Austin had grown up in the same neighborhood in Ogden, Utah. Austin was now nineteen years old and about to go on a mission. Emily was two years younger, and, in the fall, she would begin attending college at Utah State University. She'd known Austin since she was in fifth grade, when he and Jeremy had become best friends. But in all the time Austin had spent at the house with Jeremy, Austin had never paid Emily much attention. He was, of course, polite and usually said hello, and sometimes he asked about school, but the two of them had never done anything together. To Austin, Emily was just his best friend's little sister.

Maybe I really am going to marry Austin, she thought. *I'm glad to know that. I won't tell him though. No use scaring him.*

She lay in bed and tried to return to her dream, but she was too excited to go back to sleep. And then she remembered that Austin had stayed the night and was probably asleep in the TV room in the basement with Jeremy.

If I'm going to marry him, I need to get to know him better before he leaves on his mission. With that, she jumped out of bed. After brushing her teeth and doing what she could with her hair, she got dressed, then tiptoed downstairs to the TV room. It was seven-thirty in the morning, and her parents had already left for the temple. They went every Saturday morning but were usually home by eleven o'clock.

Jeremy was asleep on one couch, Austin on the other, each of them in a sleeping bag. There were some empty soft drink cans and an open pizza box with several uneaten crusts in it lying on the coffee table in front of the couches. Two acoustic guitars also lay on the coffee table.

"Howdy, Cowboy," she said softly to Austin, who was still asleep.

Not that Austin was a cowboy, but he and Jeremy sang country songs together. She had never understood how they could get away with that when neither of them had ever been within five feet of either a cow or a horse.

The whole thing had started as a joke. Acting on a dare from one of their friends, Jeremy and Austin had sung a country song for a school talent show. They were trying to make fun of western music, but apparently nobody noticed, and they became an instant sensation at school.

Jeremy already knew how to play the guitar, and Austin soon learned, at least enough to get by. They even bought a couple of western shirts and some cowboy boots and black Stetson hats to wear while they performed.

For a time they thought they might have a future in country music, but nothing turned out. And so, the previous fall, when Austin went away to USU and Jeremy to BYU, their singing career together was put on the shelf.

But now they were back home for the summer, hanging out while waiting to go on their missions. They'd been asked to sing at the Fourth of July picnic at a city park, and the night before they had been practicing for that.

Austin had always seemed to enjoy spending time at Jeremy's, where things were much more relaxed than at his house. Austin's parents were very formal and proper people, and Emily had always felt sorry for him for having to grow up with a dad who was a successful lawyer and who went by the name H. Lloyd Brunswick. His mother was so conscious of appearances that she wouldn't eat fried chicken with her fingers, even at a ward picnic. Emily noticed things like that.

It was cold in the basement, and Emily grabbed a blanket from a closet.

She wrapped it around her and sat cross-legged on the floor in front of Austin, studying his face. She'd never said anything about it, but she had always thought Austin was

5

really good-looking. Even when he was being one of Jeremy's pesky friends, she couldn't help liking him. Not even her friends knew it, but she was fascinated by the way he laughed and the way he moved his mouth when he talked or sang.

Once, when she was in ninth grade, Austin had squirted her with a hose while she was sunbathing. She pretended to be mad at him, but she was secretly thrilled to have him pay attention to her at all. Sometimes, when Jeremy and Austin would make a mess in the TV room, Emily's mom would make her clean it up, but that was all right. She would just pretend she and Austin were already married and that she was doing what a wife does for her husband and her husband's friends.

She leaned closer to him. *He really does have an interesting face,* she thought. *The face of a poet—a bad poet, one who doesn't make much money selling his poems and who has a certain sadness about him.*

She wasn't sure where the idea about poets had come from until she remembered that her parents had made her watch the opera *La Boehme* one night on public television as a part of family home evening. At the time she thought it was dumb, thinking that if these people would sing less and go out and get a job, they'd all be better off. But something had remained from the experience—the romance of being a starving poet living in a ghetto with friends as bad off as you.

Austin had prominent cheekbones and a long narrow face. It made him look as though he wasn't getting enough to eat. He also had thick, dark brown hair, which he was now keeping cut short in preparation for his mission.

She used to think he was conceited, but now that she was going to marry him, she decided to think of him as being sure of himself.

She was pretty certain Austin's folks considered themselves superior to everyone else. And there were good reasons for them to think that. For one thing, they lived in the biggest house on the nicest street in the ward. Austin's mom wore dresses to Church that made her look as if she were going to a fancy dinner party, and his dad always wore expensive suits and commercially laundered shirts and highly polished shoes. He was on the high council, and she went from one leadership position to another, in Relief Society and Young Women. Their oldest son was at Harvard, studying for his MBA, and their next oldest was in the honors program at BYU. Their biggest embarrassment had been when Austin hadn't been accepted to BYU because his grades weren't good enough. Emily wondered if Austin's mother blamed Jeremy for that. Too much country music.

I'll never be good enough for Austin's mother, Emily thought. *But what do I care? I don't like her very much anyway.*

Austin, my love. She had a hard time even thinking it without laughing. *This isn't easy,* she thought, *making the adjustment from being Jeremy's little sister to Austin's one and only true love.*

She wanted this to be like the prince who walks in on Sleeping Beauty, falls in love with her, and kisses her. Except this time she was taking the prince's part. Even so, she decided it probably wouldn't be a good idea to try to kiss him, especially with Jeremy nearby. She was sure he would tell on her.

Another problem was that Austin's mouth was slightly open. A thin line of saliva had run down his chin and dripped onto the floor. She didn't judge him harshly for that. She herself had awakened before to find drool on her pillow, but, even so, she wished she hadn't seen it happening to Austin. It kind of took some of the magic out of the moment.

Part of the problem—being in love with Austin—was that she'd known him a long time. He hadn't always been cool.

He used to be awkward and pick at his face a lot. But now he'd begun wearing longer shirts that didn't pull up so you could see his underwear when he bent over. And it had been a year or so since he and Jeremy had prided themselves on making gross bodily sounds.

Since coming home from his first year at USU, Austin did seem more mature to her. *If he's made this much progress in one year, just think what he'll be like after he returns from his mission,* she thought.

Scooting closer, she tilted her head sideways, parallel to his, to see what it might be like to wake up in the morning and see him lying next to her. She wanted it to be romantic, but it wasn't. For one thing, she was still put off by the saliva on the floor.

She tried scooting a little closer to see if it made her feel more romantic toward him. She tilted her head and closed her eyes and then opened them slowly. "Good morning," she whispered. She puckered her lips and moved closer as if she were going to kiss him.

"Emily, what are you doing?" Jeremy grumbled.

She turned around. Jeremy was sitting up in his sleeping bag. She wondered how long he'd been awake and what he'd seen.

"Nothing," she said, moving quickly away.

"Don't give me that. You were doing something."

"What was I doing?"

"I'm not sure, but it wasn't . . . normal."

"I was just waiting for Austin to wake up because I've decided to cook you two some breakfast."

"You don't know how to cook breakfast."

"I do so."

"Fine, then, go cook it. When it's done, we'll eat it. Just don't stare at people when they're sleeping. It's creepy. I mean, how would you like it if you woke up and somebody was sitting there watching you sleep. When he wakes up, I'm going to tell him what you were doing."

"Please don't, okay?"

"Well, I might let it go this time. But that breakfast better be good, that's all I can say."

She hurried to the kitchen to cook breakfast. *This will be the first meal I'll cook for my future husband,* she thought. *And he'll be gone for two years so it better be good, something he'll remember while he's away.*

She'd never been much of a cook. There was no need to learn in their family. Her mother was a great cook and prepared most of the food. And, in fact, her mom didn't like people messing things up in what she called, "my kitchen."

Emily rummaged around in the refrigerator, looking for something to fix. She decided she'd make bacon and eggs and pancakes.

She fried the bacon first, so the smell of it would fill the house. She set the cooked bacon aside, then worked on making pancakes. At first she had the frying pan turned on too low, and the batter was too thick, so the pancakes turned out anemic looking, with the insides still runny.

She thinned the mix and turned up the electric frying pan. The first batch would have turned out okay, but she flipped them too soon, so they landed in a wrinkled heap in the pan. She scraped them out and tried again.

By the time she'd figured out how to cook pancakes, she'd run out of batter, and the garbage can was filled with her mistakes. She stirred up some new batter and started over again.

Working patiently, she made fifteen really good pancakes, almost eight for each of them. She didn't want any because she'd gotten filled eating scraps from what she'd thrown away.

At first she was going to cook the eggs sunny-side up,

but she broke two of the yolks, so she decided to make scrambled eggs.

The hot chocolate went okay, except that she spilled half a cup taking it out of the microwave. She threw some paper towels in the microwave, promising herself to clean it up later.

Finally everything was ready. She went downstairs to announce breakfast, but Jeremy and Austin were still sleeping. She had no patience with that. She began pulling the bottom of Jeremy's sleeping bag. "Breakfast is ready."

He held onto the sleeping bag and pulled it up to his chin. "We need to sleep a little longer."

"No, you've slept long enough. Everything is getting cold. I'll be upstairs waiting."

"What's wrong with you, anyway?" Jeremy complained

"You can sleep after you eat breakfast."

"What's going on?" Austin asked sleepily.

"My crazy sister has cooked breakfast for us."

"What for?"

"Who knows why she does anything? Anyway, she wants us to eat now. You okay with that?"

"Yeah, sure. If you think about it, it's nice of her to do that."

"Yeah, I guess. Let's go eat."

Emily was hoping the boys would compliment her on her cooking. Instead, they ate hunched over, their heads down, not even talking.

Finally, Austin asked, "Can I have some more pancakes?"

That was the chance she'd been waiting for. When she returned from the kitchen, she laid her hand softly on his shoulder and leaned close to him, letting her long blonde hair brush past his ear as she forked a couple of her best pancakes onto his plate. "Have all the pancakes you want, Big Boy," she said, in what she hoped was a seductive voice.

Jeremy was staring at her, not quite sure what was going

on. "Get me some more pancakes too while you're at it," he grumped.

She went back into the kitchen, got a couple of pancakes, went around to Jeremy's side of the table, and lobbed them onto his plate. Then she sat down next to Austin.

A short time later Jeremy went to go take a shower. That left Emily and Austin alone.

She took his plate back into the kitchen and dished up the rest of the scrambled eggs, five strips of bacon, and the last of the pancakes, then returned to the dining room and set the plate in front of him. "Here, why don't you finish this up?"

"I'm pretty full already."

"You're a growing body," she said, then quickly corrected herself. " . . . A growing boy . . . that's what I meant. A man, really, if you think about it, a young man about to serve a mission. Who knows how they'll feed you in the mission field? They might not have bacon where you're going, so eat all you want. And not every country has pancakes. Some countries don't. Ecuador I think . . . no pancakes. I heard that once." She felt like a complete airhead, rambling on like that, but she couldn't seem to stop.

"Is something wrong?" Austin asked.

"No, nothing, why do you ask?"

"You have kind of a wild-eyed look about you. And the way you're talking, it's sort of like you're about to go over the edge."

Her voice became high and strained. "The edge? Really? I haven't noticed." She wiped at the perspiration that was gathering on her forehead. It was time to change the subject.

"Where do you think you'll serve your mission?"

"Illinois."

"Really? How can you be sure?"

"I've already received my call."

"Right, I knew that," she said, feeling stupid. "So you're pretty sure, then? I mean, they could change their mind."

"They don't change their mind once you receive your call."

"No, of course not. When are you going?"

"Two weeks. And then two weeks later, Jeremy leaves."

"Two weeks? That doesn't give us much time then, does it?"

He looked at her with a puzzled expression.

She winced. "Excuse me. What I meant was it doesn't give you much time to get ready. That's what I meant."

"It gives me two weeks."

"Yes, that sounds about right."

She needed an excuse to sit with him, so she decided to have some breakfast, but when she went into the kitchen, all the good food was gone. Watching to make sure Austin couldn't see her, she fished through the garbage can under the sink, looking for reject pancakes that weren't too bad. When she found one, she put it on a plate then took it in the dining room and poured syrup on it.

"Where'd you get *that* one?" he asked.

"Not every pancake can be a masterpiece," she said.

He glanced at the misshapen, burnt pancake. "How many you got in there like that?"

"Not many."

"I can't believe you went to so much work for us. That was really nice."

She melted under his smile. "Thanks. That really means a lot to me."

She didn't want him to leave her and go down and watch TV. She decided to get him to talk about himself. "What do you hope will happen on your mission?"

"I don't know. I'd like to do as well as my brothers did."

"In what way?"

"Well, Cameron led the mission in baptisms four months

in a row, and then he was called to be mission assistant. And Stephen was a zone leader for almost a year. Before that, he led the mission in baptisms for three months."

"They did really good then. Are you hoping to match that?"

"Well, yeah, I'd like to."

"I'm sure you will."

"When I come back from my mission, you'll have caught up with me in school."

"I know."

"What are you going to study?"

She was surprised he wanted to know. It made her like him even more. "You'll probably think this is dumb, but someday I want to be a news anchor for one of the major networks."

"Really? What made you decide that?"

She started to blush. "I'm not sure if I should tell you or not. I've never told anyone."

"You can tell me."

"Promise you won't tell Jeremy?"

"I won't. I promise."

"When I was growing up, people made fun of me."

"How come?"

"I just didn't fit in. It was partly my looks."

"You've always looked okay to me."

"I have a high forehead," she said. "It makes me look smart."

"You are smart."

"I know. I've always been smart. It wasn't just that, though. In seventh and eighth grade I had a lower voice than most of the boys in my class. And I had the habit of asking really tough questions. One time in eighth grade this boy gave a talk about his science project. I kept asking questions he couldn't answer. Finally, he started to cry. I got him to admit that his dad had done the whole project and that he didn't know anything about it. The only people who liked me in school were the science and math teachers." Her voice trailed off. "I spent a lot of time feeling like a complete misfit."

"I've always liked you."

It made her heart race to hear him say that. "I know, but that's just because I was Jeremy's little sister."

"So what made you think about becoming a news reporter?"

"Last year, one of my teachers told me he thought I'd be a good news anchor. So I started watching the news more. What I really liked was in-depth interviews with world leaders. I kept thinking, I could do that. So I'm going to give it a shot."

"Good for you. Does it ever worry you there's a lot of competition for something like that?"

"I'm not too bad-looking, and I'm smart, and I can talk to people." As soon as she said it, she turned red. "I'm sorry. I shouldn't have said that. You must think I'm really conceited. I've never said that to anyone, but you asked."

"What you said about yourself is true. You are good-looking, you are smart, and you can talk to people."

She blushed again. "Don't tell Jeremy though, okay? He'll make fun of me."

"I won't tell him if you promise not to tell anyone about me wanting to be a mission assistant on my mission."

"That's not a bad thing."

"No, but still, it's not something you're supposed to be wishing for. It's just that with my brothers having done so well, it's almost expected I'll follow in their footsteps. Not that my folks would ever say anything like that. But the way I look at it, somebody's got to be a leader on my mission, so why not me?"

"Sure, you'd be really good."

14

There was a lull in the conversation. They could hear the shower going.

"Jeremy takes long showers. You'll be lucky if there's any hot water left."

"I can always go home."

"No, don't do that," she said much too quickly. She started to blush again. "Let's talk some more."

"What about?"

"I don't know. Whatever you want to talk about."

"I just can't believe I'm talking to you like this," Austin said.

"You mean like we're equals?" she asked.

"Yeah, I guess that's it."

"I know what you mean. I've always thought of you as just one of Jeremy's friends."

"How do you look at me now?"

"Different than I used to. I even had a dream about you last night."

"No kidding? What did you dream?"

"Oh, you know, just the usual," she said, aware she was blushing again.

"You want to tell me about it?" he asked, grinning.

"No, not really. It's a little embarrassing."

"You could tell me."

"Probably so, but I'd rather not."

"Sure, I understand," he said. Then they were silent for a few moments.

Austin sighed. "Can I tell you something?"

"Sure."

"I'm not sure I even want to go on a mission."

"Why not?"

"I'm not sure if I'm doing it because that's what I really want to do, or if it's just to please my mom and dad, or just because it's what my brothers did. Sometimes I feel like my whole life has been planned out without anyone asking me what I want to do. You know what? I didn't really earn my Eagle rank in Scouting. My mom did most of it. That's not right, is it? Eagle Scout, returned missionary, college graduate, then law school, marriage, some kids, and then maybe they'll want me to run for office, maybe even governor. I'm sure it's all down on paper somewhere in my mom or dad's files." He paused. "That's why I liked singing cowboy songs with Jeremy, because it wasn't in 'The Plan.' My mom hated me doing it."

"Did she ever tell you that?"

"No, in our family we don't say things directly. We beat around the bush. All she said was that she thought I could make better use of my time."

He took a deep breath then released it as he rested his head on the back of the chair and stared at the ceiling. "I'm not sure what worries me the most, that I'll end up being a mission assistant on my mission, or that I won't. Either way, I'll end up feeling like a loser."

"Does Jeremy know about any of this?"

"No. That's crazy, isn't it? He's my best friend, but you're the only one I've ever told."

She smiled. "I'm glad you did."

"Why?"

"Because I want to be more to you than just Jeremy's sister. I want to be your friend."

"You are then. We'll make it official. Are you going to write to me while I'm gone?"

"I will if you'll write back."

"I will. I promise." He glanced at her. "I've watched you grow up."

She didn't know what he was driving at. "Yeah, so?"

"Well, I've noticed the changes taking place in you as you've gotten older."

She started to blush.

16

"This was a dumb thing to say, wasn't it?" he asked with a nervous smile. "I shouldn't have said that. Sorry."

"No, it's okay. You know what? I'm glad you've noticed."

They were both saved more embarrassment by the bathroom door opening. "I'm done," Jeremy called out before heading to his room.

"I guess I'll take a shower too," Austin said.

She stood up and reached for his plate. "Sure. Go ahead. I'll finish cleaning up."

"I can help out after I'm done with my shower."

"Okay, if there's anything left to do."

She worked fast because she didn't want Austin to come into the kitchen after his shower and find out what a mess she'd made. The first thing was to hide the evidence of her botched attempts at making pancakes, so she quickly hauled the kitchen trash to the big can in the garage. Then she filled the dishwasher and turned it on.

It was not only Austin she needed to clean up for. She had to hide what she'd done from her mother.

After putting things back in the refrigerator and wiping down the counter, Emily jumped into the car and drove to the store where she bought eggs, bacon, and pancake mix with her own money. If she hadn't, her mom would have asked, "Where did all the bacon and eggs go?" And then Emily would have to say she'd cooked breakfast for Austin and Jeremy. Then her mom would say, "You cooked a pound of bacon and a dozen eggs for three people? That was supposed to last a week."

The house had to be returned to its original state, or her mom would keep asking questions until Emily admitted that she'd had a few failures in the process of cooking. And then her mom would tell her that they weren't rich enough to waste food and lecture her that she should have cooked hot cereal instead because it was a lot cheaper. As far as her mother was concerned, hot cereal was the answer to every breakfast need.

Her mother was the boss of the house and of the family. Her dad's role was to stand next to his wife and nod his head. Because he seemed weak, Emily didn't have a lot of respect for her father. At times he seemed invisible. He went to work, he came home, he did odd jobs around the house. Emily never went to him for permission to do something, and even if she had, he would have told her to ask her mother. She never asked his advice either.

Her mother was the general. Everyone else in the family, including her dad, was a private.

For these reasons, over the years Emily had built up a lot of resentment against her mother. At times, lately, they had hardly been able to talk to each other. In one of their little arguments, her mother had said, "I know why this is happening, Emily."

"Why?"

"Because there are two women in the house now. This is nature's way of saying it's time for you to go to college."

At the time Emily didn't understand fully what her mother was saying, but now she was beginning to.

Emily couldn't imagine admitting to her mother that she'd made breakfast because she'd had a dream that she was going to marry Austin someday. She wasn't sure if her mother would make fun of her or try to talk her out of the idea. Either way, it would be more than Emily could stand.

Austin and I had a nice talk, and he told me things he's never told anyone else. And I told him about my hopes and dreams for the future.

She smiled. It was a good start.

The two weeks before Austin left on his mission passed quickly. Emily tagged along when Austin and Jeremy sang for the Fourth of July entertainment in the park. After the

18

boys finished performing, some girls they'd known in high school came up and made a big fuss over them. All Emily could do was stand in the background and wait for everyone to leave. But two of the girls stuck around. After a time, Austin and Jeremy and the two girls took Emily home and then the two couples went to one of the girls' houses.

Emily went to Austin's farewell too. But, once again, Austin's older friends and classmates monopolized his time. After the sacrament meeting everyone was invited over to Austin's big, fancy house for lunch. Again, Emily tagged along but ended up in the back of the crowd.

The girls fussing over Austin were all older than she was. Some of them had been away to college too. She couldn't compete with them. They were equals with Austin, and she was just Jeremy's little sister. She resented that fact, but there didn't seem to be much she could do about it.

Most of the girls there hugged Austin at least once, some, every time they saw him. But Emily couldn't even get close to him. There was always a crowd of friends around him, laughing about their experiences in high school or at college, and talking about how this person was doing on his mission and who'd gotten engaged.

When it became evident that Austin wasn't going to pay any attention to her, Emily decided to take action. She pushed through the crowd around Austin and said brightly, "Well, Austin, I need to go now. How about a good-bye hug?"

When Austin went to hug her, she melted into his arms and stayed there for as long as she could, which was until she heard one of the older girls say, "Oh, isn't that sweet? Even Jeremy's little sister is going to miss you, Austin. She must have had a crush on you all these years. I bet you never knew that, did you?"

Hearing that made Emily mad, so she took Austin's face

in her hands and kissed him on the lips. He seemed startled
and backed away.

"What's going on here?" one of the girls asked Jeremy.

"I have no idea."

Emily left and walked home. She knew Jeremy would
tell their parents that she'd kissed Austin. But she didn't care.

She wasn't Mommy's little girl anymore.

2

I am so good! Emily thought as she watched a video clip of herself presenting the evening news the Utah State University campus TV station.

Her freshman year of college was officially over. She'd finished her last exam on Friday but decided to stay over until Monday, spending most of Saturday editing a demo-tape of the best of her news broadcasts.

Her plan was to make copies of the demo-tape and send them to TV stations across the country. If a job offer turned up right away, she'd quit college and go to work full-time. She was hoping to work in a town like Denver or Minneapolis, which would put her in position for a national network job within a few years.

It was a strange sensation looking at herself on the monitor. It was almost as if she were watching someone else—someone older, more confident, knowledgeable, and capable than herself. She attributed what she had become on camera to her teacher, David Alexander.

David Alexander had come to USU for one year as a visiting professor. Two years earlier, while still in his mid-twenties, he became a media star during the twenty-eight-day standoff at the U.S. embassy in Syria, where he and twenty-six other Americans had been confined to the embassy by armed militants. During that time, David Alexander reported the ongoing crisis in a series of feeds that got on the major network newscasts.

At the end of the standoff, the flamboyant David Alexander, flak jacket and all, walked out of the embassy, a media personality, known to millions. From there he went to work in Washington, D.C., where he covered politics with a cynical flair that endeared him to the American people.

The campus TV station was just getting started; fall semester had been the first time the newscasting class was offered. At the first meeting of the class, ten people showed up in the makeshift broadcast studio.

They had waited about ten minutes when David Alexander finally arrived, angry at not being able to find a parking place. "I shouldn't have to park three blocks away," he grumbled.

Emily and the other members of the class had all heard of him, and they were ready to be impressed by the famous news crusader. He lived up to his billing; his rumpled hair and clothes made it look as though he had been up all night, working on an important story.

In fact, wearing khaki pants, a wrinkled denim shirt, and a loosely knotted tie, David Alexander didn't look like any university professor Emily had ever known. He didn't seem very friendly, either. He fixed the waiting students with a steely gaze that seemed to say, *You're beneath contempt and lucky to have me here.*

Seeing him for the first time, Emily thought, *He must be the most conceited person in America. Does he really believe America is hanging on his every word? I'm glad he had to walk three blocks.*

But even so, she felt herself being pulled in by the power of his personality and his rugged good looks.

On the morning of the first class, while still ranting about the parking situation, he spilled coffee on his shirt, which caused him to unleash a string of swear words.

One of the class members, a young woman, got up to leave.

"Where are you going?" David Alexander challenged.

"I'm in the wrong class," she said.

"What class do you want?"

"Any class but this one," the girl said with an air of self-righteousness.

David Alexander watched her go then shook his head in disgust. "Utah," he muttered. "Why did I ever agree to come here? I must have been out of my mind."

He dunked half a donut in his coffee while he gave an introduction to the class. By the time he remembered to retrieve it, it had broken off and fallen into his coffee. He swore again. Another student, this time a young man, left the class.

He fished the fragments of donut out of his cup with a spoon and then took a sip of coffee. "If you all want to drop the class, be my guest. Do what's best for you. But before you do that, give me a few minutes of your time."

He set his coffee cup down on the table and glared at them. "I don't know if you have any interest in history, but right now you're looking at someone who knows what it's like to see history unfold. I was the one who covered the standoff in Syria. How many have seen me on TV?"

Most of the people in the room raised their hands.

"I've done one-on-one interviews with the President and most of the leaders in Congress. I've talked to heads of state, movie stars, entertainers, and serial killers. The news is my life. I can't promise you this will be like your other classes, but I can promise you I'll do my best. I've never done this before, and I'm sure I'll never do it again. But if you'll let me, I'll give you the benefit of my experience."

He's good at what he does, Emily thought. She could see

how he used his husky voice to good advantage. His skill at making eye contact made each of them feel as though he was talking just to them, and that he was sharing something with them that he'd never told anyone before.

The next time the class met, their numbers had dwindled to six students.

"I see we've lost a few more," he said. "Anyone else want to drop out?" he asked.

No one moved.

"Well, then. Let's get to work."

He had each class member read from a newspaper article, as if they were a newscaster. He had Emily go first.

She thought she was doing a good job until he called out, "Stop! Do you know anything about what's happening in the world today? When's the last time you read the *New York Times* or the *Washington Post?*"

She gave him an embarrassed smile. "Never."

"You think people want airheads reporting the news?"

"Well, no . . ."

In his animated state, he slammed his coffee on a desk, cracking the mug, which started to leak. He ignored the mess. "If you want to be a talking head and just read copy other people write, that's one thing. Any stooge can do that. But in a news *reporter,* the public wants someone with intelligence who can make judgments and give perspective. You read like you were announcing an ice cream social. Are you sure you want to take this class? There's still time to drop and take something you're better suited for." He gave a dramatic pause. " . . . like social dance, for instance."

That infuriated her. "I'm in this class to learn. Teach me what I need to know and I'll get better," she spat back at him.

"You're sure you'll get better? I'm not. Right now about all you're good for is to make coffee."

"I don't know how to make coffee," she shot back.

He threw up his hands. "Why me?" he muttered, then stormed to the back of the room to cool down.

Who do you think you are to talk to me like that? Don't tell me what I can or can't do. That's up to me to decide. I'll show you.

Because David said she ought to, Emily began reading the *New York Times.* The first time she picked it up, she was amazed at how big the paper was. *Do people really read all of this?* she wondered. But because she was afraid of disappointing him, she forced herself to spend four hours, reading the whole thing.

She also watched every news show she could find on TV to see what she could pick up from the best in the business.

At the time they started the class, the campus TV station wasn't even on the air, but by midterm, they'd received the necessary FCC authorization to begin broadcasting.

When she enrolled in the class, Emily's dream was of becoming a news anchor, but under the influence of David Alexander, she changed her focus. What she really wanted to be was an investigative reporter—out in the trenches, digging out the essence of a story and then reporting it on the air.

But there was little opportunity to do that in Logan for the campus TV station. All she could do was learn how to write news stories and then read them on the one broadcast the station did each day. Fortunately, though they were all older than Emily, none of the other five remaining students in the class had any interest in being on the air. That meant Emily was the one assigned to give the evening news every day at five-thirty.

On her first day she showed up at two o'clock to get ready for the newscast. She was wearing a dress she usually wore to church.

David took one look at her and ordered, "Go home and change."

"What for?"

"You think people want to get their news from a prom queen?"

"I'm not a prom queen," she shot back at him.

"Then don't dress like one." He walked to the coffee machine to pour himself a cup of coffee.

She followed him. "I never know what you want."

"No, apparently you don't. Excuse me, I need a cigarette." He picked up his new coffee mug and turned to walk out of the studio.

She had had it with him. "Don't you walk away from me! If you have something to say, then say it!"

He stopped in his tracks, turned around, and glared at her. "What?"

"I said, if you've got something to say, then say it."

His thick eyebrows raised and he smiled. "My gosh, there's a real person in there, after all. Okay, you want to talk? Let's go outside and talk. I really do need a cigarette."

She stood next to him under the eaves during a cold, steady rain that was threatening to turn to snow.

He offered her a cigarette.

"No thanks."

He lit up. "You're right. It's a disgusting habit. Go ahead and say it. I know you're thinking it."

"It's a disgusting habit."

He took a deep drag on the cigarette and then slowly let it out. "You sound like my mother."

"You have a mother?"

"I do. She lives with me just outside Washington."

"Just the two of you?"

"Just the two of us. And a cat. She has the cat, that is. I don't like cats."

It was the first bit of personal information he had volunteered. Standing there watching him smoke his cigarette, she studied the face America had grown to trust.

"I can't believe I'm standing here talking to David Alexander," she said. She immediately regretted saying it because it made her sound awestruck, which in many ways was true, but not what she wanted to convey. She wanted him to treat her as his equal.

He shrugged his shoulders. "It's like everything else. You prepare in advance. You work up to it a little at a time. And then when your big chance comes, you just go in there and do the best you can."

"That's what I want to do someday."

He seemed surprised. "No kidding? I thought you were taking this just to get an easy elective."

"Not at all. I want to take over your job someday."

"Well, at least you've given me fair warning," he said with a chuckle as he let his cigarette drop to the ground. He put it out by grinding it into the pavement. "Sorry for coming down so hard on you. From now on, I'll try to watch that."

"It's okay as long as you're honest with me. I just want to get better."

"So . . . we've got an agreement then?" he asked. "Honesty above all?"

"Sounds good to me."

"Okay, let's get to work."

She went back to her apartment and went through the things in her closet, trying to find something David might approve of. Concluding she didn't have anything really appropriate, she settled on a long-sleeved, white, turtleneck sweater and a pair of black pants, then came back and practiced her delivery.

At six o'clock, when she finished the newscast, David Alexander said, "That wasn't too bad . . . for the first time, that is."

She knew he was trying his best to be kind, but she no longer needed that from him. "Let's go have a cigarette," she said, mimicking him.

That was the first time she'd ever seen him be delighted by anything.

Outside, they found it was now snowing. The one good thing was that the wind wasn't blowing, so they were able to stand under the eaves and stay dry.

With a skeptical look, David offered her a smoke, then grinned when she refused it.

"I didn't think so," he said, lighting up his own.

After a moment, he said, "Viewers expect us to cut through the rhetoric and tell them what's really happening. That's why they watch. Because they trust us to tell them the truth."

"How did I come across today?" she asked.

"Like a nice girl reading someone else's thoughts. You don't convey any conviction or mental toughness."

"How do I do that?"

"By questioning everything. You can't just accept what people tell you. You have to be ruthless enough to ask the really hard questions."

She thought about his answer. "I'll work on it."

"That's my girl."

"I'm not your girl."

"I know that."

"Then don't say it. Oh, and also, don't expect me to learn to make coffee for you, either."

He started laughing. "Who are you? And what did you do with the nice girl who used to work here?"

"If you want toughness, then that's what you'll get. You don't scare me anymore."

"Really?"

"Really. And while we're at it, I can find things you could work on too, you know. Like the way you say your name, for instance."

"How do I say my name?"

She mimicked his dramatic delivery. "This is David . . . Alexander."

She returned to her voice. "I know that's how you start your news broadcast, but you don't need to do that all the time, okay?" She mimicked him again. "This is . . . David . . . Alexander . . . I'd like a large supreme with anchovies. And that's the end of the story."

"You are *bad!*" he roared with delight.

"Also, is it okay if I point out when you're being rude? Or would it be like telling Moses he has manna stains on his robe?"

David must have felt he'd been human enough for one day because he fell back to his usual self. "You work hard, and you can say anything you want to me."

It was only a three-credit course, but Emily worked harder on it than any other class. She started coming in early in the morning to practice giving the news.

She and David developed a good working relationship. He became a little more agreeable, while she became mentally tougher. She would not admit it to anyone, but she also began to think about him all the time. In the morning she wondered if he would approve of the way she was dressed. Through him she became more aware of her voice. When she was around him, he pointed out every time her voice reverted to that of a bewildered teenager who was out of her league. "You can have mental toughness, but if you sound like a breathy teen on camera, everyone will turn you off."

And then there was eye contact. "Look at me when we're talking," he said over and over.

She looked at him but made the mistake of smiling.

"None of that. You're tough as nails, remember."

"Tough as nails," she said, trying to look as steely-eyed as he.

They ended up looking into each other's eyes. It was more intimate than either one intended.

He turned away first. She should have recognized that as a bad sign.

There was a spillover between what she was learning from David Alexander and the rest of her life as a student. And it wasn't always good.

As evidenced by this phone conversation: "This is Ben Christianson. I talked to you after Sunday School class."

"Oh, yes. You're the one who thinks the Book of Mormon teaches us to be against any legislation favoring gun control."

He cleared his throat. "Yes, that's right."

"I view that as an untenable position, Ben, but why did you call?"

"I was wondering if you'd care to go to the winter formal dance with me next week."

"Didn't you just break up with Colleen Turner?"

"Yes."

"You were nearly engaged to her, weren't you?" she asked. She realized she was using her newscaster's voice.

"Yes."

"And you broke up with her two days ago. Is that right?"

"Yes."

"Didn't take you long to bounce back, did it, Ben?"

There was a long pause.

Emily continued. "The way she tells it, you broke up with her because you discovered she's not a good speller. Is that right? This was after you led her to believe you were going to give her a ring for Christmas. And you broke up with her because she made too many spelling mistakes in a love note she sent you for your birthday? Am I close on this, Ben?"

He hung up.

After that, word got around, and nobody asked her out. Strangely enough, she didn't care. The boys in her classes and in her student ward seemed immature to her, especially compared to David Alexander.

Emily's brother, Jeremy, was serving a mission in California while Austin was on his mission in Illinois. Every two weeks she sent them each a letter. Actually, she often sent them identical letters.

Jeremy wrote back to her at most once a month. He seemed to be doing well, having success in finding people to teach and baptize. Austin's early letters indicated that progress was slow, but that he was sure that things were about to break open.

Over Thanksgiving break, she baked cookies and sent them to both of her missionaries.

As time went by, any special feeling she once had for Austin faded. She began to think of him more as a cousin than a potential boyfriend.

She tried to tell Jeremy and Austin about David Alexander, but she always tore up what she'd written about him because when she read it to herself, it sounded almost as if she were falling in love. And she knew that wasn't true. It was just that at the moment, David Alexander was the most important person in her life.

That's all.

She knew that if she admitted to having feelings for him then she would have to deal with the fact that he wasn't a member of the Church. And that was something she didn't want to face.

In January, Emily was hired on a part-time basis to continue working at the station. She took a reduced class load so she'd have more time to devote to learning from David Alexander.

In February, he suggested she'd look better on-camera if she had her hair cut. He even went with her to the hair stylist to make sure it was done right. He also went shopping with her and helped her pick out a black pantsuit, which he said made her look more professional. Maybe that was true, but when she wore it to classes, she noticed boys paid a lot more attention to her, so she wasn't totally convinced it was because she looked more professional.

In March, a benefactor gave the college some money to buy a remote unit, so the station could do on-the-scene coverage of breaking news stories. That was an exciting thing for Emily. There weren't that many sensational news developments in Logan, but there were some automobile crashes, a fire at an apartment complex, and even a robbery and a brief hostage situation at a fast-food place. David knew a lot about how to play to the camera and tell a story, and he coached her on how to do reports from the field.

"Look," he said to her. "Even though you've just arrived on the scene, you have to give the impression you've been there from the beginning and that you're on top of the story."

"How do I do that?"

"A lot of it is in the tone of your voice. You can't seem overwhelmed by the situation or too excited. I'll give you some tapes of my feeds from Syria to look at."

The long Logan winter finally came to an end, and spring broke through.

In May, on a Monday, just before the end of school, David approached Emily. "What would you say if I asked you to have dinner with me on Friday night?"

"Is this a hypothetical question?"

"For now it is."

"If you were to ask me, I'd question your motives. If this were an attempt to come on to me, I would view that as unethical and a clear violation of the teacher-student relationship. That would make an interesting on-air exposé, don't you think?"

32

He winced. "It would not be for that reason."

"What would the reason be then?"

"I'll be leaving soon. I thought it might be nice for us to get together and talk."

"I see. Would this be business or pleasure?"

"Most likely, a little of both."

"And where would we be eating?"

"Wherever you want."

"So, what are we talking here, a couple of hours?"

"Yes, I suppose so. Why are you giving me such a hard time?"

"I was once told not to trust anyone."

He smiled and shook his head. "I've created a monster. You'll go with me then?"

"Yes, under the conditions we've discussed."

"Will you wear the black pantsuit?"

"What is this, *Fantasy Island?*" she teased.

It was the first time she'd seen him blush.

For the rest of the week, she could think of little else besides their Friday date. She told herself that it wasn't because she was in love with David—that she was only flattered by his attention. But she was also becoming aware that he liked her much more than he cared to admit.

They ate Chinese food at a restaurant in Logan. Emily had never eaten there before, but the hostess and their waiter treated David like an old friend. He told Emily he ate there two or three times a week.

They got to the restaurant before the dinner crowd arrived, so they had the place pretty much to themselves. After glancing at the menu, Emily let David order for her.

Remembering how arrogant he had been when they first met, it surprised Emily to find David looking at her as though he were some love-struck boy. A few months before, she probably would have lowered her gaze, but not after being tutored by him for a year.

While waiting for their food, she asked, "Why are you looking at me?"

"I was just examining my creation," David responded. "Before I met you, you were Emily–1. But now you're Emily–2. I've made you what you are today. So, I was just looking at my handiwork. I did a pretty good job."

"You may not think so in a minute."

"Why's that?"

"Because I have some questions I'd like to ask, if that's all right."

"And if it isn't?"

"Then I guess we'll just sit here and stare at each other."

"All right, go ahead."

"Are you married?" she asked.

"No, not now. I was once, but it didn't work out. Laura and I got married when we were still in college. When I graduated and took the assignment in Syria, she continued on at school. I was gone a year. By the time I got back, she'd met someone else and wanted a divorce. So we did it as painlessly as possible."

"Any children?"

"No."

She nodded. "All right. One other question. Why did you leave Washington, D.C., to come here?"

He winced. "I came here for the skiing."

"How many times have you gone skiing since you've been here?"

"Are you kidding? All the time. Skiing is my life."

"I can verify that, you know."

After looking around to make sure nobody could hear, he leaned forward and rested his elbows on the table. "If I tell you, will you promise to keep it confidential?"

"Yes, of course."

He gave a troubled sigh. "I got an anonymous phone call one night from someone, tipping me off that a congressman

34

was involved in the acquisition of some key real estate near a downtown redevelopment district in his home state."

"What was wrong with that?" Emily asked.

"It was an insider's deal. The politician used his prior knowledge to take unfair advantage of the situation, and he made a lot of money on the sale of the property he bought."

"What did that have to do with you?"

"Well, when I found out about it, I didn't have any hard evidence that he had been tipped off—only the anonymous phone call. Then I did something a newscaster should never do."

"What?" Emily asked, wide-eyed.

"I hated this guy. He had embarrassed me a couple of times by snubbing me when I tried to contact him. I decided to get even."

"How?"

David didn't answer for a moment. When he did, he spoke softly. "I planted some evidence, so I could use the story."

Emily was amazed. "That could have got you sent to jail."

"It would have, except the night before the story was to air, the network found out I had set the guy up. My boss was furious. At first he fired me, but I begged for another chance. He told me he'd consider hiring me back if I'd take a year off to think about what a blunder I'd nearly made. He'd gone to school here, so he wrangled the college into letting me get the campus station up and running. That's why I turned up here."

Emily didn't respond, but just sat, looking at him.

"What?" he said.

"What you did was wrong," Emily said.

"I know," he said. Then after a moment, he added, "It's not something you would have done, is it?"

"No."

"Why not?"

She shrugged her shoulders. "It's the way I was brought up."

"You're a Mormon, aren't you?"

"Yes."

"Well, you're a good representative for your church."

Emily thought about that. She hesitated, then asked, "Would you like to know more about what I believe?" She immediately regretted doing so. What interest would a man like David Alexander have in her beliefs?

He shook his head. "No. Thanks for asking, though. I'm not a very good candidate for religion."

Their waiter brought them each a bowl of hot and sour soup. "This will knock your socks off," David said.

She took a taste. "Wow!"

He laughed. "Exactly. It clears your sinuses. It also guards against colds and flu. And not only that, it will guarantee you a plentiful posterity."

She laughed. "Sounds good, except I can wait on the last one."

"You and me both, kid."

They spent the rest of the meal in light conversation.

After they had finished eating, the waiter brought the check and a couple of fortune cookies. David gave Emily first choice, and then they cracked them open.

"How do they know these things?" David asked, handing his fortune to Emily to read. It said: "You will receive good news."

She read hers but didn't offer to share it with David.

"What does yours say?" he asked.

"Nothing. Just something stupid," she said, wrinkling up the little slip.

David reached across the table and took Emily's closed fist in his hand. Slowly, he pried her fingers open and took the fortune from her. It read: "Look for a new romantic interest in your life."

After reading it, David looked into Emily's eyes. He didn't say anything for a moment, but when she looked away, he said, "I don't suppose there's any place we can go now, is there?"

"You mean, like to your apartment?"

"Something like that."

"Probably not."

"Not that I have anything in mind," he said.

"No, I'm sure you don't."

"So, basically, this is it?"

"We could go to a movie if you want."

"I don't like to go out in public. Too many people recognize me."

"Poor baby," she teased. "Admit it, David, you love the recognition, don't you?"

"Not always."

"I'm not sure I believe that." She looked at the clock on the wall. "Your two hours are up."

He shook his head. "I have something I want to say."

"Okay, what is it?"

He leaned forward and spoke confidentially. "What if I were to admit there's a possibility that . . . well . . . that I can't get you out of my mind?"

Be careful, she thought, *this has no future. Play the skeptic. It's what he's taught you.*

She raised her eyebrows the way he'd coached her. "Then I'd ask if you've ever considered how old you are compared to me?"

He cleared his throat. "I'm twenty-seven . . . well, actually, I'll be twenty-eight next month."

"I'm eighteen. That's ten years. That's a big difference, don't you agree? When you were a senior in high school, I was in the second grade. How come you didn't invite me to your prom, David?"

"All right, there's an age difference, but you act much older than your age."

"That's because you've coached me."

He took her hand. "Do you have anyone in your life right now?"

"Not right now. I've scared them all away." She told him how merciless she'd been when Ben asked her out earlier in the year.

"So there's nobody?"

She thought about Austin. "Well, at one time I thought I might end up marrying my brother's best friend, but I've pretty much given up on that now."

"How come?"

"I won't even see him for another year. And, also, right now I'm hoping for a career in broadcasting, at least until I'm twenty-five or thirty. Then I might get married and settle down."

"Maybe I'll still be around then," he said.

"Maybe so, but, to be honest, it wouldn't do you any good."

"Why not?"

"When I get married, it's going to be in a Mormon temple to someone who believes the way I do."

He gave her one of the crooked smiles she had found so alluring and cleared his throat. "Well, it looks like I've pretty much made a fool of myself here, doesn't it?"

I should tell him how much he's meant to me. I should tell him I've spent nearly every waking hour wondering what he'd think about what I wore or how I did my hair or how I looked and sounded on camera. I should tell him I started reading the New York Times *and* The Wall Street Journal *just so I can talk to him intelligently. I should tell him I know his every gesture, the way he raises his eyebrows when I've done something he approves of, how he softens his penetrating gaze sometimes when we're together. I should tell him I've often wondered if this is what it's like being in love.*

But she said none of those things. And at her door, she said, "Thanks for all you've done for me."

He tossed it off. "I didn't do much. Your hard work made it happen."

In a gesture of professional equality, he shook her hand. "The next time you have hot and sour soup at a Chinese restaurant, I hope you'll think about me."

"I promise," she said, quickly turning to go into her apartment. The last thing she wanted to do was to cry in front of David Alexander.

I need to get back to reality, Emily thought. Instead of making copies of her demo-tape, she had just been sitting, daydreaming. She planned to send copies to TV stations in Denver, Minneapolis, Seattle, Boise, and Salt Lake City and needed to get them in the mail.

At the beginning of the school year, she'd had a hard time watching herself on video, but David had insisted she critique herself every day by studying the videotape of her newscast.

He had been right. Looking at herself had at first been painful, but doing so had helped her get rid of nervous gestures and improve her on-camera poise. She had in fact become conscious of everything she did, as though a camera were recording her every action—even the simplest of tasks, such as putting on her makeup, walking to class, stopping to talk to a friend, or even taking notes in class. The camera in her mind was always just ten feet away, dedicated to recording every movement she made.

Sometime in March, she had realized that she liked what she was seeing when she looked at herself, either on videotape or through the eyes of the camera in her mind.

It wasn't that she was completely satisfied with everything.

She could think of plenty of things she would have liked to change about herself. For one thing, she was five-foot-six, but would have preferred to be a couple of inches taller. Girls her height had to work harder to be noticed by guys. Sometimes she also wished her hair weren't blonde. Mainly because she believed that brunettes were given more respect than blondes.

But in spite of that, when she looked at herself on camera, she was mostly pleased with what she saw. It was not something she ever talked about, but she did look good. Not so much beautiful as radiating a sense of self-confidence, competence, and what David called *integrity*. *I'm as good as people I see on the national news,* she thought. *It's only a matter of time before I'm there too.*

If Austin could see me now, she thought, *he wouldn't believe how much I've changed. It's like David says—now I'm Emily–2.*

The segments from the demo-tape ended. When she got up to retrieve it from the VCR, she saw David Alexander standing in the doorway. "What's this?" he asked. "A meeting of your fan club? Looks like you're the only one who showed up."

"I thought you'd left town already."

"I was gone for a few days, playing tourist, but now I'm back again. I'm leaving tomorrow for Washington. I'll be back on the air this Wednesday. Will you watch me every night?"

"You know I will. You're my hero."

"Yeah, right. So you made a demo-tape to send out?"

"That is correct."

"Against my advice to finish college first?"

"I can't let this go, David. It's the most exciting thing in my life right now."

"What kind of a price are you willing to pay for this dream of yours?"

"Whatever it takes."

"Do you have any idea how many demo-tapes major market stations get a year from people like you? Hundreds. Most of them are never even watched. So what makes you special?"

"I'm very good."

"Who told you that?" he asked.

"You did."

He scowled. "When did I ever tell you that?"

"Well, not directly, but one time you told me that newscasters in markets like Seattle and Portland aren't much better than me."

"And you took that as praise?" he asked.

"It's as much praise as you ever give anyone."

"Let me tell you something. The chances you're going to get a job by sending out demo-tapes are very slim. I still say you ought to stay in school."

"I want to at least try to get a full-time job in broadcasting. If nothing comes of it, then I'll come back to school in the fall."

"Have you talked to your parents about this?" he asked.

"Not really."

"You should. If you won't listen to me, at least listen to them."

"They won't care. I've got to work this summer anyway. Why not do something that really interests me?"

He threw up his hands. "All right, this is against my better judgment, but if you're really serious about this, then come back and see me in a couple of weeks. I know some people. We'll make some calls, and I'll take you around to some stations, and we'll see what comes of it. If you want, you can stay at my place. It's got way more room than I need. And my mother would enjoy some company. You'd have your choice of four different rooms. There's some rooms I've never been in. We'd probably never see each other."

"You'd help me get a job?"

"Yeah, I guess maybe I could do that. After all, I created you, so I might as well put you to good use."

"It'd be so great to work in Washington, D.C.!"

"You're out of your mind if you think that." He looked at his watch. "I've really got to go now."

"I won't ever forget you, David . . . Alexander." She mimicked the way he said his name on the air.

"If you come to stay with me, don't expect much. I'm a lousy host. I spend a lot of time on the road, especially if there's an international incident. Most of the time you won't even see me. My mom's good company, though. You'd like her. And she'd like you, too. The two of you have a lot in common. She also wants me to quit smoking."

"Sounds like a sensible person."

He shook his head. "I'm still not sure that you wanting to go to work right away is a good idea. Are you?"

"I've come this far. I can't turn back now."

"Well, okay then, come out, and I'll see what I can do about getting you a job. Talk to your folks about it. If they have any questions, have them talk to my mother."

"They won't have any problem with it."

He smiled. "Are you crazy? Of course they'll have a problem with it. Anyone who's seen *My Fair Lady* would know what's happening here."

"What *is* happening here, David?"

He didn't want to say any more, but, while opening the door to leave, he said softly, "'I've grown accustomed to your face.'"

He turned and bounded down the stairs.

3

Austin had been on his mission for one year but didn't feel much like celebrating.

He was, at that moment, at a zone conference listening to his new district leader, Elder Hastings, explain the secrets of his success. Elder Hastings and he had been in the MTC together just over a year before, but Hastings had become the superstar of the mission. *I was better than him in the MTC, so what happened?* Austin asked himself.

Elder Hastings continued. "Number one: be prayerful. Number two: work hard. Number three: follow the mission rules. Number four: . . ."

What is going on? Austin thought. *By now I should be one of the top baptizers. Or at least a district leader. But I'm nothing. What am I doing wrong?*

Austin had grown up listening to his mother read letters from his older brothers while they were on their missions. He'd seen the look of pride on her face when her sons were called as district or zone leaders. He remembered the day he came home from school and his mother had proudly announced, "Guess what? Cameron made mission assistant!"

At first, Austin's letters home had been full of news about how hard he was working and about the success he and his companion were about to have. But then, gradually, in the face of continuing futility, his hopes began to fade. The success his brothers had experienced was somehow eluding him. No baptisms meant no leadership opportunities.

He wondered what his mother was telling people about him when they asked. Maybe something like, "He's keeping busy." But even that wasn't the truth. He wasn't keeping busy. That was part of the problem. His first companion had been about to go home and had not been that concerned about working hard. They had spent a lot of time at members' homes and did very little teaching. And they'd had no baptisms.

Elder Briggs, his current companion, had health problems—an inner ear condition that caused him to get nauseated when he got out of bed. The best thing he could do when that happened was to just stay in bed and hope it would soon pass.

Elder Hastings continued. "If you'll plan your work and then work your plan . . ."

Austin groaned inwardly. It seemed so unfair that he should be forced to listen to Elder Hastings talk about his success. In the MTC, Austin had been the acknowledged leader in their district, much more so than Elder Hastings. Now, when the mission newsletter came each month, it was a painful reminder of his lack of success. He was not named as one of the elders on the Top Ten List. Excerpts from his weekly letter to the mission president were not quoted as examples of what could be done if you only worked. He was not listed as being a new district leader, zone leader, or mission assistant.

He was a nobody.

But at least the mission newsletter only came out once a month. Having Hastings as his district leader was going to be the ultimate put-down. There was nothing harder to live with than a person who'd had quick and easy success. Austin dreaded all the well-meaning advice he was going to get in the near future.

If I'd had at least one decent companion, I could have done as well as Hastings. All I need is somebody who can work hard.

Hastings was on a roll. He concluded with, "If you'll just follow these steps, you can have the same kind of success my companions and I have had."

Finally, Hastings sat down and President Merrill stood up to address the missionaries.

"Well, we've had some excellent counsel today. Thank you, Elder Hastings. There's really not that much I can add to what you've already said."

Austin winced. *Hastings will be mission assistant within three months. Just my luck,* he thought bitterly.

The meeting ended half an hour later. During lunch, President Merrill began interviewing missionaries.

Austin dreaded the interview because he had so little to report. While waiting, he went to the Primary room and sat at the piano and played hymns he'd learned in high school when he was the priesthood pianist.

After a while, Hastings looked into the room. "President Merrill asked me to find you. He'd like to talk to you now."

Austin blushed because he was sure that Hastings must think he was a problem elder for President Merrill to specifically ask for him.

As Austin stood up to go with Hastings, Hastings stuck out his hand. "It's going to be great working with you again, Elder."

Austin nodded halfheartedly. "Maybe you can help me have the same kind of success you've had." He was being sarcastic, but he was sure Hastings wouldn't take it that way.

"Well, you can! We're in this together. If we all do our part, we can all succeed."

And if we do, that will be your ticket to being mission

assistant, Austin thought as he followed Hastings to the bishop's office where President Merrill was interviewing missionaries.

There were five elders ahead of him.

"He'll be next," Hastings said to the elders in front of Austin.

The elder who had been first in line raised his eyebrows. Austin saw the gesture. *They all think I'm a problem elder. Well, maybe I am. I haven't had any baptisms. I don't work enough hours. I'm not sure I can support my district leader. My companion and I don't get along that well, especially when he lays in bed half the day. So maybe I am a problem elder.*

He felt his face getting hot. *This is so unfair. I haven't done anything wrong. I can't help it that Briggs gets sick all the time.*

I don't care what people think, I haven't done anything wrong, he thought. And yet he'd been tempted, and that made him feel guilty. He'd thought of going jogging by himself on the days when Elder Briggs was sick in bed. It was hard for him to sit around in a dumpy apartment with nothing to do.

And then there was the time he'd looked out the window and seen the girl in the apartment next door having trouble getting her car started. He'd thought about going outside and giving her a hand. He was sure he could have gotten her car started, but being there alone with her would have been a violation of mission rules. So he let her solve her problem herself. But she was good-looking, and after that he watched her each morning when she walked out to her car. He knew that was not what he should be doing. But when he had nothing to look forward to each day except hoping that Briggs would feel better in the afternoon so they could go out and do a little missionary work, it was easy to fall into bad habits.

I wonder if Briggs told the president about the time I slugged him? I hope not. It wasn't that big of a deal. I just lost my temper, that's all. And I didn't hit him that hard.

The wait in line seemed to take forever.

"The president is taking a long time in there with Elder Rice, isn't he?" the elder behind him said to Austin. "When that happens, it usually means . . . major problems."

"Really?" Austin said. "Maybe they're just talking."

"I doubt it. Not when the president's got so many to interview." The elder paused. "How come you get special treatment?"

"My companion and I have to leave early. We have a discussion scheduled at six."

It was a lie, but Austin didn't care.

"Where's your companion then? The president will have to interview you both before you go. He should be here with you so you can leave."

Austin shook his head. He wasn't going to continue making up lies. "I was just kidding. I don't know why the president wants to interview me now."

"It's usually a problem when that happens."

"You're absolutely right. Look, why don't we save ourselves a lot of trouble. You go in and tell the president what my problem is. And then we'll both be happy. I mean, you seem to know so much. There's really no need for me to even be interviewed, is there? You pretty much know my life story."

"Hey, back off, okay? You don't need to get hostile."

"Look, I don't even want to talk to you."

The elder nodded. "I'm not surprised the president wants to see you right away. You know what? I just feel sorry for your companion, that's all."

Austin felt like starting a fight.

And that is when the president opened the door. The

elder who'd been in with the president left quickly. His face was red. *Problem elder,* Austin thought.

President Merrill smiled, shook Austin's hand, and escorted him into the office. "Oh, good! Elder Hastings found you. He gave a fine talk today, didn't he? You're lucky to have him for your district leader."

"Yes, of course," Austin said, tight-lipped.

Don't say anything. Just get through this interview as fast as possible, he told himself. He pictured the elder next in line timing him to see how long the interview took. Anything over five minutes would be taken as an indication that Austin had a major problem.

"How are you getting along?" President Merrill asked.

"Good, I guess."

"How are things between you and Elder Briggs?"

"All right."

"Really? When I interviewed him a few minutes ago, he said you nearly beat him up once in front of a housing development. He said people were watching the two of you from their windows."

"Oh, that. I didn't really hit him . . . at least not very hard. Well, okay, I might have shoved him a little. I'm surprised he even remembered it."

"What brought it on?"

"Well, you know, he gets sick some days and can't even get out of bed. That means I have to spend the whole day in the apartment. That gets old fast. One time, after two days of that, I told him I didn't care how he felt, we were going tracting. Well, we got out there, but after about fifteen minutes he said he was feeling sick and needed to go back to the apartment. That's when I told him he was doing it on purpose and that we weren't going back to the apartment. I might have shoved him a little. He fell down, and I was standing over him yelling. When we noticed people watching us from their windows, I helped him up, and we drove

48

back to our apartment. Since then, when he gets sick, I just let him be sick. So things are a lot better now."

"I appreciate your willingness to work with Elder Briggs. I know it hasn't been easy."

Austin nodded, then looked at his watch. He shouldn't stay much longer or the elders in line would start wondering what his problem was. He wanted to move this along. "I'm living the mission rules, President."

"Good for you." He paused. "Are you happy?"

Austin looked again at his watch. *I've got to get out of here.*

"I guess so," he said.

"You don't look happy."

He gave a big phony grin. "Looks like I need to tell my face then, doesn't it? Look, President, I'm okay. I know you've got a lot of interviews to do. I'm doing okay. Really."

"You don't want to talk about it?"

"There's nothing to talk about. Really, I'm fine."

The president noticed him looking at his watch. "Are you in a hurry? Do you have an appointment?"

"No."

"Then why do you keep looking at your watch?"

"There are people outside."

President Merrill understood. He went to the door and told the elders in line to go to the chapel. He said he'd have Elder Hastings get them when it was their turn.

And then President Merrill returned, closed the door, and sat down. "Tell me why you're not happy."

"Is it important that I be happy? I'm keeping the mission rules. Isn't that enough?"

"That's just the beginning. There's a whole lot more than that. Tell me what's going on. I really want to know."

Austin sighed and decided he would be honest with President Merrill. He looked down at his hands. "I'm not making the progress I should be making. I haven't had any baptisms, and my mission is half over. My brothers went from being district leaders to zone leaders to mission assistants. It doesn't look like I'm ever going to have any leadership responsibilities. Everyone talks about what a good missionary Elder Hastings is. Well, I was in the MTC with him. He was good then, but I was even better. I was the district leader in the MTC. And now he's the star and I'm a nobody. With Elder Briggs sick so much of the time, we don't work enough hours. We don't teach enough. We have no prospects for baptism. I just about go crazy when he's sick in bed. I can't leave him. I came here to work and I'm not able to do that."

He felt as though he might cry and looked away from his mission president. Finally, he said, "I pretty much feel like a failure." He sighed. "Other than that, things are going okay."

President Merrill nodded and reached for his scriptures, then read from Doctrine and Covenants, Section 18: "And if it so be that you should labor all your days in crying repentance unto this people, and bring, save it be one soul unto me, how great shall be your joy with him in the kingdom of my Father!"

The scripture brought no comfort to Austin. "Right now it looks like I could go my whole mission and not even have one baptism."

"What if that one soul were Elder Briggs? Or what if it's yourself? Wouldn't that count too?"

Austin shook his head. "Probably not." He felt a rush of emotion, and he hated himself for feeling it. "The truth is, President, any way you want to look at it, I don't measure up. You know that, and I know that, so let's not try to hide the fact from each other."

"If you're doing what the Savior wants you to do, how can that be considered not measuring up?"

"I came out here to teach and baptize. Well, I haven't had any baptisms. Doesn't that make me a failure?"

President Merrill stood up and came around the desk. Facing Austin, he put his hand on Austin's shoulder and looked him in the eye. "When I was a little boy, some days I used to pretend I was a fireman, or the next day I might pretend I was an Air Force pilot, but at the end of each day, I'd take off my fireman hat or I'd put away my model airplane, and then I'd still just be a boy."

That's just what I need, Austin thought sarcastically, *another story about him growing up on a farm in Idaho.*

"This is similar to our situation. We are disciples of Jesus Christ who, right now, are missionaries. You could become a district leader, Elder. You're certainly of the caliber of person who would make a good district leader. But even if that happens, you will still be a disciple of Jesus Christ who also happens to be a district leader. And when you're released from your mission, you'll be a disciple of Jesus Christ who just happens to be a college student or a gas station attendant or whatever it is you choose to do with your time."

Austin was staring at the carpet, just waiting for the interview to be over.

President Merrill reached out and touched the tip of Austin's chin with his forefinger and lifted it until Austin was looking directly into President Merrill's eyes. "Elder, the Savior couldn't love you any more now, if you were a district leader or a zone leader or an assistant to the president. I have assigned you where I believe the Lord wants you to serve. Don't second-guess the Savior. Serve him the best you can in the position you are in and then just trust the Lord to make it turn out the best for the kingdom."

Austin fought to control his emotions. He felt love emanating from the president, and so he listened with his heart.

"I know it's not easy being Elder Briggs's companion. You've lasted longer than his last four companions. Elder Briggs is hoping he can serve out his entire mission. If he does, it will be because of you. Try to work with him the best you can. If you'll do that, I promise you, you'll be blessed for it."

Tears welled up in Austin's eyes as, for the first time in months, he felt appreciated. It was a great relief to know he had the president's respect and confidence.

The president continued. "Try to think about the Savior more. Try to reach out to others the way the Savior would. If you do that, everything will change. He is our Guide, our Example, and our Redeemer. Look to Him and live."

As they shook hands, President Merrill drew Austin in close and gave him a hug.

"Thank you, President," Austin said. "I'll try to do better."

"Let me know how it goes. Call me anytime you need to talk to me."

Stepping away, Austin blew his nose and wiped his eyes. The trick was not to look as though he'd been crying. Elders would pick up on that and believe the worst, and then privately be merciless.

He opened the door and walked swiftly down the hall, hoping to get somewhere he could be by himself for a few minutes.

As he walked past the kitchen, he saw two women from the ward who were preparing lunch. They were working alone. After watching them for a moment, Austin cleared his throat and asked, "Do you need any help?"

"Why, yes, we do. We were supposed to have four women come and help, but two of them haven't shown up yet. Could you cut the Jell-O into squares and put them on a plate on top of a bed of lettuce?"

"Sure, no problem."

"Thank you so much. How considerate of you to offer. I've been preparing lunches for these conferences for three years, and you're the first elder to offer to help in the kitchen."

Austin didn't know why, but hearing her say that brought

52

tears to his eyes. He said nothing but washed his hands in the sink and went to work on the Jell-O.

It was the perfect place for him at that moment. The two women ignored him as they talked about their families, and the elders avoided him because they didn't want to help out. So it left him time to himself to collect his thoughts.

In a way he found it strange to be doing this. His dad never helped in the kitchen. Maybe his father thought that was woman's work.

From now on, I'm not going to worry what my dad thinks or what my mom thinks or what impossible goals I might have set for myself before my mission. Instead of setting goals to baptize so many people, I'm going to set a goal of trying to put the Savior first in my life. He treated others with compassion. I'll try to do the same thing. Even Elder Briggs. That's the only goal I can set on my mission that can carry over after my mission.

Austin smiled at how precisely he had measured and cut the Jell-O into squares. It meant that everyone would get the same amount. That is the way it should be. Strangely enough, even though all he was doing was cutting Jell-O into squares, he felt happy to be giving service.

He felt a lot better now.

4

Emily woke up at seven in the morning but church wasn't until eleven.

She stretched then relaxed, choosing to stay in bed and let herself wake up slowly. For the first time in months, she had no papers or exams to worry about and no Sunday School lesson to prepare for church that day.

The apartment normally housed four girls, but because it was the end of the semester, Molly, in the other bedroom, was the only other one still left. The other two had left for home after their last final exam.

It seemed like such a luxury not to have to get up and to be done with school for an entire summer. And, if she got a job working at a TV station, maybe forever.

She rested her hand on her stomach and felt it rise and fall with each breath. *I wonder if I've lost any weight,* she thought. *I feel so skinny. Maybe it's just because I'm lying down. I'll have to weigh myself when I get home.*

She fantasized being the next Jane Pauley or Diane Sawyer, influential, trusted by viewers, able to examine important issues of the day, smart, intelligent, and with a little help from makeup experts, beautiful too. When she found corruption in government, she would reveal it. When she found heartwarming stories of ordinary people who did extraordinary things, she would let the world know. If there were health warnings that needed to be made, she would sound the alarm.

She remembered something David Alexander had said, "Reporting the news is like standing on a riverbank during a flood and describing what comes down each day. Every day is different. There are high points and low points, but whatever it is, you're there telling the world what you see."

She retrieved David's business card, studied the phone number he'd given her, thought about calling him, but then decided against it. *If I wait another day or two, maybe he'll call me.*

She decided to take a shower. Because she didn't have girls at the door clamoring for her to hurry up, and because she didn't have to be anywhere for hours, she could take her time. That was also another luxury she hadn't enjoyed since coming to college in the fall.

As the water cascaded over her, she faced away from the spout, lowered her head and let the water drum on the back of her neck. It was better than a massage.

A cloud of warm mist filled the room giving it a mysterious air as if it were fog. She grabbed the tube of shampoo and, using it as a microphone, assumed her newscaster's voice, "The swamp monster has gone back into the swamp, but I've gone in to get him. Authorities say that dense fog in the region is hampering their search for the half-man/half-frog creature who, it is believed, brutally killed a night-watchman last night." She put her hand to her throat as if someone were choking her, then dramatically slumped over.

If she got a job working for a national network, she wasn't sure if she'd use her real name or not. "This is Emily Savage . . . This is Emily . . ." She paused. She knew there had been a TV news personality named Jessica Savage, so she couldn't use that. But she liked the combination of Emily, which seemed quite feminine, and the word *Savage.*

She tried to come up with variations. "This is Emily Beast for CBS news . . . This is Emily Barbarian for CBS news . . . This is Emily Maniac for CBS news . . . This is Emily Homicidal for CBS news . . . This is Emily Nightmare for CBS news . . ." She started giggling.

She might have gone on much longer, but the hot water started to turn lukewarm, so she got out and started drying. She'd had so much fun in the shower that she grabbed the shampoo tube again. "This is Emily Wolf . . . This is Emily Coyote . . . This is Emily Badger . . . This is Emily Rhino." She started laughing but stayed in character, doing the interview. "I'm sorry. It's just that sometimes I crack myself up. This is Emily Delusional."

Molly called out through the bathroom door. "Emily, who are you talking to?"

"Nobody, I'm just playing TV announcer." She opened the door a crack. "Do you need to get in here?"

"Well, yeah, for just a minute and then I'm going back to bed." She walked in. "Gosh, you've really steamed up the place, haven't you?"

"Yeah, sorry. It's the longest shower I've ever taken. It's so good not to have to rush around to get ready. I'm done in here for a while. Help yourself."

In her room, Emily took her time getting ready for church. She examined the reflection of her face in the mirror attached to the door. *What else can I do to improve the way I look?* she thought. She couldn't decide if she should color her hair, which was fine and silky and blonde. She called it *blonde,* but a boy in high school once told her it was the color of a field of hay stubble. It wasn't exactly a compliment, but at least it was accurate.

She felt happy and contented that school was over. She had a good chance of getting straight A's. The next day, before leaving to go home for the summer, she'd mail out her demo-tapes to TV stations. That might open up some possibilities for her, but even if it didn't, there was still a good chance that David could get her a job working in Washington, D.C.

David is falling in love with me, she thought. *Serves him right for being so mean to me in the beginning. It's flattering, but I have no intention of doing anything about it. Except it means I have power over him. Imagine that—little old me having power over the rich and famous David Alexander.*

It doesn't matter, though, because Austin's my one true love. She smiled at the thought because since coming to school she'd spent very little time thinking about Austin. But at least she'd continued to write him, which wasn't that much trouble since she'd been sending him the same letter she sent to her brother.

She looked in the closet for something to wear, but there wasn't much choice. Because of doing last-minute term papers and cramming for finals, she hadn't done a wash for well over a week. She found a long-sleeved white blouse in the back of her closet. It had been a Christmas present from her aunt. It was too big for her, and was much too flouncy for Emily's taste. She thought it made her look like a Gypsy.

After she got dressed and put her makeup on, she went in the other bedroom to wake up Molly. "Hey, sleepyhead, it's time to get ready for church."

Molly just moaned and rolled over.

Emily sat on Molly's bed. "Come on, you know you've got to do it."

"Just ten more minutes."

"No, c'mon, it's time."

Molly was a cowgirl from Soda Springs, Idaho. She used little makeup and wore the same blue denim dress to church every Sunday. She was going with a returned missionary from Ashton, Idaho, and they had been talking about getting married.

Molly stretched, yawned, and slowly got to her feet, then

padded to the bathroom. She turned to face Emily. "Brett's going to pick me up. You want to ride with us?"

"No, that's okay. It's such a nice day. I think I'll walk."

Half an hour later Emily left the apartment on her way to church. It was a beautiful morning, with the temperature in the midseventies and a light breeze blowing. The sun was warm on her cheek, which reminded her she was looking forward to getting a tan during the summer. It wasn't easy for her to do because of her light complexion, but she thought if she consistently sunned ten minutes a day she might be able to get a little color.

She thought about her weight again. She'd heard that the camera adds about ten pounds to a person's appearance, and from what she'd seen she believed it. Maybe she'd go on a diet over the summer, when it was easier to lose weight by eating more fresh fruits and vegetables. But if she did decide to diet, she for sure wouldn't tell her mother about it. Emily's mom thought Emily looked fine and had never understood when Emily worried about her weight. It was just one more thing on which they had disagreed.

Even so, Emily was looking forward to being home again and to letting her mom take care of her. While living away from home for the first time, she'd found out how much work it took to do the things she'd always taken for granted when she lived at home—buying groceries, cooking and cleaning up afterward, and washing and ironing clothes. It would be nice to give some of those chores back to her mom.

What if I do get a job and don't spend the summer at home? What if I never come back to school? Am I really ready to be on my own?

The weather was so pleasant that Emily was almost sorry when she reached the institute building where church was held. She was early. The meeting wouldn't begin for twenty minutes.

She went in the chapel and sat down to wait. She spent a few minutes reading her scriptures and then went out into the hall to get a drink of water. The water was cool and pure and tasted good.

Returning to her seat, she closed her eyes. *It's so quiet and peaceful here,* she thought.

She remembered that she'd forgotten to pray before she left her room and felt guilty because she'd had plenty of time. *It's because school is over,* she thought. *I don't have any impossible deadlines to meet or any hard exams to study for. I'm out of my routine. That's why I didn't pray. I should have, though.*

She closed her eyes and began to whisper a prayer, but she stopped when some people began coming into the chapel. She didn't want them to think she was weird.

There weren't that many at church that Sunday because the semester had ended, and most of the students had already left for home.

After church, back at her apartment, Emily was glad to get out of her church clothes. She changed into jeans but continued to wear the blouse she'd worn to church. For comfort, she didn't tuck it in and left the sleeves unbuttoned.

She was alone in the apartment. She figured Molly had gone with Brett to visit his grandmother who lived in Smithfield. She didn't mind. It was nice to have the place all to herself. She fixed herself a sandwich then started to sort through folders from school. By four in the afternoon, she had a garbage sack full of old papers she was going to throw away. After that, she took a nap until five, then woke up just as Molly returned.

"You want some supper?" Emily asked.

"No, you go ahead. We had a big lunch, so I'm not hungry now. I think I'll take a nap for a while."

Emily got up and looked for something to eat. The

cupboard and fridge were pretty much bare, but she did find a package of Ramen noodles.

She turned the electric burner on to high and put the water on to boil before sitting down to read the Sunday issue of the *New York Times*.

She got so interested in an article on the front page that she forgot about the pan on the stove until she heard the water vigorously boiling and sloshing over onto the stove. She stepped quickly to the range, and when she reached to remove the pan from the red-hot burner, the right tail of her blouse brushed against the glowing coil and caught fire.

She didn't panic at first because it was only a small flame. She brushed at it with her hand to put it out but that only fanned the flames. Within seconds, the flame raced up the right side of the shirt, and then the whole front of the blouse was on fire. She could hear the "whoosh" of the flames as they rushed upward. At first there was no pain, just the sensation of heat on her skin. But in a moment, the pain was beyond anything she'd ever experienced. Not just on the surface, like burning a finger on an iron; this was much deeper. Each breath she took carried flame-heated air and airborne contaminants into her lungs, searing her mouth and lungs.

The polyester fabric not consumed in the fire melted and formed a hot, gooey substance that stuck to the skin on her arms, chest, and stomach. It felt as though the blood under her skin was boiling.

In full-blown panic, Emily screamed again and again.

Molly came running into the kitchen and saw Emily engulfed in flames. "Oh, Emily!" she screamed, but stood for a moment, not knowing what to do. Then she tackled Emily, pushing her to the floor and slapping with her hands at the burning fabric, trying to smother the flames. Panicked, Emily fought to get free and struggled to her feet, still screaming.

Molly tried to get what was left of the smoldering fabric

off Emily by pulling it over her head, but as she did so, the flames caught Emily's hair on fire.

"Aaagh!" Emily screamed as the fire licked at her ears, face, and scalp.

Molly fought against being overwhelmed by panic, knowing that if she didn't do something fast, Emily would die. *Water!* she thought. She knew it would take too long to fill a bucket. Emily might be dead by then.

Spotting the spray attachment on the sink, she grabbed it and turned on the water. "Don't move, Emily! I'm putting out the fire!"

Molly started on Emily's head and then moved down until the fire was put out. The molten fabric adhering to Emily's arms, chest, and stomach cooled and stuck to the severely damaged skin.

Emily slumped to the floor, wracked with pain and in shock.

Molly grabbed the phone and dialed 911. "My roommate just got burned in a fire! You've got to come right away!"

Writhing on the wet floor, Emily was trying to get enough air into her lungs.

"My name?" Molly cried out. "Why do you need to know my name? I'm telling you my roommate is dying!"

Emily felt as if there were a heavy weight on her chest preventing her from breathing. *I'm not going to make it,* she thought. *I'm going to die. I just hope I can live long enough to tell my mom and dad I love them.*

Molly finally calmed down enough to give the 911 operator the needed information. She hung up the phone and got on her knees beside Emily. "They're on their way, Emily. Just hang in there, okay?"

Emily wanted to thank Molly, but the pain was so severe that it took all she had just to breathe. She wasn't ready to die, but she almost wished she could because of the pain.

Molly was crying. She grabbed a dish towel and began

wiping at some of the water around Emily. "The ambulance is coming right away, okay?" she blurted. "They'll be here any minute."

"I think I'll need to have someone look at this," Emily whispered.

"I know. They'll take you to the hospital."

She still wasn't getting enough air, but trying to breathe more deeply brought intense pain to the burned areas of her stomach and chest.

She never heard any sirens, but after what seemed a long while, the room was suddenly full of strangers—a policeman, firemen, and paramedics.

"What's her name?" one of the paramedics asked.

"Emily," Molly said.

"Emily, I'm Devon. We're going to get you to the hospital, so they can take good care of you. Okay?"

She tried to answer but all that came out was a moan.

Devon cut her burned shirt away from her body so it wouldn't pull at the skin when they moved her onto a stretcher.

"Is she going to be all right?" Molly asked.

"We just need to get her to the hospital, that's all."

They started down the stairs, carrying Emily on a stretcher. Even though they tried hard to be gentle, each step caused her intense pain.

They got her in the ambulance and started for the hospital. "Don't tell my parents about this," she whispered to Devon.

"They need to know, Emily."

She didn't want her mom and dad to worry. But even so, she remembered back to the time when she was little and fell off the monkey bars at a playground. She had broken her wrist, and she remembered how her mother had held her on her lap and kissed her to "make it all better" while waiting for the doctor to see them in the emergency room of the hospital. She desperately wanted that kind of comfort now.

It was a short ride to the hospital. Emily was wheeled directly into the emergency room, where on a count of three, she was gently lifted onto an examination table. Having been alerted by the paramedics, the members of the medical staff were ready for her, and she was immediately surrounded by a doctor and two nurses.

The doctor, in his midthirties, took charge. "I'm Dr. Sullivan. We're going to check you over to see how you're doing." He addressed one of the nurses, "Get her vitals," he said.

While one nurse was checking her blood pressure and heart rate, the other placed an oxygen mask over her mouth and nose. She was having trouble breathing, and getting the oxygen helped lessen the panic she'd been experiencing, feeling that at any minute she might die. They also started an IV in a vein in her left arm.

After a few minutes, Molly came rushing into the emergency room. Emily asked her to get someone to administer to her, and Molly left to go make the phone calls.

Emily wanted to know how badly she'd been burned. She raised her head and saw that her chest and upper right arm were covered with large and very wet blisters. She lay back down again. *This is worse than I thought.*

The few times Emily had been burned, her mother had always used Neosporin ointment on the burn. She thought the nurse would bring a big tube of the stuff and apply it to her burn. But that didn't happen.

She felt herself going in and out of consciousness. One time when she woke up, she realized the doctor was talking to someone on the phone. It sounded as though he was asking for advice. *Oh, great, he doesn't know what he's doing,* Emily thought.

Holding the phone to his ear, Dr. Sullivan stepped to

Emily's side. He lifted the sheet that was loosely covering her and said, "Well, the burned area is over her right arm, the right side of her face, her neck and chest . . . I'd say twenty percent . . . third degree. Her pulse is steady, but we're still trying to stabilize her breathing. Yes, we've done that . . . Yes, we've done that . . . No, not yet. I wanted to talk to you first. All right, we'll do that. What else? . . . All right, we'll prep her and get her ready for the flight. Thanks for your help."

As soon as Dr. Sullivan got off the phone, he ordered morphine for Emily. Then he spoke to her. "Emily, we're going to AirMed you to the burn center at the University of Utah in Salt Lake City. They'll take good care of you. We're going to try to keep you comfortable until the helicopter arrives, okay?"

Perhaps because she'd been watching reruns of *M*A*S*H* on TV, Emily pictured a military helicopter, where the patients are strapped onto a stretcher outside the helicopter. *What if I move the wrong way and fall?* she thought.

A nurse came and administered morphine through Emily's IV.

Maybe it was the morphine, but the image of the helicopter ride became more and more distorted in her mind. She pictured a cot dangling from a helicopter, without any straps, and that she'd have to hold on tight for the entire ride, and that if she passed out or lost consciousness then she'd roll off and fall to her death.

I should have just used the Neosporin and stayed home, she thought. *It might take a couple days longer to heal, but at least I wouldn't be facing a helicopter ride.*

Molly returned. "I called the bishop. He's on the way."

"They're going to put me on a helicopter," Emily slurred.

"Yes, I know."

"I don't want to go. I'm afraid I'll fall out." Talking took more strength than she had.

"You won't fall out."

"I'm not sure I can hold on the whole time."

"You won't have to hold on."

"If I don't hold on, I'll fall."

"No, really, it's going to be okay."

"I don't want to go. It was a mistake to come here."

"You have to go to the burn center, Emily."

She closed her eyes. *What's the difference? One way or the other, I'm going to die.*

"I want to talk to my mom and dad," she said.

"All right, let's do that now," Molly said, asking a nurse for a phone Emily could use to talk to her parents.

A short time later, with Emily giving her the number, Molly made the call.

"Hello. Is this Emily's mom? Hi. This is Molly, her roommate. She's been burned. I'm here with her in the hospital. She wants to talk to you. Hold on, I'll put her on."

Molly placed the phone by Emily's good ear.

"Mom? . . . I got burned . . ." She felt her strength ebbing away. "Mom, if I don't make it, I just wanted to say . . . I love you. Tell Daddy I love him too, okay? Okay . . ."

The effort to talk was too much.

Molly took the phone. "Hello? This is Molly again. Well, the doctor hasn't said, so I don't know what to say, but it's pretty bad. I know they're going to fly her by helicopter to the burn center in Salt Lake City."

Molly stayed by her side, and for that Emily was grateful, except for a thought, which, like the fire, started small but was threatening to grow out of control. The thought was, *If Molly had sprayed me with water when she first came into the kitchen, I might not even be here now.*

"They probably won't let me ride with you, but I'll find someone to drive me down to the burn center," Molly said.

"Don't bother," Emily said.

"Don't bother? Are you serious? I love you, Emily. You know that. There's not anything I wouldn't do for you."

Gasping to get enough air, and wanting someone to blame for the agony she was going through, Emily took two deep breaths and whispered, "Then why did you wait so long to put out the fire?"

She might as well have struck Molly across the face for the hurt it caused. "I tried," Molly blurted out. "I didn't know what to do. I'm sorry. I did the best I could."

What does it matter now? I'm going to die anyway. "I'm sorry. I shouldn't have said that," Emily said.

Shortly after that two men were ushered by a nurse in to where Emily and Molly were. "I'm here to give a priesthood blessing," the older of the two said. "I brought my son."

"You're not Bishop Cherington," Molly said.

"Well, I was, up to a few weeks ago. You know what? I bet you wanted my nephew. He was recently called to be a bishop on campus."

"Why did you come when you don't even know Emily?" Molly asked.

"I never turn down a request to administer to someone."

"Please give me a blessing," Emily said weakly.

He bent over close to her. "Is there some place on your head we can put our hands?" he asked.

"I don't know."

"She was burned on her right side," Molly said. "I think here on the side, by her ear, might be okay."

"We'll be very careful," Brother Cherington said.

His son performed the anointing, and then Brother Cherington and his son gave Emily a blessing, barely touching the left side of her head with their fingers. She could hardly feel them. Brother Cherington blessed her body that it would heal and prayed that those who would treat her would make the right decisions and be able to use their skills to help her recover.

When they finished, Emily could breathe better. *Is this from God or is it from what the doctors did?*

After the blessing was over, a nurse entered the cloth-draped enclosure. "The AirMed helicopter is just minutes away."

Molly leaned near to Emily. "You okay?"

"I'm afraid," she said softly.

"Afraid of the helicopter ride?"

"Yes," she whispered.

"I'll tell them to take special care of you."

Emily's mind felt cloudy, almost as if it were detached from the rest of her body. The pain was still there, but it didn't have an edge like before. *It must be the morphine,* she thought.

A few minutes later two strangers appeared at her side. "Emily, I'm Garth, and this is Jordan. We're from AirMed. We're here to transport you to the burn center at the University of Utah."

"She's afraid of riding in a helicopter," Molly said.

Garth smiled. "Emily, don't worry about a thing. I'll hold your hand the whole way so you won't be scared."

It was time for Molly to say good-bye. She was crying as she leaned down. "I love you, Emily. I'll come visit you."

Garth and Jordan switched gurneys and rolled her out a door and then out to where the helicopter was waiting.

Emily was placed inside the helicopter, and a second later, the doors were closed. She was relieved to discover there was no way she could fall out.

Garth was true to his promise and held her hand the whole time. He talked about his son who had graduated a year earlier from Utah State University. It was hard for her to concentrate on what he was saying.

During the flight, Emily drifted in and out of consciousness. The morphine only dulled the pain; it didn't make it go away, but it seemed to her the flight took no time at all. The next thing she knew, they were passing over a mountain and she could see the lights of the city far below.

"There's Salt Lake City," Garth said. "We'll be there in just a few minutes. They'll take good care of you there. They're the best in the business."

"Do they have Neosporin?" she asked weakly.

5

The burn center staff at the hospital was ready for Emily the instant she was wheeled in. A male nurse who looked more like a football player than a health care provider seemed to be in charge. He was wearing hospital greens, and his long red hair was tied back in a ponytail. "What's her name?" he asked Garth.

"Emily Latrell."

"Emily, everyone here calls me Red. Probably because of the color of my hair, right? So it's easy to remember. You need anything, you call me, okay? Emily, you're in ER at the University of Utah Medical Center in Salt Lake City. The first thing we want to do is to check you over to see how you're doing. Okay? We'll start with your vital signs, and then we'll draw some blood for tests. You just relax and we'll try not to hurt you."

She was transferred onto another gurney, after which Garth and Jordan said their good-byes.

She found herself surrounded by a crowd of people, all of them peering and poking at her. To her, they were a mob of cruel tormentors, determined to inflict pain and embarrassment on her. Every movement, every breath, every puff of air sent her way was painful. She wished they would just give her another shot of morphine and put her in a dark room, close the door, and leave her alone.

Instead, they gave her oxygen to help her breathe, started another IV solution, and checked her blood pressure again. Next, two people lifted the sheet to examine the extent of her burns. After a few moments, one of them said, "I'd say twenty percent . . . third degree."

"I agree."

A short time later they gave her more morphine. It was such a relief to have the acute pain turn into a dull ache.

"Are you cold?" someone asked.

"Yes."

They brought heated blankets and put them on the parts of her body they weren't treating at the time.

Two nurses began the painful process of carefully cleaning the burn wounds. After doing so, they applied antiseptic ointment and bandaged the areas of her chest, stomach, and arms that had been burned. The two of them were as gentle as possible, but everything they did caused more pain.

When the process was completed, Red took charge. Before pushing her gurney out into the hall, he said, "Emily, we're taking you upstairs to the burn unit. Your traveling days are over for a while, okay? No more exciting ambulance rides. No more sight-seeing tours in a helicopter. You can just hang out with us for a while, okay? We'll take real good care of you."

They took an elevator ride to the fourth floor, then Red wheeled Emily through some automatic double doors into the burn unit. They ended up in a large open area with a nurses' station in the middle and patients' rooms surrounding it on all sides.

"We're giving you our best room to start out with," Red said. "Of course, some complain because it doesn't have a door, but that's so we can keep a close watch on you."

The last thing they did before they let her rest was to

70

record her weight, using the built-in scale in her hospital bed.

An hour or so later, her parents were brought in to see her. Because Emily hadn't seen herself in the mirror, she studied their expressions when they first saw her. Her mother's reaction was hard to read, but her dad turned away, so Emily knew it was bad.

Her mother tried to keep up a brave front, but Emily could see tears in her eyes. "How you doing, Baby?"

"Okay, I guess," she said.

Her dad was having a hard time even looking at her. "You had an accident cooking? How'd it happen?" he asked.

"We don't need to know that right now, do we?" her mother said crossly.

"No, of course not, you can tell us some other time," her dad said.

They talked some more and then a male nurse approached. "I need to cut your hair."

"Emily, they need to cut your hair," her mom said.

"I heard him," Emily answered, irritated that her mother felt the need to repeat everything.

The nurse turned on the electric razor.

"How short are you going to cut it?" Emily asked.

"Actually, I'm cutting it all off. Doctor's orders."

"Just leave it," Emily said. "My mom can trim it where it's burnt."

"The reason we do this is because we need to be able to see everything that needs treatment. We don't want your hair hiding areas that were burned."

Working slowly and taking great care not to hurt her any more than necessary, the man cut all the hair off the right side of her head, so that where she'd been burned, she was completely bald. He cut the hair on the left side of her head too, but not quite so short. It left her looking like a three-year-old who had chopped at her own hair. Then he

71

gathered up all the clumps and put them in the trash. "Okay, that's it. Thanks," he said on his way out.

"We should sue them for malpractice," Emily said.

"What for?" her dad asked.

"For cutting all my hair off."

"I'm sure they know what they're doing," her mother said.

"Sure, they do," her dad said. "Are they giving you something for pain?"

"Yeah, morphine."

"They're giving you *morphine!*" her dad said.

The next time Red came to check on her, Emily's dad said, "Is it really a good idea to be giving her morphine?"

"It must be all right or they wouldn't do it," her mother shot back.

"But what if she becomes addicted to it?" her dad argued.

"It's never happened yet," Red assured him.

Even after Red left, her dad was still fretting. "Why not something else besides morphine? I mean, there must be something else that'd be just as good, something that's not habit forming."

"They must know what they're doing. I'm sure they don't need you to set them straight," her mom answered.

Emily grew tired of having her parents there. They continually bickered, and they kept asking her questions that she couldn't answer. She felt as though she needed to entertain them, but it was hard for her to think clearly. She was also still having difficulty breathing. Every word she spoke came with a price tag on it. She wished they would leave, but they were determined to stay the night at her bedside. She felt miserable and depressed and wanted to just be left alone so she could feel that way without someone trying to talk her out of it.

Halfway through the night, her parents went to the lounge where they could sleep on recliners. Emily was relieved to see them go.

In order to accurately monitor the amount of urine her body was producing, she had been catheterized. At first, she was afraid of leakage, but everything worked the way it was supposed to. She was surprised at the interest the staff took in what came out of her body. They carefully measured it and recorded the results. *I'm like their science fair project,* she thought.

It seemed strange to her that she was producing any urine because she hadn't had anything to drink for hours. Then she realized it was because of the IV that they kept constantly running. *They're pumping fluids into me like crazy,* she thought. *It's a good thing I don't have to get up every time. I'd no sooner get back to bed than I'd need to get up again.*

The night seemed to last forever. She normally liked to sleep on her side or her stomach, but they kept her lying flat on her back, and she only slept in snatches. The morphine, which was administered through a port in her IV setup, dulled the pain but kept her feeling kind of numb and floating. Even so, every movement she made was painful.

Throughout the night, nurses came and left and returned again. She overheard their conversations. One male nurse explained in great detail the best way to buy a used car. It was like watching a bad movie on television and not being able to turn it off.

Everything seemed a little distorted, the walls not quite square, the pictures crooked, the conversations unreal.

She thought about what had happened to her, trying to find the place where the accident could have been avoided, beginning each scenario with *If only I had . . .*

At first it was easy. If only she hadn't worn the loose, polyester blouse to church . . . if only she hadn't decided to cook noodles for supper . . . if only she'd had tuna sandwiches . . . then this never would have happened. Or if, even though it was a Sunday, if only she'd eaten at some fast-food place.

Her mind raced. She couldn't stop the process. She kept thinking of alternatives, even imagining at one point that she wouldn't have been burned if she had made a different choice when she'd eaten supper with David Alexander. In her delirious state, she heard him ask again, "Is there some place we can go now?"

She knew the right answer, the answer she'd been taught to give. But this time, because she was in pain beyond anything she'd ever thought possible, this time in her mind she said, "Yes, David, let's go back to your apartment."

In her fantasy, he was surprised at her answer and gave her a big grin and told the waiter, "We've decided to postpone dessert until we get home."

That's where two paths presented themselves. Go home with David, and I don't get burned. Or tell him no, and end up here. The decision seemed so clear to me then, but now it doesn't. Nothing seems very clear to me now.

If I'd gone to his apartment, then everything would have changed. He would have asked me to marry him, and I'd have flown out with him on Saturday instead of making a videotape to send out. And I'd have met his mother and moved into their house. And tonight, instead of me lying here in a hospital bed, he'd be arranging for me to work as a newscaster.

Is it ever right to make a wrong decision? Right now it seems like it could be. One thing's for certain—I'd give anything not to have ended up in this place.

What would have been so wrong with living with David if it would have spared me this?

We'd have ended up getting married anyway, so what would be the harm?

The next morning, Emily opened her eyes to see Red

talking to a tall woman, who looked to be in her late twenties. Watching the easy manner they had with each other, Emily assumed the two were old friends.

After a few minutes, Emily heard Red say, "C'mon, I'll introduce you to her."

The attractive woman wore her brownish, copper-colored hair cut stylishly short, and she smiled pleasantly as she approached Emily's bed.

"Emily," Red said, "this is Brooke. She's what we call a child-life specialist. I used to think she and I would get married someday, but then she went and married some no-account bum who can't even hold down a decent job."

Brooke shook her head and smiled warmly at Emily. "Don't believe him. My husband, James, is an attorney."

"I rest my case," Red said, rolling his eyes.

"I'll tell him hello for you," Brooke said, chuckling.

"You do that. Well, I'll leave you two alone."

Brooke pulled up a stool and sat down next to Emily's bed. "How you doing?"

"I've been better."

"Do you need anything?"

"Not really. You say you work with children? I'm not a child."

"I know you aren't, but my role is to give you someone to talk to, and maybe answer your questions."

"Okay," Emily said.

"Oh, also, we have some CD players and some CDs that people have donated, in case you'd like that. And a few posters that people have dropped by for us to use. But, come to think of it, most of our posters are probably too young for you. What year in school are you?"

"I just finished my freshman year at Utah State University."

"Well, that's great. What are you majoring in?"

"Communications. I want to be a TV newscaster some-day."

"Good for you."

"Do you know who David Alexander is?"

"Doesn't he do TV news?" Brooke asked.

"Yes." She paused. "I worked with him all last year. After I get out of here, I'm going to move back to Washington, D.C. He's going to get me a job doing the news."

"Sounds exciting."

"David taught me so much. He told me once that he felt like he'd created me. And in many ways I guess that's true. Sometimes I feel like I'm his age, that he gave me the bene-fit of his experience. He said that when I came to him, I was Emily–1, but after being with him I became Emily–2."

"All this happened your freshman year?"

"Yeah."

Brooke had an easy pleasant laugh. "The only thing I remember from my freshman year was how smelly chem lab was."

"David Alexander and I became very close. And then, later, he sort of fell in love with me. He hasn't said that in so many words, but I could tell what was going on."

"How could you tell?"

"When he asked me to stay with him and his mother so he could see about getting me a job, he said something about the musical *My Fair Lady,* about the way he felt about me."

"What did he say?"

"He said, 'I've grown accustomed to your face.'"

For a fraction of a second Brooke winced but then quickly recovered her composure.

"You know, I think *My Fair Lady* is my favorite musical."

"Do you have a mirror? I want to see what I look like."

Brooke nodded. "That's no problem. What do you think you look like?"

76

"Pretty bad, because my dad couldn't even stand to look at me."

"Before you look at yourself in the mirror, we need to talk about a few things. Is that okay with you?"

"I guess so."

"Every time we do this I'd like us to talk in detail about what you're seeing. The reason for doing that is that some areas may not look very good right now, but they are going to get better with time. For example, in some areas you may notice some swelling, but that's going to diminish as time goes on. And then, in other areas, you may see some pinkness that looks like a bad sunburn. But that too will heal in time. So we'll point out those areas. And then, we'll point out some areas that were damaged so extensively they're not going to heal by themselves. For those areas they'll be doing skin grafts. So even those areas will improve as time goes on."

"Just let me see myself in the mirror."

Brooke nodded. "Of course, but, remember, it's better if we take our time and talk about what you're seeing. Here's the mirror."

Emily took one look at herself and gasped. She felt like crawling into a hole and dying. After a brief glance, she handed the mirror back to Brooke.

"Tell me what you saw," Brooke said.

Emily started sobbing. "It's awful."

"But it's not all the same, is it?"

"I don't know."

"Can I show you what I see?"

"No, just leave me alone. I don't want to talk to you anymore."

Brooke nodded. "Sure. I'll come back later."

As soon as Brooke left, Emily was sorry she'd sent her away.

Fifteen minutes later, Brooke returned. "How are you doing?"

"Show me what you see," Emily said.

Together they looked at the areas damaged by the fire. Slowly and with great patience, Brooke helped Emily to learn to make a distinction between skin that would heal in time and the areas that would probably require skin grafts.

"Anytime you'd like, we can do this," Brooke said. "That way you'll be able to see the progress you're making."

Emily nodded. Even though her injuries were over-whelming, there was something about Brooke's confident reassurances that made her feel better about her situation. "Thank you."

"You're quite welcome. Is there anything else I can do for you?"

"You said you had a few posters that people have donated. Could you put one or two of them on the wall for me?"

"Sure, let me go see what we have."

She returned a few minutes later with a poster of a beach. "This is Hawaii. My husband and I went there on our honeymoon. It was great, but he got sunburned real bad. So, once again, I had to fuss over another burn patient. Red nearly died laughing when I told him. He said it was my punishment for going to Hawaii without him."

"Would he really have gone with you and your husband on your honeymoon?"

"Gosh, I don't know. Knowing Red, he might have. Let's ask him the next time we see him."

Emily found it easy to warm up to Brooke, who laughed easily and smiled a lot. Her optimism was infectious, and she clearly got a lot of joy out of her work. All that made it easy for Emily to trust her.

Brooke pinned the poster to the wall where Emily could see it without turning her head. "I also brought some music for you to listen to. It's nice to have it on real loud when you're in the tank room. I didn't know what you like, so I just grabbed some of them." She shuffled through the stack. "We've got some Bach, we've got some country western, we've got some rap. What would you like?"

"It doesn't matter."

"Well, I'd say go with the Bach then. Red likes country western and hates classical music, so I like to get everybody to choose classical."

Emily thought about the friendly way Red had talked to her the night before. "I choose country western."

"Country western? Oh my gosh! This is mutiny in the ranks! Red will be gloating about this all day!"

Brooke inserted the disk in the CD player and tested it to make sure it worked and handed it to Emily. "There, I think you're set. Before I leave, we need to talk about what's going to happen today."

"Okay."

"First of all, they're going to come and change your bandages. They'll do that right here in your bed. And then Doug, he's the physical therapist, he'll come and do a little work with you. Probably all he'll need you to do today is raise your arms up. The reason for that is that when you get burned, the skin tends to tighten up, so you have to keep stretching it so it doesn't heal that way. Okay so far?"

"I guess so."

"All right. Look, if you ever have any questions, let me know. I may not know the answer, but I'll find out from one of the nurses or a doctor and then let you know."

"Okay."

"There's a couple of other things I need to talk to you about."

"Go on."

"When a person has been burned, the body goes to work right away to repair the damaged tissue. That takes a tremendous amount of energy. You couldn't possibly eat all the food your body needs to make you better. So they have a machine that can feed you twenty-four hours a day, but to get it to work they'll need to run a tube through your nose down to your small intestine."

Emily was astounded. "You're kidding, right?"

"I know it sounds awful, but, the thing is, the feeding system will allow you to get the nutrients your body will need to heal."

"How long will I have to keep the tube in?"

"Well, that depends on how things go. I'm not a nurse, you know, but it's often until just before a patient is released."

"How long am I going to be here?"

"Rather than give you a specific time, you need to think of it in terms of goals that need to be achieved before you're released."

"What kind of goals?"

"You'll be released when all your surgeries are finished, and when you're eating enough so you won't lose weight after you leave. They'll want to make sure that your mom or someone else can help you with dressing changes, and you'll have to arrange for someone who can help you with any physical therapy you may need."

Just the idea of someone running a tube through her nose and down her throat made Emily feel queasy, but it turned out not to be as bad as she imagined. The technician who installed the tube explained that its placement was extremely critical. It had to extend beyond her stomach, into her intestine, otherwise she would constantly feel full and be unable to eat any additional food. To make sure the tube was properly located, they took an x-ray. Then they used a small skin staple to fasten the tube in place, just below her nostril.

Later that day, two nurses came to change her dressings.

Working carefully and applying very little pressure, they gently rubbed the burned areas with a washcloth, removing some of the most severely damaged skin. They called the process *debridement* and told Emily that they would do the same thing every time they changed her bandages.

Then a nurse gave her a sponge bath and expertly changed the sheets without getting Emily out of bed. Finally, Doug, the physical therapist, came and briefly had her exercise her arms. All that activity left her feeling drained and exhausted.

Her mom and dad spent all day with her, leaving her bedside only when the staff came to work with Emily. As evening approached, Emily suggested they go home to Ogden, rather than spend another night in the hospital with her. They agreed.

"I wish I could be here with you every day," her dad said, "but the thing is, I'm probably going to have to get back to work in the morning." He paused. "Your mom will be here all day, and I'll come to see you every day after I get off."

One thing Emily held against her dad was that he had always been in the background, always too busy at work, always with a reason why he couldn't be more involved in her life. Even though she really didn't want her parents hanging around, she resented his excuse.

That's the way it had been all through school. She'd always gone to her mom for help. There had been an incident in junior high, in the cafeteria, when a boy had grabbed her and kissed her. She'd pushed him, but all he'd done was laugh and walk away. When she got home, she told her mom and dad what had happened. What she wanted was for her dad to go to the boy's house and get mad and start yelling and warn the boy never to do that again.

That's what she wanted. What she got was a phone call made by her mother to the principal demanding the boy be expelled. Her father did nothing except go to work and let Emily's mom take care of it.

This is no different than the way it's been all my life, she thought. *When things get tough, my dad excuses himself and goes off to work.*

It wasn't that he had that great of a job. He worked as the produce manager at a large grocery store in Ogden. Emily viewed it as a dead-end job, leading nowhere. *But he prefers that over me,* she thought. *He always has, and he always will.*

Tuesday was a carbon copy of Monday, except that they got her out of bed and sitting up in a chair for part of the time.

In the afternoon, Molly, her roommate, came to visit. Molly tried to be up-beat and positive, but couldn't completely hide her shock at seeing the condition Emily was in.

Emily, who had learned to picture what she would look like when viewed on TV, let the camera pull back to take in the full view of what she had become—scarred, bandaged, immobile, and pathetic.

"I'm sorry it took so long to get down here to see you," Molly said.

"It's no problem."

"I got you some flowers, but they wouldn't let me bring 'em in. So next time I'll get you silk flowers."

"You don't have to get me anything."

"Are they taking good care of you?" Molly asked.

"I guess so."

"I couldn't sleep at all Sunday night. I just kept going over what happened. I feel bad that it took me so long to put out the fire."

Emily was exhausted, and it took more effort than she could muster to carry on a conversation. "You did the best you could."

"That's what Brett said. He told me he's proud of me for what I did."

"I can see why."

"There's one other thing," Molly said. "I'm not sure if I should even bring it up with you like this."

"What is it?" Emily slurred.

"Last night Brett asked me to marry him."

"What did you say?"

"Well, I told him yes. He gave me a ring. Want to see it?" Molly held the ring so Emily could see it without moving.

"It's very nice."

"We've got so much to do before the wedding," Molly said. "Sending out invitations, planning the reception. My mom said she'll help me make the dress."

Exhausted by the day, Emily stared at the ceiling and wished she had the nerve to ask Molly to leave.

And then she fell asleep. When she woke up, she was happy to discover that Molly had left.

On Wednesday morning, Dr. Beiser, her attending physician, dropped by to see how she was doing. After checking her over, he said, "We need to talk about tomorrow."

"What's going to happen tomorrow?"

"It'll be a busy day. We'll be doing your first surgery. We're going to do two things: first, we're going to do what we call a deep debridement to completely clean up the worst of the burned areas; then, we're going to harvest some good skin from your bottom so we can use it to do a skin graft. On Friday, we'll attach the new skin to the damaged area. Once the new skin takes hold, you'll be well on your way to getting out of here. That's what you want, isn't it?"

"Yes, that's what I want."

"Do you have any questions?"

"I can't think of any right now."

It amazed her how often she couldn't think of any questions until after Dr. Beiser left. Sometimes she wrote them down and asked him when she saw him again. Or sometimes she just asked Brooke.

One of Emily's cousins came to see Emily later that day. Feeling physically and emotionally exhausted, Emily didn't welcome the visit. Bethany was only a junior in high school, and she and Emily had never been close.

Bethany came in to Emily's room, chewing gum. "Oh, my gosh, I hardly recognized you. You look awful."

Is this the way it's going to be on the outside? Emily thought.

"So, you got burned, right?" Bethany asked, smacking her gum.

"Yes."

"I know exactly how you feel. This morning I burned my head with a curling iron."

Emily closed her eyes and gritted her teeth.

"So are they going to fix you up like before? I hope so. I saw this guy once at a mall. I guess he'd been burned. Anyway, he was like his own freak show. Megan, my friend, goes, 'Probably the only time he feels really comfortable is Halloween, except he doesn't even need a mask.' Well, I know that wasn't very nice, but I had to laugh anyway."

Bethany may have realized she'd gone too far. "But you won't end up looking that way, right?"

"I'm really tired now, Bethany."

"Yeah, sure, well, I just wanted to see how you're doing, okay?"

"Right, thanks," Emily replied. She knew it was rude to do so, but Emily didn't say anything else, hoping Bethany would get the hint and go away.

"Well," the younger girl finally said, "I hope you get better soon."

Left alone, Emily began to fantasize again about David Alexander. *If he knew I was here, he'd come and visit me. There must be new techniques some place. Maybe back East.*

Some hospital where it's not so painful and you don't need to stay a month to get better. David would find out, and he'd get me in there, and I'd end up the way I was before all this happened. And then David would let me stay in his house for as long as I wanted. And I wouldn't have to go outside and meet people until I was feeling better. He could help me because he's rich and because he loves me. And if he'd do that for me, I'd marry him. And after a while he'd want me to work with him on a national network news program. And we'd be happy.

Because there was very little else to look forward to, the fantasy grew until Emily finally asked a nurse to show her how to make a long distance call on her room phone.

She remembered the number he'd given her. After three rings, he answered with an impatient, "What?"

She had planned on using her broadcaster's voice. She hadn't used it since she'd been admitted. Instead, she had reverted to talking in a breathy whisper to try to lessen the pain, and because she had gone to shallow breathing to avoid stretching the wounds around her chest and ribs.

"Hello, David, this is Emily," she said, hating it that she sounded like a little girl.

"Emily! Are you in town?" he asked enthusiastically.

"No, I'm in Utah. I'm in the University of Utah Medical Center. I was burned in a fire."

"That's awful," he said. "How are you getting along?"

"Not too good."

"I'm sorry to hear that."

"David, could you do something for me?"

"Of course I will."

"Could you find out if there's some new technique for treating burn patients that's not so painful and has better results? There must be, somewhere. I mean, you live back East where they do research on things like that. I don't want it to hurt so much, David, and I don't want to have any scars.

There must be some place where they can do it better than they're doing here."

"Well, sure, I can check around and see. But how would you get from there? Can you travel?"

Her voice became even more like a little girl's, and more desperate. "No, but maybe you could charter a plane and fly me out there."

"I see," he said softly.

I need something to bargain with or he's not going to do it, Emily thought.

"David, if you'll help me, and get me to a place where they can fix me up without so much pain, then I'll marry you. You'd like that, wouldn't you?"

There was silence on the other end of the line.

"David, I know you love me. I mean, you as much as told me so when we had dinner together. You asked me to go back to your apartment with you that night. You remember that, don't you?"

"Nothing happened," he said, suddenly on the defensive.

"I know."

"So, tell me again what you want from me," he asked.

"You were in love with me, David, I know you were."

"I'm in the middle of a meeting, Emily. I'll call you back later." He hung up.

The next day a small bouquet of flowers arrived, along with a note, which read, "All of us at *Evening News* wish you a speedy recovery."

That was the last she ever heard from David Alexander.

6

Emily couldn't sleep. She dreaded what was going to happen to her the next day. She knew she'd be unconscious during the surgery but, still, she feared what they were going to do to her.

She wasn't sure of the exact procedure for deep debridement, so as she imagined it, it became more awful each time. She pictured them scrubbing her injured skin with steel wool, the way her mother scrubbed a dirty pot.

Earlier in the day she'd complained to Brooke about ruining good skin to use as donor material for a skin graft.

"It's not going to be that bad, Emily," Brooke had said.

"Then why don't you let them do it to *you?*"

"You're right. But look at it this way. It's the quickest way to get healthy skin to replace the most badly burned areas of your body."

"How do they do a skin graft?"

"They attach the harvested skin over the debrided area, and the body does the rest. Isn't that amazing?"

"But what if it comes off?"

"They'll have you stay in bed three or four days to limit your movement."

Emily slept for a while but woke up again around four in the morning. She lay awake, watching as the darkness of the night slowly changed to the dull gray of the approaching day, a day of pain. *This is too much. How can I get through this? Everything I took pride in about me is gone, and there's nothing left.*

She thought back to the shower she'd taken the morning of her accident, of how wonderful it had been to have the water hitting the skin on her back and neck and shoulders and arms. She replayed in her mind how happy she'd been then, so full of hope for the future, so content with who she was, and so unaware of how blessed she was. She remembered clowning around in the shower, pretending the shampoo tube was a microphone, hoping for fame and fortune in some distant future, never realizing that even to be able to take a shower was a great blessing.

She thought about how independent she had been before the accident, when she didn't need help to wash herself or to go to the bathroom, when she didn't have people monitoring the amount of liquid that went in and the amount that came out. Being in the burn center had turned her private acts into public ceremonies.

She'd heard stories about people who kept family members hidden in the house. *That's the way I'll end up, shut away in a back bedroom, never going out except at night, afraid to come out for fear someone will see me. No job, no marriage, and no friends, my skin will still be raw with open wounds that will never heal, and I'll grow old, useless and unloved.*

Emily–1 is gone. Emily–2 is gone. What's to become of me now?

I can't get through this by myself. I need something to hold onto, something that will keep me going. I need some reason to keep living, because right now, if I had my choice, I would choose to die.

I need something to hope for. Something, anything.

She had met a girl once in high school who told her that

she'd turned her life over to Jesus. The girl had made her uncomfortable. She wasn't sure why. Maybe it was because Emily didn't want to turn her life over to anybody. She wanted to be the one in charge. Also, the girl wasn't a member of the Church, and so, the idea seemed foreign to Emily. It didn't seem like something Mormons did.

What was her name? It was very unusual. It was a grandma's name, like Faye or Nadine or Mable. It wasn't any of those but it was that kind of a name.

When she talked to me that one time, she stood too close and she spoke too enthusiastically. And she had bad breath and wore no makeup and stood so close she nearly pinned me against my locker.

She said that she'd given her life to Jesus. Well, Mormons don't do that. Mormons work hard and do what's needed to get the job done. That's what Mormons do. That's what I've always done.

But this is different. I can't make it through this by myself. I've tried and it's just too hard.

Every day I wonder if I'm over the worst part yet, but I never am.

All my life, when something's gone wrong, things have always eventually gotten better. But I'm not sure that happens with this. The worst is always ahead of me.

All the things that used to work don't work anymore.

What was that girl's name, the one who said she'd given her life to Jesus?

She always had her shirt buttoned all the way to the top button. And her hair was always matted down. And she had bad breath . . .

She had bad breath, and she stood too close, and her clothes were drab and ordinary, and she bragged about never watching TV, and she wrote religious slogans on her notebook, and she bragged that she left religious pamphlets in the bathroom. And she stood too close and she had bad breath and she talked about giving her life to Jesus . . .

And I walked away from her. And I can't even remember her name.

And now I am trapped with nowhere to go. And the only thing I can remember is a girl who stood too close and had bad breath and her hair was matted down and she asked me to give my life to Jesus.

What did that girl mean when she said she'd given her life to Jesus? Is that something they only do in other churches?

Give my life to Jesus? Sure, why not? He's welcome to it. I have no use for it now. Maybe he can make something of it now, because I can't.

I'm going to be the freak show they keep locked in her room so she won't scare little kids. Emily–2 is gone.

What would it mean to give my life to Jesus? How would my life be different? What difference would it make?

A passage of scripture came to her mind. *Come unto me, all ye that labour and are heavy laden, and I will give you rest.*

Oh, I need that so much, she thought. *I need to rest. I need someone to take my burden, and to carry it for a while, because I can't. It's too much for me.*

When she tried to think about giving her life to Jesus, the memory of the girl from school standing too close, speaking with too much fervor, her eyes glistening with emotion, kept getting in the way.

I don't want to be like that girl, she thought. *What did she mean when she said she'd given her life to Christ?*

Before my accident, how much did I think about the Savior? Oh, sure, during the sacrament, I tried to think about him. But even that was hard. There were always other thoughts coming into my mind. I think I'd try to remember that he'd suffered for my sins. But it's hard to remember every mistake I'd made the past week, every thoughtless comment, every time I passed by someone who could have used my help.

And yet in the sacrament prayer we promise to remember the Savior. I haven't done very well at that. Oh, I think about him, but not always. I don't even know what that would be like. How practical is it to think about him all the time?

Why is it the only person I've met who thinks about him all the time isn't a member of the Church, has bad breath, and isn't anyone I'd ever want to spend time with?

But now I can't do this alone.

Maybe I should try it. Maybe I should always remember him. Maybe I should keep his commandments. Then maybe I can have his Spirit to be with me.

Maybe I should do what I've been promising to do all this time.

What do I even know about the Savior? What is in my heart about him? I remember he cleansed ten lepers. That's a skin disease. He just said the word, and they left and as they walked away, their skin healed up. They must have been so happy. And yet only one returned to thank him. I would have run back and fallen at his feet and thanked him over and over again.

In the Book of Mormon it says he visited people after his resurrection. After he talked to them, he asked if there were any sick among them. And they were brought to him and they were all healed.

He was supposed to leave them, but he didn't. He couldn't just walk away. He had too much compassion not to help. When he looked into their eyes, they knew he loved them. He loved the sick, he loved the lame, he loved the blind, he loved the crippled.

He must love me too. He must know that I'm here. He must know that I'm thinking about him right now.

He must love me too. And if I'd been in that group of people in the New World that he visited after his resurrection, he'd have healed me, wouldn't he? He'd have looked into my eyes, and I would have seen the love in his eyes for me, and he'd have placed his hands on my head, and said a prayer. And when he removed his hands, my skin would have been restored to the way it was before the fire.

He would have done that for me then. I know he would. But what can he do for me now? Whatever he can do for me, I want him to do it. Whatever blessing he has for me, I want to claim it.

Lying in the gray light of early morning, she remembered a verse from the song "Away in a Manger." It had always meant a lot to her, but she usually didn't think about it except at Christmas. She mouthed the words.

Be near me, Lord Jesus; I ask thee to stay
Close by me forever, and love me, I pray.
Bless all the dear children in thy tender care,
And fit us for heaven to live with thee there.

That's what I want; that's what I need! That's what I must have if I'm going to survive this. Stay near me, Lord Jesus, I ask thee to stay close by me forever and help me, I pray.

She closed her eyes and thought a prayer. *Father in Heaven, please help me. I need you to help me get through this. It's so bad for me now.*

Your son Jesus Christ came into the world to save us, and he's done that for me. I know I've been forgiven for some of my sins. Mainly the ones I felt the worst about. But I need more than that now. I need him to take my pain, or at least make it so I can take it without wishing I were dead, because lately I've been wishing I had died in the fire. That's how bad it is for me now. Every time they move me it hurts so much I think I can't stand it anymore.

Father in Heaven, when the morning comes, when it hurts the worst, I will say a silent prayer. Please help me. You said you wouldn't give us more than we can take. Well, I can't take this, so please take some of the pain and heartache away. I will try to always remember your son, Jesus Christ, and keep his commandments.

Please, Father, help me get through this day.

She tried to come up with an image of the Savior that she could hold in her mind against the pain that was sure to come. She rejected the paintings she'd seen that showed him before a large group of people because she didn't want to feel like she was just one in a large crowd. She wanted to feel assured that he cared about her personally. She remembered a painting of him with a little girl on his lap. That was more of what she wanted. Except she wasn't a little girl. She would be a sophomore in college if she ever returned. And it was hard to imagine the Savior holding someone her age.

She wanted an image she could call to mind when the pain was the greatest. After some effort, it came to her.

She saw it as if it were a painting. She was sitting on a chair in the middle of a room surrounded by mirrors. She was wearing a brilliant white Sunday dress, and she looked the way she had before the fire. Except her head was bald, the way it was now.

Jesus stood behind her, holding his hands just inches above her, as if he were going to place them on her head and give her a blessing. And in the mirrors, the image of the two of them was repeated many times, in an endless progression of whiteness and beauty.

She looked at the Savior's face in the mirror. His attention was focused totally on her, and she could see in his eyes the love he had for her. She knew that he would give her a blessing every bit as wonderful as any blessing he had ever given anyone.

It was a marvelous image, and she vowed to keep it before her always.

Father in Heaven, please help me to know you love me,

and that Jesus Christ loves me, and that you hear my prayers, and that some good will come from this.

Please help me get through this day, and all the days that will follow. In the name of Jesus Christ, amen.

7

It was seven o'clock in the morning, but Austin had already been up for an hour. He'd taken his shower, gotten dressed, and spent thirty minutes studying his scriptures. After that he'd said his prayers and then gone into the kitchen to fix breakfast for Elder Briggs. They'd found that if Elder Briggs had something to eat a few minutes before getting up, he seemed to do better.

Austin knew the other missionaries would make fun of him if they knew he was serving his companion breakfast in bed. But Austin didn't care. The main thing was to try to keep Briggs healthy so they could get some work done.

Austin touched Elder Briggs' shoulder. "Elder, it's morning. I brought you something to eat," Austin said.

Elder Briggs sat up and took the tray, and Austin went in to get some water and some pills that had been recommended by a woman who ran a health food store. Briggs had been taking them for a week, and they seemed to be helping.

On the days when Elder Briggs said he felt well enough to work, they had taken nothing for granted. Every minute was valuable because they didn't know how long they could go before Elder Briggs would feel sick and need to return to their apartment.

Because they had no guarantees on how long their work day would be, they began to plan better, asking members for referrals instead of trying themselves to find people to teach. They also began praying that in spite of their weaknesses and limitations, the Lord would use them to bless others.

After a month of doing these things, Austin began to see his companion in a different light. By trying to imagine himself in Elder Briggs' place, Austin had become more compassionate, more tender, and more accepting of his companion's limitations.

They began to find some teaching opportunities.

Elder Briggs's health also began to improve. He was now able to work nearly every day, as long as he took it easy and didn't overdo it. By the end of the month, they were thrilled to have three people committed for baptism and two other families taking the missionary discussions.

Then one day, when they returned to their apartment for lunch, Austin found a letter telling him he was being transferred.

As he read the letter, all the feelings he'd had in the past about being a failure as a missionary, especially in comparison to his brothers, came flooding back. *I'm never going to have any baptisms,* he thought bitterly.

"I've been transferred," he said numbly to Elder Briggs.

"No, not now! Not when we're doing so good."

Austin couldn't hide his disappointment. "Can you finish up teaching the Wilcox family? And the Jones family . . ." Each name brought a new heartache that he wouldn't be there to see them baptized. " . . . And the Tremontons . . . and the Evanses . . . and Cory Jensen . . ."

"I'll take good care of them. But where are you going?"

Austin hadn't yet looked at his new assignment. He read quickly through a note President Merrill had penned, explaining the transfer. He said that one of the elders assigned to teach Vietnamese families in Chicago was going home because of a family emergency. "I'm asking you to fill in until he returns. I realize you don't know Vietnamese, but maybe you can pick it up. But even if you can't, Elder Billingsley needs a companion. Thank you. I appreciate the good you've done with Elder Briggs. Yours in Christ, President Merrill."

In his new area, Austin served as the silent partner to Elder Billingsley from Tucson, Arizona, who had learned Vietnamese in the MTC. Austin tried hard, but it wasn't an easy language to learn, and the people they taught spoke so fast it was hard to pick out any words he could understand.

When the next mission newsletter came, he learned that Elder Hastings had been called to serve as mission assistant and that Elder Briggs was to serve as district leader. The new medication seemed to have given Elder Briggs his health back, and Austin was happy for his former companion.

But that didn't mean that Austin didn't feel left out. Once again, others had been promoted ahead of him. However, he decided not to dwell on what might have been. *If this is what the Savior wants me to do, then I'll do it. It doesn't matter where I serve.*

In a letter home he told his folks about the people he'd helped prepare for baptism before his transfer. His mother wrote back: "I don't think it's right for you to do all the work and then for somebody else to come in and take the credit. Would you like your father to talk to your mission president to make sure it doesn't happen again?"

Austin answered the letter the same day he received it. "*Please* don't contact President Merrill. I am happy to serve wherever I'm asked."

Austin was unknown to most of the newer missionaries. The elders in his district knew that he worked hard and studied the scriptures with great enthusiasm, and they might have noticed, but probably didn't, that at every zone conference, he often went to the kitchen and helped out whenever he wasn't in meetings.

Elder Hastings, now serving as mission assistant, was at the next zone conference Austin attended. Apparently Hastings didn't realize Austin was in that zone, because when called on by President Merrill to speak, Hastings began by saying that he wanted to share an experience he had had while serving as district leader. Austin perked up.

"There was one area in my district that hadn't had a baptism in over a year and where the set of missionaries only worked about half the time. Well, we went in there and told them the same thing I'm telling you today, about first, you plan your work and then you work your plan. I began calling around every night to find out how each companionship had done that day. In a short time, things turned around, and in that area where there hadn't been a baptism for over a year, last month, they had four, and they are expecting more this month. Not only that, but one of the elders in that area, who hadn't been working all that hard, is now the district leader. So it just shows what you can do if you really decide to plan your work and then work your plan."

Austin smiled to himself; he had no ill feelings, but he couldn't help thinking: *Hastings is going to go through life thinking the sun rises in the morning just because he's planned it that way.*

When it came time to bear his testimony, Austin had nothing to brag about, so he chose to talk about his hero. "I was reading this morning in the Book of Mormon, about when the Savior, after he'd been resurrected, visited the people. They'd endured a horrible storm and earthquakes and had survived aftershocks. They'd also experienced a day with no light of any kind. It says they were talking to one another about what had happened, when they heard a voice . . ."

Austin opened his scriptures and began reading: "'And

they cast their eyes round about, for they understood not the voice which they heard; and it was not a harsh voice, neither was it a loud voice; nevertheless, and notwithstanding it being a small voice it did pierce them that did hear to the center, insomuch that there was no part of their frame that it did not cause to quake; yea, it did pierce them to the very soul, and did cause their hearts to burn. And it came to pass that again they heard the voice, and they understood it not. And again the third time they did hear the voice, and did open their ears to hear it; and their eyes were towards the sound thereof; and they did look steadfastly towards heaven, from whence the sound came. And behold, the third time they did understand the voice which they heard; and it said unto them: Behold my Beloved Son, in whom I am well pleased, in whom I have glorified my name—hear ye him.'"

Austin finished reading and looked over the pulpit at his fellow missionaries. "Have you ever wondered why the voice came three times? Why at first was it so soft they could not make out what was being said? Have you ever wondered about that? I have."

He wasn't sure anyone was paying any attention. Other elders had talked about their success as if that were a testimony.

Austin continued. "I can't say for sure, but I don't think this was some sound technician going, 'Testing, testing, testing.' I think we can assume that Father in Heaven is perfectly capable of adjusting the sound level so everyone can hear him.

"There were little children there who'd been terrified when the earthquakes came and when there was no light. Could it be that Heavenly Father didn't want to scare the little children, so he deliberately spoke very softly at first, so the children wouldn't be afraid?"

From his place on the stand behind Austin, Elder

Hastings leaned forward and whispered, "We don't have much time left."

"Take as long as you want," President Merrill corrected.

Austin continued. "If Father in Heaven is so sensitive that he is willing to repeat himself three times just so he won't scare little children, then he is also gracious enough to bless us when we try our best to serve him. It really doesn't matter where we serve. All that matters is that we do our best and try to pattern our lives after the Savior. Nothing else matters. Not even how many baptisms we get on our mission or whether we're a district leader or a zone leader or a mission assistant. Those are not our goals. Baptisms are even secondary to our main goal. Our main goal is to serve the Savior with all our heart, might, and strength."

After he said it, he heard Hastings whispering to President Merrill. *Hastings probably wants to refute that,* he thought.

But President Merrill let it stand.

Julia Brunswick, Austin's mother, liked to anticipate and plan. That was evident in her love of redecorating. She'd redecorated every home they'd ever lived in. With her, it was never just move in some new furniture or knock out a wall. Everything was planned out well in advance, down to the tiniest detail.

She liked to do that with her family, too. And so her husband, Lloyd, was not surprised when one morning at breakfast she said, "We need to think about the kind of girl Austin is going to marry."

"Can't that wait until he gets home from his mission?" he asked.

"If we're going to have any say at all in it, we need to start thinking about it now."

"Isn't it up to Austin who he marries?"

100

"Well, of course, but there are a few things we can do to help the process along."

"Like what?"

"I think we ought to be on the lookout for girls he can date."

"Do you have someone in mind?"

"Not yet. But he'll need someone who will help him in his career and be a good mother for our grandchildren. It wouldn't hurt, either, if she were poised, talented, and looked like she could be the wife of the governor of Utah."

"I don't recall Austin ever saying he wants to be the governor of Utah."

"It doesn't hurt to set your sights high. I'll be looking for someone for Austin, and you can look, too, in your stake calling. We need to set it up well before he comes home."

As she did in home decorating, Julia worked first on paper. She established some guidelines. The girl Austin was to marry would need to come from Utah. That would increase the chances the couple would live in Utah. Her father needed to be a professional—either a doctor, dentist, or an attorney. She herself should at least be a junior in college. Girls younger than that were not mature enough to fully invest themselves in their husband and children. She also needed to be talented in singing, or possibly play a stringed instrument, such as the violin, viola, or cello.

Once she had her list, Julia went to work trying to find girls who would qualify. She was always on the lookout.

Her plan was, once she decided on the girl of her dreams, she would start dropping brief hints about the girl in her letters to Austin. She would have to be subtle about it, but she could plant a few seeds.

In the midst of all this planning, while in the grocery store one day, she ran into Emily's mother, who told her how Emily was doing at the burn center.

"I should write Austin and tell him she's there. I'm not

sure he knows yet. Maybe if he wrote her a card, it would cheer her up."

"Oh, I'm sure it would. I really think she had a crush on him before he left on his mission."

"So I've heard," Julia said, recalling the stories Austin's friends had told about how Emily had thrown her arms around him and kissed him on the day of his farewell. It was time to change the subject. "How is Jeremy doing on his mission?"

"Oh, he's doing great. He was just called to be mission assistant."

"Really?" Julia said with a raised eyebrow. "How nice for him."

"Well, it's more responsibility, and it takes him away from what he most likes to do."

"Which is?"

"Teaching the gospel," Jeremy's mother said.

"Oh, yes, of course. Austin is doing well, too. The mission president had so much confidence in him that he asked Austin to learn Vietnamese and work with the Vietnamese refugees in the Chicago area."

"That must be a challenge."

"Oh, yes, I'm sure it is, but you know Austin. He loves a challenge."

Leaving the store, Julia felt upset that Jeremy was doing so much better than Austin was. *It's not fair,* she thought.

By the time she wrote her next letter to Austin, Julia had zeroed in on the person she had chosen for him to marry. Her name was Meredith Vance. She was the youngest daughter of the man many thought would be the next judge appointed to the Supreme Court of the state of Utah. The Vance family had moved into a house four blocks away—in an adjoining ward. Meredith was quite beautiful and also very poised. She was first chair cellist in the BYU Symphony Orchestra, and, she was majoring in family science.

Meredith was, in a word, *perfect*.

To condition Austin to the idea of dating Meredith, Julia planned out what she would say in each of her letters to him, from now until he returned from his mission. Her praise of Meredith's virtues could be no longer than one paragraph and had to be buried in the middle of the letter, so as not to tip him off.

To make sure her campaign went well, Julia sat down and wrote out all the segments about Meredith she would include in her letters to Austin until he came home.

In her first letter, she described Meredith's spirituality. Because she didn't want to cloud the issue, she chose not to convey the news that Emily had been burned in a fire and was in the burn center. *I'll wait until next week to tell him about Emily,* she thought.

I hired him an algebra tutor in junior high. I helped him earn his Eagle. I don't mind helping him find a wife, too.

I just want him to be happy.

8

When Emily woke up, she found her mother and father in her room. As soon as she opened her eyes, her mom stepped to her bed. Her father had been dozing in a chair, but he quickly got to his feet when he heard his wife's voice.

"Hello, sleepyhead, how are you feeling?" her mom asked.

"I'm not sure." Emily could hardly move because of the gauze dressings. "What day is it?" she asked. The feeding tube in her nose and throat made it difficult to speak, and her voice was hoarse and raspy.

"Monday night."

"Monday?"

"Yes. They did a skin graft on Friday."

"They say it went very well," her dad said.

"That's good," she said, still confused that it was Monday.

She wanted to be more responsive, but it seemed as though her mind could only process one thought at a time. And the thought it couldn't let go of was *It's Monday?*

Her parents stayed for a while but then, because she kept falling asleep, they said good night and left.

The next morning Brooke came to look in on her.

"Well, looks like you made it. You're looking good.

Everyone's really happy with how things went on Friday. Way to go, girl."

"It went okay then?" she asked.

"Very well from what everyone says. Looks like the graft is taking hold, so we're all pretty happy around here."

"That's good."

Brooke studied Emily's face. "You ready to do some work?" she asked.

"What kind of work?"

"Let me explain what's going to happen between your skin graft surgeries. Each morning you'll go to the tank room where they'll remove the gauze dressings and then put you in a tank of warm water for a few minutes. Doug will be there to help you exercise your arms and legs. After that, they'll check how your graft is doing, clean the burn wounds, and probably do a little more debridement. Then they'll apply a fresh layer of medication to the wounds and wrap you up again in clean gauze. You okay with all that?"

"I guess so." Emily said tiredly.

"That will take care of the mornings. After lunch, in the afternoons, you'll probably end up doing some more physical therapy. And then in the evening they'll do another dressing change. So you're going to be busy."

"Looks that way."

"But I have to tell you, everyone here is excited about how well things have gone for you so far."

"I'm glad," Emily said, but she was thinking, *I need to get ready.*

After Brooke left, Emily closed her eyes and, in her mind, prayed for help to be able to get through the day. *Please help me, Father in Heaven. I can't do this by myself. Please let me take advantage of what the Savior has done for me. Please help me stand the pain. Please, dear Father, please help me. Please help me.*

She thought about the Savior's life and tried to recall

again the miracles of healing he had performed. She also pictured herself in the room of mirrors with Jesus about to give her a blessing. *If I think about Jesus Christ and trust him to take away my pain, then maybe I can get through this,* she thought.

She would have liked to have more time to prepare herself, but an hour later they came to get her.

After transferring her from her gurney to the stainless steel washing table in the tank room, Red and Doug began removing the dressings. She tried not to cry out but sometimes she couldn't help herself.

"I'm sorry, Emily. I know it hurts," Red said. She could tell they were trying to be gentle, but whatever they did and no matter how slowly they worked, it all hurt.

Emily kept her eyes closed and prayed. That seemed to help.

After a while, she opened her eyes and, as if for the first time, really looked at Red and Doug. Doug was older than Red, almost completely bald, wore a handlebar mustache, and looked as though he hadn't had much sleep. Red was taller and bulkier than his partner, and he had freckled, hairy arms. She could tell by the set of his mouth and the way he was grimacing that he hated hurting her.

"Red?" she said.

"Yes?"

"Thanks for your help," she said.

He nodded his head.

"I just want you to know I'm grateful to you for caring. You, too, Doug."

Doug smiled. "Thanks, Emily. That's real nice of you to say. I know this is painful, and I wish we didn't have to hurt you, but the way to healing is through pain."

"I know."

As they continued removing the dressings, she went through the words to a song. She found herself saying over and over again in her mind, *Be near me, Lord Jesus, I ask thee to stay close by me forever, and love me, I pray.*

She felt a warmth come over her that wasn't just that of the warm, humid air they maintained in the tank room. It came from somewhere else, and, although it didn't totally take away the pain, it made it easier to handle.

She looked forward to lunch because that meant they'd be done with her for a while. But even lunch was a challenge. She wasn't very hungry, but they brought her more food than she'd ever eaten at one time in her life.

She took a few bites and then pushed her tray away.

The nurse who had delivered her lunch came back to check on her progress. "You have to do better than that," he said.

"I can't. I'm not that hungry."

"You have to eat if you want to get better. Your body needs the nutrients to repair itself."

"Okay, I'll try."

He was a bit overweight himself, and he grinned when he said, "Boy, what I'd give for permission to eat more."

She forced herself to eat and drink, but there was still enough on her tray for two or three others.

There were two large plastic trash containers in her room. When nobody was looking, she pulled one of them close to her and buried some of her food under the trash.

Her trick wasn't discovered, and that made her happy.

Two days went by.

Emily had a secret, but she didn't know whom to share it with. Her secret was that her faith in Jesus Christ was helping her get through her pain.

When she woke each morning, she would go over in her mind each activity of the day that would bring her pain, and then she would pray, whispering the words. "Father in Heaven, you said you'd never give us more than we can bear. Well, this is more than I can take. Please help me." She asked for help when her dressings were changed, help when she went through physical therapy, help on a day when a skin graft was scheduled, and help afterward, when she was confined to bed and had to remain in the same position for hours.

After she had prayed, she tried to think about the Savior's life, and how he had shown compassion for those who suffered hardship or pain.

She had asked Brooke to get her a Bible and look up a passage, which Emily then memorized. She said it to herself over and over again through the course of a day.

Come unto me, all ye that labour and are heavy laden, and I will give you rest.

Take my yoke upon you, and learn of me; for I am meek and lowly in heart: and ye shall find rest unto your souls.

For my yoke is easy, and my burden is light.

As each day progressed, she thought frequently about the pains the Savior had endured. She pictured him in the Garden of Gethsemane suffering for the sins of the world, himself amazed at the depth of the agony he was enduring, crying to his Father for relief. She pictured the angel who came to comfort him at that time. She pictured the mockery of his trial and the cruelty of the Roman guards who placed a crown of thorns on his head, then jammed the cruel points into his scalp. She pictured him being scourged with a whip and then being forced to haul the heavy cross piece through crowded streets while being mocked by the crowds that gathered to watch him struggle up the hill Golgotha. She pictured the nails being driven into his hands and feet and then his being lifted up upon the cross. And she thought about his agony as he hung there.

He suffered for me, so that I would not have to suffer. He took upon him my sins. I know he loves the whole world, but now I feel very strongly that he loves me. He knows me by

108

name. He knows where I am and what I'm going through. He has the power to help me get through this.

Then a warm feeling would come over her. It wasn't that the pain necessarily diminished, but she would feel a power to endure it. The sense of being loved would wash over her, and the relief would bring tears to her eyes. Then she would give a prayer of gratitude and try very hard to keep that feeling through the hardest parts of her day.

She did not tell the nurses because they would have an explanation, but, because it would be purely medical, it wouldn't be the right explanation. Brooke had become a friend. She was there consistently, explaining what the doctors and nurses were too busy to explain, providing help and assistance however she could. But Emily did not even tell Brooke about her secret.

Each morning, as she prepared herself mentally for the day's activities, she tried to picture the Savior: how he looked, how his voice would sound, what it would be like to look into his eyes. And when she did that, she experienced a tender, comforting presence. *He loves me,* she thought.

For the first time, she felt the reality of the Savior's love for her, not in some general way, but in a personal way— that he knew about her accident, that he knew she was undergoing great pain, and that he cared about her and would bless her.

It was, more than anything, something she felt, and felt deeply. She had always believed he was the Savior of the world, but, now, she knew something else: that he was *her* Savior, *her* advocate, *her* champion, and, yes, *her* friend. *I want to be his friend. I want to live so I'll merit that honor. I hope he will always be able to count on me. I know now that I will always be able to count on him.*

She found it difficult to explain any of this. She tried once with her mom and dad.

"Jesus is helping me get through this," she said.

"Of course he is, dear," her mother said.

"No, you don't understand. I mean he *really* is. I mean, *personally* helping me."

"He helps everyone," her dad said.

"He is my Savior and my redeemer. He is helping me get through this."

"You bet, he is," her dad said, as if he knew what she meant.

"You don't understand. It's like he's near me. He loves me. He really loves me. I'm sure of it."

"He loves everyone."

They still didn't understand.

Her mother gave a sideways glance at her dad. "She's under a lot of medication. It might be clouding her thinking."

Emily gave up trying to describe what she had discovered. What she was feeling was sacred to her, and she could not bear to have other people dismiss what she was feeling or attribute it to the medications she was taking. It was real, but she decided it was also deeply personal.

No one will ever understand what the Savior and Father in Heaven are doing for me. But I know. And I am so grateful. I will always be grateful.

I thought I had lost everything in the fire, but that's not true. I gained something too. From that loss comes me, Emily–3.

The next morning Brooke was with Emily when Dr. Beiser came by to examine her. When he was done, he said, "You're making good progress, Emily. Today we'll be fitting you for a burn scar support garment. Around here, we call them a *Jobst,* but that's just a brand name."

"What does it do?"

"It keeps constant, gentle pressure on the damaged

areas, and that keeps the scars from getting thick. Thick scars are less flexible and more unsightly."

"How long will I have to wear it?"

"Probably about a year and a half."

"Everywhere I go!"

"Yes, that's right. I know that seems like a long time, but, believe me, they do help."

Later that morning, the nurse who measured her for the pressure garment showed her a picture of what it would look like. The model in the picture, a young woman, was smiling. Looking at the brown, skin-tight sleeve, Emily thought to herself how phony the picture was. *I'll bet she's not even really a burn victim,* she thought.

The nurse explained that the pressure garment Emily would be wearing would come in three separate pieces: the top, a sort of tight-fitting turtleneck sweater that would cover her neck, chest, arms, and stomach; a pair of shorts, needed to protect donor sites where skin had been harvested for skin grafts; and a kind of a hood that would cover her chin, cheeks, and most of her head.

Learning to wear the compression garment was just one more thing. It was exhausting, thinking about all that she had gone through since her accident, and it never seemed to end. Every day brought something new: confronting the shock of seeing the damage done to her body, enduring debridement, going through the surgery, having to have her dressings changed, learning to live with a tube that ran up her nose and down her throat, doing the physical therapy, and enduring the daily pain. It was all more than it seemed possible to endure. The best thing about learning to wear the compression garment was that it was one of the last things she'd have to do before getting out of the hospital.

That night her home ward bishop came to visit her. At first sight, Bishop Ingersol, who taught biology at Weber State University, did not appear to be athletically gifted. His slim build and medium height hid his skill at racquetball, which he played nearly every day during his lunch hour. When he was younger, he had been ranked among the best players in Utah. And even now, in his late thirties, he kept open a standing invitation to the youth in his ward, that if they could get over ten points in a game that went to twenty-one, he would buy them a milkshake.

While in high school, Emily had noticed that the most rebellious boys in the ward seemed to get no more than eight or nine points in their first games against Bishop Inger-sol. He kept them coming back by saying, "I think a couple more games and you'll get that milkshake." With each game came encouragement to live gospel standards. Often they managed to win the coveted milkshake just before they left on their missions.

Bishop Ingersol explained something to Emily that her parents had already told her—that the members of the ward had all been fasting and praying for her that day. He had come to tell her the news as he himself was about to end his fast.

"Thank you, Bishop," she said. "Please thank everyone for me."

"And we've put your name on the prayer roll in the Ogden Temple. So, every hour that the temple is open, people will be praying in your behalf."

Emily had heard of that but never thought it would be something she would need in her life. Imagining those prayers made her cry. The tears welled up in her eyes, and she looked toward her bedside stand for a tissue. Bishop Ingersol quickly plucked a couple from the box and handed them to her.

Neither of them said anything for a few moments. Then Emily said, "Can I tell you something, Bishop?"

"Sure, anything. What is it?"

She thought he'd understand, but even so, she hesitated.

Finally, she said, "When I pray for help and think about Jesus Christ, it doesn't hurt as much."

Bishop Ingersol thought about that for a moment, then said, "There is no one more compassionate than the Savior. In fact, there's a scripture that tells us that. Have you got your Book of Mormon here?"

"I couldn't look it up anyway. It's hard for me to do any reading."

"I'll write it out for you," he offered.

"You don't have to do that," she said.

"I know, but I'd like to."

Bishop Ingersol excused himself to find a Book of Mormon and something to write on. Fifteen minutes later he returned.

"One of the hospital service volunteers found me some poster board and a marker," he explained.

He had hand-lettered the passage from Alma 7:11–12, in large enough print so Emily could read it from her bed:

And he shall go forth, suffering pains and afflictions and temptations of every kind; and this that the word might be ful- filled which saith he will take upon him the pains and the sicknesses of his people. . . . and he will take upon him their infirmities, that his bowels may be filled with mercy, accord- ing to the flesh, that he may know according to the flesh how to succor his people according to their infirmities.

The next day was similar to the day before except one of the physical therapists had her sit up in a chair and then try to walk. She was surprised by how weak she had become and how hard it was just to stand up and move her legs.

"That's real good," he said. "But can I make one sugges- tion? Most people, when they walk, swing their arms. You're holding them stiff. It makes you look like a robot."

113

"It'll hurt if I do that."

"I know, but try it just a little bit."

She tried again, this time with a tiny bit of arm movement.

"Good girl. We'll just keep working on it."

Every few days Brooke and Emily repeated the ritual of using a hand mirror to look at the damaged areas. Each time Brooke would ask, "What do you see that looks different?" And each time, Emily would try to point out areas where she thought improvement had taken place. But things progressed slowly, and it wasn't always easy to see a change. She was discouraged the healing wasn't going faster.

She decided to talk to Brooke.

"Sometimes I wish I'd died in the fire."

Brooke nodded. "I bet you do feel that way sometimes."

Emily was surprised that Brooke didn't try to talk her out of the way she was feeling.

"But you didn't die, Emily. So, what kinds of things are you going to do to get through this?"

"I don't know what it will be like when I leave here. I'm afraid people will make fun of me."

Brooke nodded. "I can't tell you that's not going to happen. Maybe we should talk about how you're going to cope with it, if it does happen."

"This never ends, does it?"

"But just look at all you've accomplished since you've been here."

Emily was in no mood for a pep talk. "Just leave me alone, okay?"

9

Later that day Emily broke down a little and confided in her mother her fears that she was going to be scarred forever. Then, after her parents returned from supper, her dad waited only a few minutes before bringing up the subject. He cleared his throat and said, "Your mother says you're worried about your face and neck and . . . uh . . . chest."

Emily was mortified, immediately wondering how many people her folks would talk to about her. She could just imagine what they would say—to people in the ward, people at work, people in the check-out line at the store—they'd all know; they'd all be talking about her.

Have you heard about the Latrell girl?

Oh, yes. Isn't it sad?

Emily couldn't stand the thought.

"We'll pay for whatever you need, even if the insurance won't," her dad was saying.

She looked closely at him. Tears were brimming in his eyes.

She couldn't handle it. "I'm really tired. Can you go now?" she said.

"Sure, whatever you want, Princess."

I'm not anybody's princess, she thought. *I'm a freak show.*

The next day, her roommate Molly dropped by the burn unit with a wedding announcement. After visiting for a few minutes, Molly said, "You know, I really wanted you to be in my wedding line, but, uh, . . . I mean, with you being burned . . ."

"Don't worry about it," Emily said.

"I'd love it if you could at least come to the reception."

"I don't think so."

"Will you be out of here by then?" Molly asked.

"I hope so."

"Then come. All our friends from college will be there."

"It'd be better if I didn't show up."

"Why do you say that?"

"I wouldn't want to freak out your guests."

"Don't say that, Emily. You're more important to me than any of them. Please come."

"I'll see how it goes," Emily said, certain though that she would not attend.

Molly was full of cheerful talk about her wedding plans and where they'd spend their honeymoon and where they'd live after the wedding. Although Emily tried to be happy for her, it was like hearing someone talk about visiting a new and inviting country when you know you're never going to make that trip.

I will never be married, she thought bitterly. *Who would want me now?*

She remembered how as a little girl, she and her friends would play getting married, pretending to walk down the aisle and dreaming about wedding gowns, cakes, flowers, and photos. In her childish games, she'd never put a specific face to her groom. It was just as well.

Whoever he was to be, I hope he has a happy life. She felt like screaming. *Just because I wanted to have a stupid bowl of noodles on a Sunday afternoon, I will never know what it's like to be cherished by someone. And I'll never have any children.*

Because she was no longer in critical condition, Emily was moved to another room the next day. Brooke showed up to see how she was doing.

"How are things going today?"

"Just great."

"You want to talk about it?" Brooke asked.

Emily thought about it. She shook her head.

"Would it be helpful to talk to someone who has had a similar experience?"

Emily thought about it. "I don't know. Maybe."

"I'll see what I can arrange."

The next day was Brooke's day off, but another child-life specialist, a young woman named Angelica, showed up shortly after lunch with a visitor.

"Emily, this is Elizabeth Gneiting. I'd like you to talk to her. I'll leave you two alone for a while."

Elizabeth was an attractive woman in her midthirties. She wore her hair long and was smartly dressed in a navy blue business suit and a white blouse, buttoned high on her throat. She was carrying a day-planner and a cell phone.

She stepped to the side of Emily's bed.

"Brooke tells me you're worried about how you're going to look," Elizabeth said. She spoke in a businesslike, professional way, and Emily wondered if she were a doctor or an attorney.

"I *know* how I'm going to look. I just don't like it."

"What happened to you?" Elizabeth asked.

Even thinking about the fire made Emily feel ill. She didn't want to describe it. Instead, she just said, "I got burned in a cooking accident."

Elizabeth nodded her head. "I was using gasoline to strip

some furniture in my basement when the water heater ignited the fumes. Stupid, huh?"

"You were burned?" Emily asked.

Elizabeth bent toward Emily and lifted her long brown hair away from her face and neck. "Take a look," she said.

Emily studied Elizabeth's face. The skin was a little red, but smooth and soft-looking.

"It looks good." Emily said.

"Thank you, but you wouldn't have said so five years ago. That's when it happened. I spent nearly two months being treated in this facility—going through all the things you are."

"But how badly were you burned?" Emily asked. "I mean, look at me. Was it this bad for you?"

Elizabeth nodded. "When I first saw myself, I wanted to die. I didn't think I'd ever be normal. But that's the thing about this place. They never give up. They just keep trying to make it better. If they're willing to do that, then I think you'd better not give up either."

Emily just stared at her.

"Look," Elizabeth said. "I know all about the pain and the long nights and the fears you're experiencing. It's not easy, and only those who go through it can appreciate how hard it is. But things improve. It may never be as good as it was, but life goes on. Honest. You need to hang in there and not get discouraged. If you're willing to work with them, they can do miracles in this place."

Emily looked at Elizabeth, not even daring to hope she could look as good as the attractive and confident woman standing next to her bed.

"Do you really think so?" Emily asked.

"I *know* so," Elizabeth said. She took a business card out of her planner and put it on the nightstand. "Listen, if you ever want to talk, call me at this number, night or day. I'll always have time for you."

118

"Thank you."

"You're quite welcome. Well, I'd better go. I need to catch a plane. But, remember, call me anytime."

When her parents came that night, the first thing Emily said was, "I'm not going to be ugly." She told them about Elizabeth's visit.

During her parents' visit, her father sat in a chair and kept dozing off. Looking at him, Emily noticed that his hair had thinned considerably and was more gray than she remembered.

"You look tired, Dad," she said.

"Just getting old, I guess."

"You might as well tell her," her mom said.

Emily had never seen her father embarrassed, but he seemed to be so now. He hesitated before saying, "Well, I'm a paper boy. Isn't that something? You'd think I'd have done that when I was a kid, but, hey, I never was very good at timing."

"You've got a paper route?" Emily asked.

"Yeah, but don't picture me riding a bike from house to house—that's not what I do. I do rural delivery, so I mostly drive around and put the papers in boxes on the same posts where they have their mailboxes."

"What time do you do that?" she asked.

"Oh, pretty early."

"Tell her."

"Well, I get up at four. I'm usually done by seven, so that gives me time to go home, have some breakfast, and get to work. So it works out real well."

"But why would you do that?"

He looked uncomfortable.

Her mother answered for him. "We're concerned the insurance isn't going to cover all these medical bills," she said.

Her dad interrupted, "You don't need to worry. They'll cover all the basic costs, but, . . . well, . . . I want you to have every operation they say you should have . . . even if the insurance won't pay for it," he said.

He's doing this for me, Emily thought.

Emily had never felt close to her father. It seemed he was always at work, and when he wasn't at his job at the super-market, he spent his time doing yard work for other people. In the summer, he had hardly been at home at all, usually working until dark. He did yard work most of the time she was growing up, until he hurt his back and began having trouble lifting his mowers in and out of the bed of his pickup truck. Emily had never given much thought to why he worked so much. All she did was resent his never having time for her and wish that he were as funny and personable as some of her friends' fathers.

I've never appreciated him, she thought. *He's always been in the shadow of my mother. We put him there, and he has stayed there because he thought that was where we wanted him.*

He's always been the weak parent. I've known that since junior high school. He was always saying, "Go ask your mother." So after a while I quit even asking him. And that made him irrelevant.

He's getting older, and someday he'll die. And maybe he'll go to his grave thinking of himself as a failure because Mom and I paid so little attention to what he did for us. I've never even thanked him for what he's provided for us or for him being dependable. And now he's got a paper route. For me.

What do you wish for, Daddy? A daughter who appreciates what you do for her? Or is that too much to ask? Have you given up on that?

"Daddy?" she asked through her tears. It had been a long time since she'd called him *Daddy*.

"Yes, Princess."

"Thank you for working so hard for me."

"I wish I could do more."

"Could you give me a priesthood blessing?"

He pursed his lips and looked away. "Isn't there somebody else you'd like to have do that? We could get the bishop to come, or President Fletcher."

"No, I want you. You're my father, and I want a father's blessing."

During the blessing, Emily felt the influence of the Holy Ghost when her father rested his fingertips on her head and, through both their tears, gave her a blessing.

"Don't worry about a thing," he said.

"I won't, Daddy. I know you'll take good care of me."

As the time for her to leave the hospital approached, Emily began to realize how grateful she was for the care she had received in the burn unit.

"Red, I think you're the greatest," she said one morning in the tank room.

Red laughed. "Sure you do, Kid. How could you help it?"

"What about me?" Doug asked.

"You're the greatest, too," she said.

"We can't both be the greatest," Red said. "I think I'm just a little bit greater than you, Doug. What do you really think, Emily?"

"I love everybody here," she said. "I'll miss you guys when I leave."

Red laughed. "Look, sometime when you're missing us, just go slam the car door on your hand, and then you'll remember us, and it'll seem just like old times."

"Thanks. I'll do that."

"You ready to hurt?" Red asked.

"I'm ready. I know you're only trying to help me get better."

"I wish we could bottle that good attitude of yours. We could use more of it in this place," Doug said.

A few days later, she had her second skin graft. Again, the procedure took two days—one day to harvest some skin, this time from her thighs, and the second day to do the actual grafting.

A few days later, Dr. Beiser was examining the new skin graft. "Looking good," he said. "How do you feel?"

"I don't have much good skin left, do I? You've taken it all."

He nodded. "We'll let you heal up for a while. But you'll be having skin grafts off and on for the next year."

"I will?"

"Oh, yes. We don't give up easily. We'll probably be sending you home in a few days, but then we'll bring you back, from time to time, for more grafting as the need arises and the healing progresses."

As the time approached for Emily to be released from the hospital, she began to fear leaving the secure and supportive environment. One minute she couldn't wait to leave, and the next she would be nearly in tears at the thought of leaving Red, Doug, Brooke, and all the others who had worked so hard in her behalf. She'd also made friends with some of the other patients, and she knew she'd miss them.

There were some things, of course, to be excited about, one of them being getting some privacy back into her life. She hated having other people give her sponge baths. She was also looking forward to eating her mom's cooking and being able to go in the backyard and see the flowers and hear the birds in the morning, and even going into the kitchen to fix herself something to eat. She looked forward to being in her own room and listening to her favorite CD.

She was told by the staff that she would be kept busy at home, taking care of herself. Twice a day she would need to put ointment on the damaged areas. And, of course, she would be wearing the pressure garment all the time, except for the time she would be allowed to take it off to bathe herself.

She was given two sets of compression suits to wear. She chose a white and a blue pair for her shorts but decided on peach for the turtleneck sweater part and also for the top she'd wear on her face, neck, and head. She thought the neutral tone would most nearly match the color of her skin.

She feared going back into the world. She dreaded having people stare at her and wondered what would be said about her behind her back. Brooke seemed to understand her fears, but she encouraged Emily to go back to college in the fall, go shopping at least once a week, and to otherwise try to get back to a normal routine as soon as possible.

"That will be hard to do."

"I know, but look at what you've already accomplished. Everything we asked you to do here was hard, but you did it! If you can get through what you've gone through here, you can get through anything. You're stronger than you think you are."

Even though she was going to be living at home, Emily would still need to return to the burn center every day for physical therapy. She also still had several skin graft operations ahead of her.

Finally the day came when she was to be released. She was anxious to go, but there was always more red tape to be cut through. *It just never ends,* she thought as she and her mother received some more last-minute instructions about what they would need to do once Emily got home.

"When am I going to be released?" Emily complained.

"Real soon."

"That's what you said the last time I asked you."

"It's even sooner than that."

Emily was packed and ready to go. She was wearing the

compression garment. All that was left uncovered was part of her forehead, her eyes, and her nose and mouth. She thought the hood made her look like one of Santa's helpers.

The hair on her head was still mostly gone, but was beginning to grow back. It was more like a crew cut now. From a certain angle, looking in the mirror, she looked like a fourteen-year-old boy. That was not something Emily was especially proud of.

Her mother had invited everyone on the staff to a going-away party. And at the appointed time, everyone gathered in her room.

Emily hadn't expected a celebration, and for a moment she didn't know what to say. Finally, she said, "This is really great of you guys to see me off like this."

"You've been a good sport and kept a good attitude all the way through. You've made our jobs easier," Doug said.

"We just wish everyone who comes here could be as cooperative as you've been," Brooke added.

"I was starting to think of this as my home. I know I'm going to miss you all."

There was a cake and some cans of cold soda pop. While they ate, they remembered the good times, the jokes, the wisecracks, the long talks. And then it was time to go.

Emily said good-bye to each of the staff members. Even though it was painful to do so, she hugged them all. Pain had become irrelevant. She'd learned to put herself through pain because sometimes the rewards made it worth it—like hugging these wonderful caring people whom she now thought of as her second family.

She didn't want to leave.

"When you're rich and famous like Barbara Walters, remember us, okay?" Brooke said.

"That's probably not going to happen now."

"I don't believe that. From what I've seen, I don't think there's anything you can't do if you set your mind to it."

A nurse stuck her head into the room from the hall. "We've got an admission, ETA 85 minutes. He's being transported from Moab."

Now everyone had work to do. The staff quickly said good-bye and hurried out of the room.

Brooke stepped close to Emily and kissed her on the cheek. "Come see us anytime you want, okay?"

"Sure, I will. Thanks a lot."

A nurse pushed Emily in a wheelchair while her mom walked alongside, carrying an armful of supplies. Then the nurse waited with Emily while Emily's mom went to bring the car up to the hospital entrance.

This was the first time she'd been outside for thirty-one days, except for two times during her stay when Red had put her in a wheelchair and taken her outside, where they'd argued over which university, USU or the U of U, has the most beautiful campus.

On the way home, even though it was hot outside, Emily found she needed to have her window open. After having been stationary so long and with so many drugs in her system, the motion of the car made her carsick, but with the window open it was better.

"Do you want me to turn the air conditioner off?" her mom asked.

"No, leave it on."

"With your window wide open?"

"Yes, that's right. It's better for me if the window's open."

"Whatever you say," her mother said.

Oh great, she's mad at me already, Emily thought.

Much of what was left of the summer was taken up by daily trips from their home in Ogden to the burn unit at Salt Lake City for physical therapy. On the way home, Emily and her mom would usually go through the drive-through at a fast-food place for lunch. Once they were back in Ogden, her mother would frequently drop Emily off and then go shopping or run other errands.

She never asks me if I want to go shopping with her, Emily thought after days of never going anywhere except to the hospital and back. *Is she embarrassed to be seen with me?*

She didn't ask her mother because she was afraid her mother's response would confirm that suspicion.

One big problem was that Emily had begun losing weight. Until just before she was released from the burn unit, Emily had remained hooked up to the feeding machine. She'd also been given huge amounts of food to eat at each meal.

But with the feeding tube gone, it was up to Emily to get enough calories, and it was an up-hill race that she was losing. Within the first week, she'd lost almost ten pounds.

"You've got to eat more," her mother said.

"How can you say that? All I do is eat."

"How about if I put a raw egg into your chocolate milk?"

"That sounds awful."

"You won't even be able to taste it."

"Don't do it."

"We have to do something, or they'll put you back in the burn center."

"I'm doing the best I can," Emily protested.

"I'll figure something out," her mom muttered.

The next time her mother brought her chocolate milk, one taste was enough for Emily to know there was a raw egg in it. She waited until her mother was in the garden, then threw it down the drain and poured herself a regular glass of chocolate milk.

When members of her home ward found out she needed to eat a lot in order to help her skin heal, they kept bringing in fresh baked bread, vegetables, desserts, casseroles, and baskets of fruit. And with each gift came love and caring. Emily was often brought to tears by their generosity. Even when she wasn't hungry, she'd eat a little of whatever was brought just to demonstrate her appreciation.

Emily's suspicion grew that her mother was ashamed to be seen with her in public. She was also growing weary of her dependence on her mother for every little thing. She began to push herself and set a goal to be able to bathe, attend to the damaged skin, and dress herself with no help. Within a month, she was doing it.

I'm not going to be the spinster daughter who's kept in the back bedroom and never comes out, she thought. *I'm scared to death of going out in public, but I'm not going to just sit around here for the rest of my life. I've got to get out of this house once in a while. I've got to have a life besides feeling sorry for myself and watching television.*

For the first four weeks she was home, Emily didn't attend church, but the bishop assigned two members of the priest quorum to come to her house each Sunday and give her the sacrament. They didn't stay long, and it was never the same ones twice. Most of the boys didn't have much to say, and they would barely look at her. They just seemed to want to get the job done and get out of there.

Emily knocked on her parents' bedroom door at 6:00 o'clock on a Sunday morning.

"Come in," her mother said. Her dad was still out delivering papers.

"I want to go to church today," she said.

"Are you sure?"

"Yes, I'm sure."

Her mother sighed. "Well, we'd better see about getting you ready then."

"Thanks, but I can do it myself."

Everything took a long time, but she wouldn't let her mother help.

Fifteen minutes before church started, she was in the

bathroom, about to put on the headpiece of her compression garment. At first she had thought she'd put on eye shadow and lipstick, but since she looked like a boy, she decided the makeup would make her look more like a clown than a girl. She decided to go without any makeup.

It probably doesn't matter anyway, she thought. *The way I look, is anyone going to notice if I'm wearing makeup?*

Emily dawdled just enough to make sure she and her parents arrived five minutes after the meeting began. They sat near the back, in the overflow area. She was glad they were late. She didn't want people asking questions or staring at her. Her dress fit poorly over her compression suit, and she imagined she looked like a boy who'd gone scuba diving and had come to church with the top part of his wet suit still on.

They sang the sacrament song, then the prayer on the bread was said, and the deacons fanned out across the congregation. The deacon who served Emily's row simply handed the tray to the person on the end of the row. He didn't seem to even notice Emily.

This isn't so bad, Emily thought.

She spent the time while everyone was partaking of the sacrament looking around, trying to determine if anyone was staring at her. Nobody seemed to be. She felt relieved. While getting ready for church, she'd imagined little children going into hysterics when they saw her, but that didn't happen.

The prayer was said on the water, and trays were carried throughout the congregation.

Emily spotted two teenage girls talking to each other four rows up, but they didn't seem to be talking about her. A baby began crying and had to be carried out.

This isn't too bad, she thought. *Just like usual.*

She took the water without thinking and passed the tray along. As she did so, Emily suddenly experienced a wave of guilt.

I'm supposed to be remembering Jesus Christ and his atonement. I just renewed a promise to always remember him and keep his commandments. And what am I doing instead? Thinking of myself. I could have died, but my life was spared. Now I'm back in church, but instead of being grateful, all I've done is worry about people laughing at me. I should be concerned about what the Savior thinks instead of worrying so much what other people think.

The only thing that got me through my pain was relying on Him. He was there for me; now I can't even focus for a few minutes on being grateful.

She tried to force herself to think about the Savior, but sacrament time was almost over. Her last-minute thoughts of Jesus brought no comfort—just a feeling of frustration and guilt.

I missed an opportunity to remember the Savior. I must never do that again.

As the meeting progressed, a deacon, the bishop's messenger, came off the stand and walked to the back of the chapel. When he came to where Emily and her parents were sitting, he handed Emily a note. Bishop Ingersol had written: "We'd like to have you bear your testimony and briefly share your experience after our last scheduled talk."

She showed the note to her dad. "I can't do it," she whispered.

He put his hand on hers. "I think you should," he said.

The deacon didn't care either way; he'd done his duty. He returned to his place on the stand.

Her dad leaned over and whispered in her ear. "Just bear your testimony," he said softly.

She closed her eyes and took a deep breath, waiting to be introduced and dreading the long walk to the front of the chapel.

When the concluding speaker finished, the bishop stood at the pulpit and said, "As many of you know, Emily Latrell was accidentally burned while she was going to school in Logan. She has spent about a month undergoing treatment in the burn center at the University of Utah, but she's back with us now. Emily, we're glad to have you home. Before we close, we'd like to hear your testimony and have you tell us a little about your experience."

Emily stood up and walked slowly to the front of the chapel. She kept her eyes straight ahead, but knew that everyone was looking at her. Bishop Ingersol smiled at her as she reached the stand and walked to the pulpit. She stood there for a moment, her head lowered, feeling breathless, and not knowing exactly how to begin.

Finally, she raised her eyes and looked out across the congregation. Everyone was looking at her expectantly. Some were smiling, and a few looked as though they might be ready to cry. She had known most of these people since she was a little girl. Some had been her Primary teachers, her Young Women teachers and leaders, and Sunday School teachers. She saw their former bishop smiling at her. They were people who loved her.

She began speaking. "I'm glad to be back here with people I love . . . in my own ward . . . I worried about coming today because I was afraid people would make fun of me . . . for the way I look. The reason I'm wearing this 'elf suit' is that it helps my skin grafts heal the way they're supposed to. I know you may have questions. It's okay to come up to me and ask, but if you make fun of me, it'll make it very hard for me to want to come here every week.

"I want to thank my mom and dad for being such a support and help to me. I love them both even more than I ever have before.

"When Bishop Ingersol visited me in the hospital, he told me that many of you were praying for me and that you held a special fast in my behalf. I would like to thank you so much for that. Your prayers helped tremendously. Also, I

130

would like to thank those of you who have brought food since I have been home or have shown your love and concern in other ways. I am so grateful for all the support you've given me and my family.

"I'm grateful to my Father in Heaven and to his son Jesus Christ for sustaining me and strengthening me. They love us so much. I found that out for myself while I was in the hospital."

She felt a rush of emotion. She wanted to say more, but she didn't trust herself not to break down completely. She concluded by saying, "I know that Jesus Christ is my Savior, and that he loves me. I bear that testimony in the name of Jesus Christ, amen." And then she returned to her seat at the back of the chapel.

After announcing the closing hymn and prayer, Bishop Ingersol said a final word: "We all need to look out for Emily. We need to be careful that we don't bump into her or pat her on the back too hard, and that we give her our love and support. And let's continue our prayers in her behalf. She still has much to go through."

On Tuesday of the next week, while on their way home from physical therapy at the burn center, Emily asked her mom, "What are you going to do after we get home?"

"I thought I'd go to the mall. Do you need me to pick up anything for you?"

"No, but I want to go with you."

"Really?"

"Yes."

"Are you sure you're ready for that? People can be so cruel."

"I know that, but I still want to do it."

Her mother gave a troubled sigh. "Well, all right, if that's what you want."

"You don't have to tag along with me. We can separate

after we get to the mall and agree to meet up at a certain time."

"Why would I do that?"

"Well . . . you know . . . if you'd be ashamed to be seen with me."

"Emily! Do you really think I'd be ashamed to be seen with you?"

"I don't know."

"It's just that I wouldn't want you to get hurt because of what someone says."

"I can't live my life being afraid of what people might say."

"All right, we'll go shopping. Do you need anything?"

"I need clothes."

"What for?"

Although she hadn't said anything about it, Emily had been thinking of it for days.

"For when I return to USU in the fall."

Her mother quickly glanced at her. "You can't be serious."

"I am."

"It's much too early for you to even be thinking of that."

"I can't stay in my room like a good little burn victim. I want my life back."

"Your life can't be the way it was."

"I know that, Mother, but at least I can be in college."

"What about physical therapy? How are you going to get to the burn center from Logan?"

"There must be somebody in Logan who can do it."

"What about the other operations you'll need?" her mother asked.

"I'll schedule them on holidays."

"Why do you have to push yourself so hard?"

"Because I'm afraid that if I don't get out soon, that after a while I'll be content to stay at home and never go out."

"I'm afraid of how you'll be treated."

"I'm scared to death about that, too, but I have to at least try."

"I don't want you to be hurt."

"I know. But don't worry. I'm the master of pain."

After they got home, they agreed to leave for the mall in half an hour.

Emily lingered in the bathroom looking at her reflection in the mirror. *I look like someone who's been in a fire,* she thought. *I guess that's okay, because that's what I am—someone who's been burned in a fire.*

What will I do if somebody comes up and slaps me on the back? And how can I try on clothes if I can't lift my arms above my head?

Am I really sure I want to do this? I don't want people staring at me like I'm some kind of freak. All I want is for people to leave me alone.

Tears started to roll down her cheeks. She was eighteen years old. Everything she had grown accustomed to about her appearance had changed. It was as though she'd moved into someone else's body, and that, too, a body she could no longer rely on—a body that required hours of care every day, a body that was scarred and tender and marked with redness.

This is like being at the burn center and having to work through my pain.

Going shopping is just something I have to do.

It was not a busy time in the mall. They walked slowly to their first destination. Some passersby stared at Emily, until she met their gaze, then they quickly looked away.

They entered their first store to look for clothes.

"May I help you?" a clerk asked Emily's mother. He was in his midtwenties, a flashy dresser.

"We're looking for some slacks."

"Great. What size is your son?"

Emily turned away. *I should never have come here.*

"Actually, this is my daughter. She was in a fire."

"Oh, I'm really sorry. I've been taking antihistamines for a sinus infection. I guess I'm not thinking too clearly. Let's see, let's look over here."

They walked to a rack of pants. "What did you have in mind for her?"

"Well, something for college."

"Any particular color?"

"You can talk to me," Emily said.

"Oh, sorry. I didn't know."

After pawing through the racks, Emily finally found a pair of tan slacks she liked.

"Would you like her to try them on?" the clerk asked her mother.

Emily grabbed the pair of slacks and headed for the changing room.

"You could try them on at home, Emily, and then just bring them back if they don't fit."

"I always try things on at the store," she said, entering the changing room.

"I'd better go help her," her mother said to the clerk.

Emily stuck her head out through the curtain. "I can do it myself."

Five minutes passed.

"How are you doing in there?" her mother asked.

"I'm okay."

"Do you need any help?"

"No, I'm fine."

"Would you mind if I went to the drugstore for a minute? I need to fill one of your prescriptions."

"No, go ahead. I'll be okay."

After finally getting the slacks on, Emily looked at her reflection in the mirror in the changing booth. They were belted, but even cinched up tight, they were way too big.

134

She took them off. She would have to go to at least one size smaller.

"Excuse me," she called out.

No answer.

She looked out through the curtain. The clerk was at the counter, his back to her, talking to someone on the phone. Emily looked down at herself. Although she wasn't wearing slacks, because of the compression shorts and shirt, she'd never been more covered up in her life.

What does it matter? Everyone thinks I'm a guy anyway. She walked out to the rack, picked out a smaller size, and returned to the dressing room.

The smaller size fit better but was still a little loose. *I'll be gaining weight someday, so I'd better get these.*

She looked at the size. The last time she'd worn that size waist, she'd been in eighth grade.

A few minutes later she stepped out of the dressing room wearing her new slacks.

It was a moral victory.

The summer passed slowly for Emily. She couldn't hold a job, and she had no social life. Besides going to physical therapy, she spent some time during each day taking care of her skin grafts—rubbing ointment on them in an effort to keep the grafted skin moist, supple, and healthy. The rest of the time, she mostly hung out in the house, watching television and killing time.

Every time she applied the ointment, she looked at her scars and the deformity of her body. She felt ugly, and her condition seemed like something shameful, something to keep hidden from the world.

Wanting to prove she could take care of herself, Emily did her own laundry, washing her clothes in the washing machine but rinsing out her pressure garments by hand, rolling them in a towel to soak up the water, and hanging them on a clothesline on the back porch to dry. At first it scared her to use the stove, but she also began doing some of the cooking for the family.

In mid-July she got a letter from Utah State University confirming her class schedule for the fall term.

"Are you sure you're ready to do this?" her mother asked.

"I am. I can't stay in the house the rest of my life. I've talked about this with the staff at the burn center. They agree I should go."

"It's too soon," her mother said.

"Are you waiting for the time when I'll be exactly the same as I was before the fire? I don't think that's going to happen. Do you?"

They had a heated discussion. The more objections her parents put up, the more determined Emily was to prove them wrong, and the more certain she sounded that she could handle any problem that might come her way while at college.

Finally her parents gave their reluctant permission.

That night, alone in her room, her own doubts returned. She was haunted by every exaggerated claim she'd made to her parents.

What if they're right? she thought. *What if it is too soon?*

In a barely audible voice, to try to get some courage, she sang the song that had helped her get through the burn center:

Be near me, Lord Jesus; I ask thee to stay
Close by me forever; and love me, I pray.
Bless all the dear children in thy tender care,
And fit us for heaven to live with thee there.

And then she picked up the letter from USU and looked once again at the classes she would be taking in the fall.

10

———

Austin and his companion were teaching a Vietnamese family of four: a husband, his wife, and two grade-school aged children. On the second discussion, Austin taught part of the lesson. Even though he struggled with the language, the family encouraged him with their smiles and nods. Austin understood about half of what they said, which was a great improvement over what it had been.

When he and his companion returned to their apartment that night, there were three letters waiting for him.

The first one was from Jeremy, Emily's big brother. He told of his success in California and about serving as mission assistant. *I'm happy for him,* Austin thought. But at the same time it was hard not to compare himself with Jeremy.

It doesn't matter, he thought. *I'm serving to the best of my ability, in the place where the Lord called. Nothing else matters.*

Jeremy also wrote: "I guess by now you've heard about Emily. After a month of being in the burn center, she's finally home. She says she's going to return to school in the fall, but my mom worries it's too soon. I'm sure she'd appreciate hearing from you. I hope you'll also include her in your prayers."

Austin was stunned. He read the news about Emily over

again. He hadn't heard anything about her being burned. He would have thought his mother would have written him about it.

He vowed to buy a get-well card and send it to Emily.

The second letter was from his mom.

"Do you know your mission president's birthday? If you can find it out, it might be a nice gesture to send him a birthday card. Doing something like that is always thoughtful. Your father always sends birthday greetings to his clients. Just a thought.

"You remember me telling you about Meredith Vance? Last Sunday she played her cello in sacrament meeting. She did an excellent job. Her mother told me Meredith plays first-chair in the BYU Symphony Orchestra.

"I had a chance to talk to Meredith after church. When I told her about you learning Vietnamese, she said she had spent a week in South Vietnam last summer, providing music for the BYU Folk Dance Ensemble. She said she found the people there very kind. She told me to say something to you in Vietnamese. I wish I could remember what it was. I'll have to write it down the next time I see her."

It made Austin angry to think that his mother would tell him about a girl he'd never met, and, at the same time, neglect to inform him that his best friend's sister had spent a month in a hospital.

She's trying to manipulate me again, grooming me for when I get back so I'll fall in line and be the son she wants me to be. Just like in Scouts when she made sure I made Eagle.

The third letter was from the mission office. Austin didn't think anything about it because the elders were always getting mailings from the staff. He was pretty sure he knew what it was about. He had ordered a large-print copy of the Book of Mormon in Vietnamese for an elderly woman who had been baptized just before he came into the area.

When he opened the envelope, though, he knew it

wasn't about the Book of Mormon. It was a letter written on mission stationery. He read the message quickly, then, out of shock, sat down.

He was being assigned to work in the mission office as a companion to Elder Lambert, the mission secretary, and would be managing the commissary. Austin's first thought was, *I'll be working with Elder Hastings.*

It was almost too much to take. *Hastings is one of the most self-centered, arrogant people I've ever known. How will I ever be able to stand working with him?*

Two days later, at the mission office, Austin was being trained in his duties by Elder Nichols, who would be going home the next day. "The only bad part is you have to be in the office with Elder Twinkle Toes."

"With who?"

"Twinkle Toes. Hastings. He's sort of an office joke around here."

"How come?"

"Don't you know?"

"Not really."

"Everything good that happens in the mission, it's because of him. Everything bad that happens, it's somebody else's fault. You'll see."

President Merrill, Elder Hastings, and his companion were out of town for the day. During lunch, the office elders made some more snide remarks about Elder Hastings. Austin joined in, doing an imitation of Elder Hastings giving a talk at zone conference. It was very funny, and everyone laughed.

For the rest of the afternoon, Austin kept to himself, doing an inventory of everything in the commissary. He felt guilty for making fun of Elder Hastings—not that the arrogant missionary didn't deserve it.

He partially closed the door to the commissary and sat

down behind a stack of books, in a position where he'd be out of sight of anyone walking by and looking in.

He closed his eyes and mouthed the words to a silent prayer. *Father in Heaven, there must be a reason why you've called Elder Hastings as mission assistant. People here in the office make fun of him. I did it too, today at lunch. I don't feel good about it now, though.*

Father, in many ways, my mission has been a huge disappointment. At least compared to what I thought it was going to be. I thought I'd come here and have a lot of baptisms, but that hasn't happened. And that I'd be a leader like my brothers. It seems like I go from one bad situation to another. And just when I'm starting to get on top of things, then I get transferred.

And now I'm in charge of the mission commissary. Who cares about that? All I'll be doing is wrapping packages and sending out books and tapes the elders and sisters order. It's not all that hard. Anyone could do it. I'm stuck here. At least that's the way I feel now.

I probably shouldn't have made fun of Elder Hastings behind his back. But he brings it on himself. I'll try not to do it anymore. I'll just keep my mouth shut when others are making fun of him. And I'll do my best to do a good job in the commissary.

The next day Austin found that merely being quiet at lunch was not enough. Because his silence was interpreted as agreement, he excused himself, saying he needed to finish up an inventory of supplies, and ate the rest of his lunch alone, in the commissary.

While he was eating, he looked up the word *backbiting* in the index of his triple combination. The definition that meant the most to him he found in D&C 88:124–125: "Cease to find fault one with another. . . . And above all things, clothe yourselves with the bond of charity, as with a mantle, which is the bond of perfectness and peace."

The door was partially open, and he could hear the elders talking. They were laughing, making fun again of something Elder Hastings had said.

This is like a small, exclusive club, he thought, *and all you have to do to join is make fun of Elder Hastings, and then wink and grin at each other every time he tries to do his job. Well, it isn't right, and I'm not going to do it while I'm here. I'll do my job the best I can and stay out of everybody's way.*

Later that day Elder Hastings and his companion returned with President Merrill. The jokes ceased but there were secretive nods and winks among the office staff at things Elder Hastings said. Once again, Austin retreated to what was becoming his sanctuary.

The next morning President Merrill came into the commissary to see him. "How are you making out here, Elder?"

"Doing okay, thanks. I've taken an inventory of what we have here. And I've made up a new order form we could either mail or give out at zone conferences. Also, I've come up with a list of things we're not carrying but that we ought to keep in stock. You might want to look at this and tell me what you think."

He handed President Merrill a two-page list.

President Merrill went through it on the spot, putting a check on the items he approved. "You've been busy."

"Yeah, pretty much."

"I can always count on you to do a good job. That's one of the things I appreciate about you. I'm looking forward to having you work with us here in the office."

"Thank you, President."

The room wasn't very big, and Austin was uncomfortable being crowded in there with President Merrill. But the president made no move to leave.

"There's something you should know," President Merrill said, resting his hand on Austin's shoulder. "Heavenly Father wanted you here in the office."

"He does?"

"I don't know why, but the impression came as clearly as anything I've ever received."

"Thank you for telling me that, President."

Over the next few days, Austin made up the backlog of requests for books left over by Elder Nichols, who had apparently used the position as an excuse to do as little as possible while waiting to go home.

While Austin waited for the postman to come, he went in the commissary and closed the door. He sat on the stool and closed his eyes. *Father in Heaven, Sister Dulles ordered a copy of the Book of Mormon in Spanish. In her letter she said for me to send it right away. I'm sending it priority mail so she should get it either tomorrow or the next day. I hope that whoever it's going to, it will do some good.*

Father in Heaven, I have to know something. I'm not sure if I should even ask it. It's just that I know now that I'm not going to be some great leader in the mission, and so far I haven't had a lot of baptisms, so there's not much to brag about to Jeremy or my folks. But if I could just know that you approve of my service here, that would be plenty enough for me.

He felt a wave of warmth flood over him, a feeling he associated with the influence of the Spirit. He closed his eyes and surrendered to his tears, basking in the feeling of knowing that the Lord loved him.

Thank you, Father, that's all I needed to know.

Austin bought two get-well cards at the store, but because he didn't know Emily's exact address, he sent the cards to Jeremy and asked him to forward them to her.

On Monday afternoon of the next week, President Merrill and Elder Hastings and his companion, Elder Hathaway, left for another round of zone conferences. Once they were gone, the backbiting against Elder Hastings picked up again among the office elders.

Austin retreated further into his own work, expanding his duties to include developing software that could be used to help President Merrill plan transfers. He spent most of each day at the computer, developing and testing the software. At lunch he retreated to the commissary and ate by himself while he filled out the orders that had come in the morning mail or read the scriptures. He knew he was being a recluse, but he hated listening to the jokes about Elder Hastings and the other small talk that went on. The only contact he had with his companion, Elder Lambert, was in companion study early in the morning and when they went out in the evenings to do contacting and teach the discussions.

By the end of the week he was sure that the software he'd developed was easy to use and might help President Merrill try various options as he considered possible transfers.

He had also discovered something from reading the Book of Mormon—something he had never seen before. He was excited about it but didn't share the insight he'd had; the office elders didn't seem all that interested in scriptural insights.

On Monday night, the mission assistants and President Merrill returned from a zone conference. The next morning, during an office prayer meeting, Elder Hastings gave a report.

"Things are really going forward there. Most of the missionaries are using a daily planner I presented to them last time. It helps them focus on what's most important. The number of baptisms also jumped nine percent this month. It just shows what can happen when you plan your work and work your plan."

Austin glanced at two of the office elders. They had an unmistakable smirk on their faces.

He studied President Merrill. *He must know that the baptisms last month didn't depend on the planner Hastings made up. So why does he let Hastings carry on the way he does all the time?*

Every morning under President Merrill's direction, the office staff had a morning devotional, consisting of a song, a prayer, a spiritual thought, and an outline of the day's activities, led by Elder Hastings.

Austin was asked to give the spiritual thought. He asked everyone to turn to Mormon, Chapter 8. He read to them part of verse 5: "For I am alone. My father hath been slain in battle, and all my kinsfolk, and I have not friends nor whither to go; and how long the Lord will suffer that I may live I know not."

"That was written in A.D. 401," Austin said. "Moroni was still alive in A.D. 421. So it appears he might have spent twenty years alone, without friends or family."

Elder Hastings glanced at his watch, then began to tap his fingers on the president's desk. "That was real good," he said, anxious to get on to something more important.

"I'm not done yet," Austin said.

"Oh, sorry."

The office elders smirked at each other.

"Now I'd like you to turn to Ether, chapter 12," Austin said. "You're probably familiar with this. This is where Moroni tells the Lord he's afraid the Gentiles will mock his words. The Lord tells him that it's going to be all right. What I want to do is to read Moroni's response to the Lord. That starts in verse 29 and goes through verse 36. Elder Hastings, would you do me a favor and time me while I read?"

"Sure. I have a stopwatch feature on my watch, so that'll be no problem."

"Thanks." Austin read the verses at the pace he thought Moroni might have spoken them. When he finished, he said, "Stop. How much time was that, Elder Hastings?"

"One minute, forty-three seconds."

"Almost two minutes then?"

"Yes, that's right. Well, that was really good! Thanks for sharing. Now let's get to work."

"I'm still not done," Austin said.

Elder Hastings rolled his eyes, then catching President Merrill's stern gaze, he relented. "Okay, go ahead."

"Do you see what is happening here?" Austin asked.

Nobody said anything.

"I do," President Merrill said softly.

"I knew you would."

"Elder Hastings, do you know?" President Merrill asked.

"No, not really."

President Merrill asked each of the office staff in turn. Some of them hadn't been paying that much attention. Others had been watching for Elder Hastings to say something they could later make fun of.

A few silent moments passed.

"Tell them," President Merrill said to Austin.

"Moroni has no friends, no family, nobody to talk to. The Savior knows that Moroni could use a friend to talk to, and so he listens for nearly two minutes. That's how considerate the Savior is, how sympathetic to our needs. Do you know anywhere else where the Savior appears to someone and just *listens?* Usually, he comes, gives his message, and then leaves. But he didn't do that with Moroni—maybe because he knew Moroni was lonely."

With his voice catching and tears burning his eyes, Austin said, "Jesus Christ is gracious and kind. He honors those who do their best to serve him. I know that now more than I've ever known it before."

"Thank you for that marvelous spiritual thought," President Merrill said.

A short time later they went to work.

During the lunch hour, Elder Hastings came to the commissary.

"Can I get you anything?" Austin asked.

"No, not really."

Hastings was silent for a few moments, then he said, "That was a really good spiritual thought you gave today."

"Thanks."

"I was wondering if you'd mind if I used it for our next zone conferences."

"Sure, go ahead."

"Are you sure? You might need it sometime."

"I read the scriptures every day. There's always something new to discover."

"I read them every day, too, but I don't get as much out of 'em as you seem to do."

"Maybe it's because you're in a hurry all the time."

"That's probably it, all right." Elder Hastings nodded his head. He seemed to be on his way out, but then he stopped. "Can I ask you a question?"

"Sure, what is it?"

"You don't have to answer it if you don't want to."

"All right, what's the question?"

"Do people make fun of me?"

Austin didn't know what to say. "Why would you even ask a question like that? You've had more success than anyone else in the mission. You led the mission in baptisms for, what, seven consecutive months? Every time you've gone into an area or a district as a leader, there's always been a jump in baptisms. So why would you even care what a few slackers say about you behind your back?"

"It is happening then, isn't it?" Elder Hastings said.

Austin turned to his work. "I really don't want to talk about this."

"C'mon, Elder, we came out together. I know people are making fun of me. I can see it in their eyes. Please, help me." Austin had never seen Hastings look vulnerable before.

"All right, some people do make fun of you, but it's mostly here in the office."

"What do I need to change about myself?"

"You can't be serious. Why change? There's nobody in this mission who's even come close to what you've accomplished."

"No matter how well I'm doing, I always want to do better."

Austin had never admitted to anyone besides President Merrill the sense of failure he had about his mission. "I can relate to that."

"Maybe we could help each other."

"You don't need any help," Austin said.

"I can do better if you'll help me. What kind of help do you need?"

"I've been out here over a year and I've never had even one baptism," Austin confessed.

"Let's work together then, okay?"

"Okay," Austin said.

On the days when Elder Hastings was in town, he arranged it with the president so he and Austin could trade companions and work together. At first, because they didn't have anybody to teach, they went to libraries and fast-food places and tried to strike up conversations with people. Elder Hastings was a natural at getting people to talk to him. He was amazing to watch.

After a few days, when they hadn't had much luck, they switched to visiting members, asking them to commit to finding someone to teach. They met with a young married couple, John and Cassie Walters, who were managing her dad's trailer park.

"But we don't know anybody who's interested," John said.

"That doesn't matter," Elder Hastings said, smiling confidently. "Just set the date, and the Lord will send someone to you."

"He will?" Cassie asked.

"Sure, why not? He wants people in the Church more than we do. He'll send someone to you who's ready to be taught. I guarantee it."

In the car on the way back to the mission office, Austin said, "How can you guarantee something like that?"

"Why not? We want to baptize. Heavenly Father wants us to baptize. So why wouldn't he send someone for us to teach?"

"It's just that I wouldn't have guaranteed them this was going to work on their first try."

"With all due respect, Elder, what's that gotten you so far?"

After a painful pause, Austin said softly, "No baptisms."

"That's right, no baptisms. Well, we're about to change that."

In some ways, Austin secretly hoped it wouldn't work, and that John and Cassie wouldn't find anyone.

But two weeks later, an old high school friend stopped by to visit John and Cassie. John asked him to take the missionary discussions, and he agreed.

Three weeks later he was baptized.

The morning after the baptism, Austin and Hastings went to McDonald's for a late breakfast to celebrate. Hastings and his companion were leaving after lunch to travel with President Merrill.

"Well, now you know how it's done," Hastings said.

"Yeah, I do. Thanks a lot."

"No problem. Now it's your turn to help me."

"It's like I said before, you don't need any help."

"What do the office elders think about me?"

"I don't know. Why don't you ask them?"

"You said you'd help me. So do it. Tell me what I need to change."

Austin fiddled with his drink cup. "I'm not sure I can do this."

"Why's that?"

"Because . . . well . . . we're friends now."

"That's why you should tell me. I mean, if there's something I'm doing that turns people off, then I'd like to know what it is."

Austin took a deep breath before replying. "Well, whenever you give a talk to the elders, it comes across, like, 'Look at what I've done! Aren't I great? Why can't you all be like me?' You don't have to do that. Everyone knows who you are and what you've accomplished."

Austin wasn't sure how Hastings would take it—if he'd get defensive or try to argue his case, or else get mad at him.

"Part of my responsibilities as mission assistant is to motivate others to have success."

"I know."

"So how can I do it without appearing arrogant?"

Austin shrugged his shoulders. "I don't know. I just run the commissary."

"What would you do if you were mission assistant?"

Austin laughed. "Check to see if President Merrill had lost his mind."

"I'm serious."

While he thought, Austin placed their empty wrappers and boxes on the tray. "I'd talk about the Savior. He's the reason we're here. What he did and what he's revealed is what were supposed to be teaching. That's what I'd do—talk about the Savior."

"Every talk?"

"Every talk. Every training session. Every meeting. Always, every day."

Hastings nodded his head. "I'll try it and see how it works."

"Okay."

"Let's go."

On the drive to the mission office, Hastings looked over at Austin. "How about if we set a goal to baptize every month while we're in the office? You with your companion and me with mine?"

"Sounds good."

"We'll do it then . . ." Hastings paused. "That is, with the Lord's help, we will."

Austin smiled. He had never been so happy since he'd been on his mission.

A month later Austin was transferred out of the mission office to work with Vietnamese families again. A missionary was going home and wasn't being replaced, and Austin was the only elder in the mission who had any experience teaching in Vietnamese.

Austin was leaving behind a family of three who were on the fourth discussion and had committed to be baptized. Hastings said he'd take good care of them.

It's all right, I guess, Austin thought on the bus heading to his new area. *The president had no choice. Besides, I'm here to serve in any way the Lord wants.*

That's one lesson I've learned out here.

11

It wasn't easy, but Emily made it through her first day of classes.

One of the hardest things was enduring the stares she got wherever she went. It seemed as though everyone she passed looked at her. Her compression suit, with its hood, did look a little bit like a costume, and in a way she couldn't blame people for wondering why she was dressed like that. Still, it was hard not to feel self-conscious and something of a spectacle. She avoided making eye contact with people, but she could tell that they were staring at her.

She'd rented a locker so she wouldn't have to haul all her books in a backpack, and during the day she stopped twice by her locker to drop off books and grab some others. Then, after her last class, she decided to go home to rest.

When she got to her apartment, she was glad to find none of her roommates there. She closed the door to her room and lay down on the bed to take a nap.

At about four-thirty, she woke to the sound of voices in the living room.

"I can't believe we're stuck living with someone like her. She's going to scare all the guys off," one of the girls said.

"I hope she's not expecting us to be her nursemaid twenty-four hours a day," another said.

"Why did she even come here anyway?" another asked. "If I looked like that, I can't imagine I'd want to show my face in public."

"The point is that she's here, and she needs us. I don't mind helping her."

"Fine, then, go ahead and help her, if that's what you want, but I have better things to do than tend some freak."

Emily held the hurt in. She didn't want to embarrass her roommates by letting them know she'd heard them, so she stayed in her room, ready to pretend to be sleeping if anyone came in.

In some ways she didn't blame them and could understand why they'd feel that way about her. She *felt* like a freak. But it hurt to have them talking that way about her hurt.

She heard someone at the bedroom door but kept her eyes closed.

Then the door was quietly pulled shut. "She's here," someone hissed.

"Was she listening to us?"

"No, she's asleep."

"We'll have to be careful what we say around her."

Half an hour later Emily got up and left the apartment without saying anything to her roommates.

She went to the library to study, but it was hard to focus on what she needed to do. She thought about what the girls in the apartment had said. She didn't want to blame them for feeling the way they did; she just wished they understood what it was like for her to feel like an outcast.

She'd had a taste of that kind of misunderstanding before. While shopping in the mall at home, Emily had noticed a little girl staring at her. The child couldn't have been older than three, and Emily smiled at her and wiggled her fingers in greeting. Noticing Emily, the girl's mother quickly reached for her child.

"Come away," the mother had said, snatching her daughter's hand and quickly walking out of the store.

I didn't mind the little girl looking at me, Emily thought. *She'd probably never seen anyone like me before. But I don't understand why the mother didn't bring the girl over. I would have gladly explained what had happened to me.*

There had been other times when she had been embarrassed by people's reaction to her appearance. Once, a day or two after Emily had come home from the hospital, a group of girls from her ward dropped by her house. They were members of the Mia Maid class, and they had baked some cookies for Emily. They arrived at a time when Emily was out of her compression suit, applying ointment to the areas that had been burned.

From her bedroom, Emily could hear the young women talking to her mother in the living room. "We brought her some cookies we made."

"That's so thoughtful of you. I know she'll appreciate them."

"Where is she?"

"She's in her room."

Before her mother could say anything, one of the girls pushed open the door to Emily's room.

Emily quickly covered herself up, but she couldn't hide her neck and face.

"Oh, my gosh!" the girl said, pulling the door closed.

"What?" one of the girls asked.

"She looks so bad. How is she ever going to show her face to anyone after what happened to her?"

"Girls, we appreciate the effort you made in making the cookies," Emily's mother said curtly. "But the next time you visit someone who's sick, you might try to not leave them feeling worse than before you came."

I tried not to show how much the girl's comment hurt me, Emily thought.

But it did hurt me. And it will always hurt me. And now I'm in a position to be hurt like that over and over again.

Her tears fell on the page she was trying to read. *I'll never be able to sell this book back,* she thought.

Only people with clear skin and good eyes and strong legs belong here. I should just pack up my bags and go home and never come back. I can't fight the whole world. I thought I could, but I can't. I'm going home to Ogden. I'll just stay in my room. That's the only place where I feel safe and where I don't have to interact with people.

To blunt her disappointment, Emily had begun retreating into frequent daydreams. She had one fantasy she especially enjoyed in which she was reunited with David Alexander. She had seen him on the television evening news one night, standing in front of the wreckage from a train derailment somewhere in the South. His handsome face was framed by the burning wreckage glowing in the night behind him. With his clothing characteristically rumpled and his hair wet from standing in the rain, he was as flamboyant as ever, and seeing him brought all Emily's old feelings for him flooding back. For days after that, she couldn't get him out of her mind, and whenever she thought about her scars and all she had lost, she would retreat into a fantasy that she had never been burned and that she and David were together again.

I had a dream before my accident, she reminded herself, *but now what do I have? The world is not set up for people like me.*

She closed her book. Now that she'd decided to drop out of school and return home the next day, there was no reason to study.

She didn't want to return to her apartment or to talk to any of her roommates. She would go back later, after everyone was asleep. Then, in the morning, she'd stay in bed until they all left for classes before calling her mom to come and

154

get her. That way, she could be gone before any of her roommates returned from classes. And that would be it.

I can still take classes, she thought. *I'll take home study classes. Maybe I can get a job where I'll never have to leave my room, doing things on the computer.*

She moved to a carrel on the second level where she was out of sight but could see people coming and going, in and out of the library. It gave her something to do. After a time, she noticed a young man in a wheelchair. He did not have the use of his hands and was guiding his electric powered wheelchair by using pressure sensors on the head-rest. She watched as he tried to steer himself between two bookshelves but got hung up. He maneuvered back and forth, trying to steer himself out of the tight spot but was having little luck; the more he worked the more tightly he became wedged.

Emily watched as dozens of people walked right by him, none of them seeming to notice or care about his predicament.

Isn't anyone going to help? she thought. *Are you all just going to let him sit there? Are you all blind? Don't you care about anyone except yourself? What is wrong with you people?*

Finally she could stand it no longer. She hurried down the stairs and went to his rescue.

"Excuse me, are you stuck?"

The young man smiled and said something, but she couldn't understand him.

"I'm sorry, could you say that again?"

He smiled. "I'm playing hide and go seek with myself."

She started laughing. "Well, would you mind if I butt in and get you out of this mess?"

"That would be nice."

She got the wheelchair turned so he could make it by himself.

"Thanks."

155

"No problem. Are you a student here?"

He smiled. "Only when I study."

"What's your name?"

"Don."

"I'm Emily. In case you were wondering, I was burned. That's why I'm wearing this Robin Hood costume."

He said something else, which she couldn't understand. But she refused to just nod her head and walk away. *I'm going to keep asking until I understand.*

When she finally pieced it together and let it sink in, she realized his comment was hilarious. He had said, "What would Robin Hood do in college? Rob from the smart and give to the dumb?"

She couldn't help herself. She started to laugh. "That is so funny!"

Don laughed too, seeming to enjoy the joke as much as Emily.

After a moment, she said, "Listen, can I help you get somewhere? Where are you going?"

"Home."

"Can I walk you home?" she asked.

"I don't walk."

Emily smiled at his quick wit. "That's okay. There are some things I don't do either. I was in a fire in my kitchen. I was cooking soup."

"Soup?" he asked with a grin.

"Yes."

He said something else, but Emily couldn't immediately make it out. After two tries, she finally understood what he'd said was, "Not much of a cook, are you?"

"Not much."

They slowly made their way through the early evening light to his home. It took awhile, but not because of him. He had an amazing ability to steer his battery powered wheel-chair by making slight movements of his head.

156

"Sorry to be so slow," she said.

Don lived in a large, older home, no more than a block from campus. It had a wheelchair ramp that Don buzzed right up, onto the front porch. He asked Emily to open the front door for him, then invited her in.

"No, thanks," she said. "I'd better be going."

But, before she could leave, Don's mother came to the door.

"I thought I heard someone out here," she said. "Who's your friend, Don?"

"This is Emily," Don said, laughing. "She got me unstuck at the library."

Don's mother insisted that Emily come in. She said she was just taking a batch of cookies out of the oven and that Emily and Don could have some. Don maneuvered his way into the kitchen, and, feeling a little awkward, Emily followed him.

They ended up having cookies and milk, with Emily feeding Don and helping him drink his milk by holding a straw to his lips. After a time, Don's father joined them at the kitchen table. Like his son, Don's dad was also a jokester, and the parents made Emily feel immediately welcome. They were warm, gracious, and easy to talk to.

Emily was somewhat relieved to see that Don's parents sometimes also had to ask Don to repeat himself. It made her feel less self-conscious about having to do so herself. Don took it in stride, patiently repeating each word until it was finally understood. Or, sometimes, with particularly difficult words, he spelled each letter.

Don's neck was bent permanently backward, and he held his head at an awkward angle. His wrists were also severely bent, and his fingers were stiff and unusable. Watching him, Emily thought to herself: *He can't weigh more than ninety pounds. How does he manage? How can his parents let him go off to classes every day without being with him*

*every step of the way? And why do I feel so good being here
with him and his mom and dad?*

It was true. Since the time of her accident, she couldn't
remember feeling more at ease or less self-conscious than
she did being in that home.

When it was time for Emily to go, Don's mother walked
her to the door. "Please come and visit us again," she said.
"Don always enjoys having company."

"Well, to tell you the truth, I'm thinking of quitting school
and going home."

"How come?"

"It's hard for someone like me." As soon as the words
were out of her mouth, Emily realized how stupid they
sounded. Don's mother didn't seem to take offense, but
Emily tried to smooth it over. "I mean . . ."

"I know what you mean, Emily. It must be very difficult
to feel different from everyone else. But if you stay here,
you'll make it easier for others who are struggling, who will
come after you. At least, that's what we tell Don. He enjoys
thinking of himself as a trailblazer. You could be one too."

Emily said good-bye and then decided to take a walk.
She found herself sitting in the dark on a bench by a sidewalk, which during the day was often full of students going
to and from class.

For just an instant, she could see in her mind an image
of hundreds of boys and girls moving in a caravan on the
sidewalk, each of them disadvantaged in some way—in
wheelchairs, or on crutches, some in compression suits like
hers, some blind, others without legs or arms. But, strangely
enough, they were not college students. They were children,
boys and girls, each of them enduring some kind of disability, through birth, illness, or accident.

The words to her battle song, slightly changed, came to
her mind:

Bless all the dear children in thy tender care
And fit us for a meaningful life to live for you here.

Suddenly it was clear to her why the people she was seeing in her mind were young children. *These are the children
who will come after me,* she thought. *I must prepare a way
for them. That is what the Savior wants me to do.*

She stood up with sudden purpose. *I am not quitting. I
am staying. I will prepare a way for all the dear children who
have special needs.*

After she got back to her apartment, she called her roommates together and said with quiet determination, "Ladies,
we need to talk."

Over Christmas vacation, Emily returned to the burn center for another skin graft. It was a painful way to renew old
friendships.

Everyone was proud of her for returning to school.

"You must be so smart now," Red teased.

"I was always smart, Red. It's just that now I can
prove it."

"You're the best, Kid. You always were."

Before Emily's operation, Brooke took her around and
introduced her to several of the new patients. "Emily is one
of our real success stories. She can teach you guys a lot."

"Like what?" a twelve-year-old boy asked. He was a
twenty-percenter, like Emily had been.

It seemed so simple: "Put your trust in God. Do what the
staff says and try to work through the pain. It's going to hurt,
but it's for the best in the long run."

The boy wasn't impressed. "I've heard all that before."

"I'm sure you have, but I'm here to tell you it works."

After the operation, she was again immobilized, which
meant using a bedpan and lying still for hours at a time, with
nothing to do except think about the direction her life had
taken.

She was glad she'd decided to stay in college. Not just because of the classes she had completed but also because of what she felt she'd done to ease the way for what she called *all the dear children*.

During fall term Emily and Don had organized a new campus organization. They called it New Directions. It was a support group for those on campus with special needs. The purpose of the club was to help each other but also to present a united front from students whose needs were otherwise not being recognized.

One of their first activities was to meet with the dean of students. Emily was nervous about the meeting, but when they were invited into his office, she was proud to be joined by two people in wheelchairs, three blind students, and four hearing impaired students.

The dean seemed a little threatened. "We are doing our best to abide by the letter of the law in regard to those with special needs," he said.

"We know you are doing your best," Emily said. "And we appreciate that. We just want you to know that from time to time our members may come across something that makes it difficult for them to carry out their studies here. When that happens, with your permission, we'd like to be able to come directly to you and ask for your help. Is that acceptable to you if we do that?"

She was surprised to hear herself speaking in her newscaster's voice.

He cleared his throat nervously. "Yes, of course. We want to do everything we can to meet federal guidelines."

"We're not speaking about federal guidelines," Emily said. "We just want to have our needs met. May I ask you something?"

"Sure."

"Do you have kids?" she asked.

"Yes."

"How many?"

"Four."

"And are they all healthy and well?"

"Yes, they are."

"That is wonderful. You must feel very blessed."

"Yes, I do."

"Try imagining one of them ending up like one of us. And then ask yourself the question, 'What would I want the university to do for my son or my daughter?' If you ask yourself that question, I think you'll look at things much differently. The truth is, sir, we are somebody's son or somebody's daughter. And we want an education as much as anyone here on this campus."

To his credit, the dean of students became a strong supporter of any requests made to him by their group.

Heavenly Father, she prayed as she lay immobilized in her hospital bed, *I'm doing my best to help you bless all the children in thy tender care. Thank you for helping me with my efforts to show my thanks for what you did for me when I was here the first time.*

When Emily returned to school for winter term, having friends from New Directions helped her feel more at home.

She and Don went to the school's winter formal together. Before the dance, they ate dinner at Don's house, just the two of them in the dining area, with his mom serving as chef and his dad as their waiter.

After Don and Emily finished eating the main course, Don's dad cleared away the dishes and then brought out an elegant chocolate pudding. Emily invited Don's parents to have dessert with them.

Don and his folks told Emily about some of the humorous things that had happened to Don as a result of his disability as he was growing up.

"Tell her about the leaf," Don said with a smile.

Don's mother laughed. "When Don was thirteen, he went to handicap camp. He rode up with the others in a school bus. The window next to his seat on the bus was open, and a leaf blew in and landed on Don's lap. When Don said, 'I caught a leaf,' someone thought he'd said, 'I can't breathe.' Everyone panicked. They stopped the bus, and the whole staff gathered around him, trying frantically to see what the matter was. They even carried him off the bus to get him some additional air. The whole time he was trying to explain what he'd said, but it wasn't until he started laughing that they listened long enough to finally understand what he'd said."

At the dance, Don and Emily danced every dance, he in his wheelchair and she next to him, moving in rhythm to the music. Afterwards, at his door, she kissed him on the cheek. "I suppose you'll tell everyone that I kissed you, right?"

He laughed. "It will be all over campus by tomorrow."

"I hope so, Don. Thanks so much for a wonderful evening."

Don's mom and dad gave her a ride home. When she walked into her apartment, two of her roommates and their dates were there.

"I saw you at the dance," one of the guys said. "I think it's great you'd go there with the guy in the wheelchair."

"Oh, Emily's always doing stuff like that," one of her roommates said.

That made Emily mad. "Doing what kind of stuff?" she asked.

"You know, feeling sorry for people like Don."

Emily couldn't let that pass. "The truth is, there's no one I would rather spend time with than Don. He's funny, he's cheerful, he's considerate. What more could any girl want?"

"Someone who can walk might be nice," the girl said.

"Oh, can't he walk? I didn't notice," Emily said.

Emily was happy, and the winter and spring terms passed quickly. She kept busy and did well in her classes. Because of her compression suit, her closest friends called her Robyn Hood, but she didn't mind. It was a sign they accepted her.

Two weeks before the end of school, as she was looking forward to going home for the summer, Emily was asked to meet with her bishop. The interview was scheduled for Sunday morning a couple of hours before church. She thought he might be going to call her to teach Relief Society in the fall, and she was comfortable with that.

But she was totally unprepared for what it really was.

"Please sit down," Bishop Cameron said as she entered his office. He had a round face and only a narrow band of short hair around his otherwise completely bald head. Because he was six-foot-five and weighed over two hundred and fifty pounds, he had spent most of his life trying not to intimidate people. He did that by speaking softly and displaying a wonderful smile.

"Will you serve in any calling that the Lord has for you?" he asked.

Thinking she knew what it was, Emily said, "Yes, I will."

"Good for you." He paused. "I went to the temple earlier this week."

That's nice, Emily thought, wondering where this was going.

"While I was there, I prayed to know who Father in Heaven wants to serve as Relief Society president when school begins again next fall. He let me know you are his choice. I don't have to ask you if you'll accept, because you just said you would, but what I need to know is, who would you like to be your counselors?"

163

Emily gasped. "There must be some mistake. You can't have me for your Relief Society president."

"Why not?"

"Well, it must be obvious, isn't it?"

"Not to me. Not to the Lord."

"Oh, please, not this, Bishop, anything but this."

"I've never been more certain about anything than I am of this calling."

Emily asked for a tissue and planted her elbows on his desk and cradled her head in her hands as the tears flowed freely. After a minute she sat up and faced the bishop. "The girls will not accept me, and they will make fun of whatever I do or whatever I say."

"If that is true, then why does the Lord want you to serve in this position?"

"I don't know."

"I don't know, either. Will you accept this call from him?"

She nodded her head but then burst into tears once again.

"Who would you like to serve as your counselors?"

Through her tears, Emily asked him for his counsel, and after discussing several of the girls, she chose two young women she thought might have been called as the president. They were both beautiful, capable, well liked, and faithful. In her mind, they were better qualified than she was, but when she told the bishop that, he smiled and told her that's the way he'd felt about his counselors too.

When she left the bishop's office, she went to the back row of the room where they were to hold sacrament meeting. She hoped she could manage not to be noticed for the time being.

What if they won't sustain me? she thought. *What if they're ashamed of me to be their Relief Society president? What if they won't come to our meetings because they can't*

164

stand to look at my face? What if they laugh at me behind my back?

There were tears in her eyes as the bishop announced the opening song.

Oh, dear Father, let me feel your love and the Savior's love. Don't make me face this alone. You were with me in the hospital. Please be with me now.

After the opening prayer, the bishop stood up. "We have some ward business. It has become necessary to release, with a vote of thanks, the following . . ."

Emily said a quick prayer.

"We have called Emily Latrell to serve as Relief Society president. Emily, will you please stand?"

A girl near the middle of the congregation audibly gasped.

Everyone turned around to look at Emily.

Don't look down, Emily told herself. *This is not your church. You didn't ask for this. This is the Savior's church. He is the one who called you to this position.*

She and her counselors were set apart during Relief Society meeting. She hoped she could just turn the time over to the teacher for the lesson, but there was no lesson prepared. There'd been a mix-up in signals. Before leaving the room, the bishop suggested Emily take some time to talk to the sisters. There were thirty minutes to fill.

Standing before the young women in her ward, Emily felt very self-conscious. It was bad enough to have to wear the compression suit, but at least it covered up the worst of her scars. She wondered what they would say if they could see the other places where she'd been burned. In some ways it was her secret that she kept hidden from the world.

Looking at the room full of young women, it occurred to her, *They may have things they wish to hide too, less visible but just as deep and just as painful.*

To give herself time to gather her thoughts, she called on

the former Relief Society president to bear her testimony. And then she asked her newly sustained counselors to respond. They said all the right things, and it was easy to see they were going to be well accepted by the young women of the ward. That didn't bother Emily. That's why she'd chosen them.

But now it was her turn. She asked for a tissue and five appeared in outstretched hands. She wiped her face and then tried to smile through her tears.

"I can understand if some of you were shocked that I was called to be Relief Society president. Believe me, you weren't as shocked as I was."

There was some nervous laughter in the room.

"The most important thing I can tell you about myself is that I love the Savior." Her voice caught, and she had to stop because she was afraid she might lose control of her emotions.

A long moment passed while she tried to gain her composure. Finally she was able to go on. "I'm grateful that he has looked beyond my scarred exterior to see into my heart."

Once again, she had to stop. She said a silent prayer for help.

"I'll do my best to serve you. And I ask you for your support."

Suddenly a feeling of calm came over her. She smiled. "Oh, one other thing, don't feel sorry for me. One nice thing about the way I am now is I don't need to spend a lot of time deciding what shade of eyeshadow to use."

It was the perfect thing to say. The girls, many of them through their tears, began to smile. Emily smiled back. *It will be better for me not to take myself too seriously. I'll take their problems seriously, but not my own. And that will help both them and me.*

They'd run out of tissues, which meant it was time to close the meeting.

12

One last interview with President Merrill was all that remained of Austin's mission. He had been invited, along with two other missionaries who were also going home, to the mission home for a farewell dinner with President and Sister Merrill. Elder Hastings was one of the three, and Austin enjoyed being with him again. He was sure that, no matter where their paths might lead them, he and Elder Hastings would always be friends.

Thinking back on their early experiences together, it was surprising to Austin that he would think of Elder Hastings as a good friend. But both of them had changed a lot as a result of their mission experiences. *He doesn't brag about himself like he used to,* Austin thought, *even though he's accomplished so much on his mission.* Austin smiled. *I taught him that.*

The subject during dinner got around to courtship and marriage. "Do you have someone waiting for you?" Sister Merrill asked Elder Hastings.

"Yes, I do. We've known each other since high school. Her name is Elizabeth. I can hardly wait to see her. Of course, we won't be getting married for at least two years. She'll be leaving on her mission in two weeks."

"She's going on a mission?" Sister Merrill asked.

"She is. It's going to be tough waiting for her, but in a way I think it's good. It'll give me time to finish college and get into dental school."

"It sounds as though you have things really planned out," Sister Merrill said.

Austin broke out laughing. "Don't say it, Elder," he teased Elder Hastings.

"Don't say what?"

"Plan your work, work your plan."

"What about you, Elder Brunswick?" Sister Merrill asked Austin.

"I'll be going back to school at Utah State University this fall."

"Anyone waiting for you?" Hastings asked.

"Not really."

After supper, President Merrill interviewed the missionaries who would be leaving the mission field the next morning.

"How do you feel about your mission?" President Merrill asked Austin.

"I'm grateful for the experience. I've learned a lot."

"What have you learned?"

Austin tried to think how to say what he had felt in his heart for many months. After a moment, he said, "That, above all else, we are disciples of Jesus Christ, and that we must always remember that, and try our best to represent him well." Austin paused. "That's about it, President. That's not much for two years, is it?"

"I disagree. I think it's a great deal. Some people never learn that. I'm pleased you have."

"Thank you, President. Thank you for all your help." Austin stood up to leave.

President Merrill motioned for Austin to sit down. "Don't go yet. There's something else I need to say." Leaning forward and resting his elbows on his desk, the president said,

"Elder Brunswick, every elder fortunate enough to have had you for a companion is now an excellent missionary. In that way you've blessed this mission a great deal, and will continue to bless it, long after you've left."

"Thank you, sir."

"Just one more thing. I believe that if the Savior had an important job to be done, he could not do better than to ask you to do it."

Because it came from a man he loved and admired, Austin took that to be a high compliment. Already feeling emotional about his mission coming to a close, Austin didn't trust his voice to respond. Instead, he just smiled at President Merrill.

"Before you leave, could I give you a priesthood blessing?" President Merrill asked.

In a quiet voice, Austin said, "Yes, sir, that would be an honor."

During the blessing, Austin experienced a feeling of peace and happiness. He felt the Spirit affirming that Father in Heaven had accepted his offering of the past two years.

On Sunday, near the end of his ward's sacrament meeting, Austin stood at the pulpit to give his homecoming report. The audience was filled not only with ward members but friends and relatives who had come to hear him speak.

He looked down at his notes, trying to decide what to leave out. It was nearly time to close the meeting. His parents had taken longer than they'd planned on, but he didn't mind. What he had to say could be said in just a few minutes.

Instead of sharing mission experiences, he simply bore his testimony of the Atonement and of the mercy and goodness of the Savior. He expressed his gratitude for the chance to serve a mission, and then he sat down.

His mother leaned over to him. "You should have talked longer," she whispered.

"It was time to close the meeting," he said.

"Oh, that doesn't matter. They always run late for missionary homecomings."

"I said what was the most important."

"You should have told about when you worked in the mission office, helping your mission president get organized."

Austin smiled and shook his head but didn't say anything.

After sacrament meeting, his friends, with the exception of Jeremy, who still had a couple more weeks left of his mission, came to the front of the chapel to congratulate him. Some of the girls who had been there for his farewell two years earlier weren't there to give him a welcome-back hug because they had married since he'd left.

His friends and family skipped the rest of the meetings and went to Austin's home for a buffet lunch. It was an elaborate meal, provided by a caterer Austin's mother had hired to prepare the food.

Gradually the crowd thinned out, until finally only the members of Austin's extended family remained. Austin started hauling the folding chairs they'd rented out to the garage.

"Why are you putting them in the garage?" his mother asked.

"I thought I'd return 'em tomorrow," Austin said.

"You can return them today. They're open Sundays."

"I just think it'd be better to return them tomorrow."

"Whatever for?"

"Because today is Sunday."

"They're already paid for, so it's not like we're purchasing anything from anybody."

"I just think it'd be better to wait until tomorrow."

His mother paused. "I'll ask your dad to take them back then, if you can just stack them in the trunk of the car."

Austin bristled, but did as he was told, and then escaped to his room to read the scriptures and write in his journal.

That Sunday, Emily had to make a choice. She could either go hear Austin report his mission in sacrament meeting, or she could attend burn camp, sponsored by the University of Utah burn unit and funded by private and corporate donations. The Utah burn camp was the only one of its kind in the nation, and was a six-day, river-rafting trip.

It was an easy choice. She went where her heart was; she went to burn camp.

On that Sunday they met at the hospital at 6:30 in the morning. The participants were organized into groups and introduced to the adults who would be their counselors for the week. The counselors consisted of burn unit staff, firemen, and adults who themselves had been burned.

"So you came after all," Red said.

"I did, Red. How could I pass up a chance to spend more time with you?"

He smiled. "Good for you. It's going to be great!"

"How many years have you been doing this?" she asked.

"Gosh, I guess it's been five years."

"You take vacation time to go?"

He shrugged his shoulders. "Where else could I have this much fun?"

He started to move off to talk to another old friend. "Red," Emily called out after him.

"Yeah, what?"

"I think you're pretty awesome."

"Not really." He made a pass of his hand at the ones who were going to burn camp. "Don't you see? These are my kids."

Emily watched him go from one former patient to

another, giving high fives and paying attention to each of them. *He has a way of making everyone feel special,* Emily thought. *He's one of my heroes. I wonder if he knows how much we all love him.*

Brooke, now a new mom, came to see them off and to show off her baby girl.

Emily was asked to be a junior counselor and was assigned Natasha, a thirteen-year-old girl who had been burned about five years earlier. Her burns were similar to Emily's, except on the left side of her body instead of the right.

From her seat in the back of the bus, Emily watched as each camper climbed onto the bus. Words began to tumble into her mind. As the bus pulled out and they began the long ride to the river, she took a notebook and a pencil from her backpack and began working to put her thoughts on paper. After several revisions, she finished writing a short poem:

> *We are the shadow children,*
> *The silent ones,*
> *Shy beyond our years.*
> *The children of dusk, the forgotten ones,*
> *Touched by flame,*
> *We turn and embrace the pain.*
> *We are the shadow children,*
> *The silent ones,*
> *Shy beyond our years.*

As the bus trip continued, Emily watched a transformation take place in the children who were there for the first time. They began the trip being quiet, shy, withdrawn, and self-conscious, but they ended up behaving like any other group of kids embarking on a grand adventure—excited, noisy, and full of fun.

Each day they rafted down the river, stopping in late afternoon to set up camp, prepare their evening meal, and sing songs and make up skits around the campfire.

On the third night, gathered once again around a campfire, they each told their story. Each could relate to what all the others had gone through.

Emily was one of the last to speak. She put some more wood on the fire, then turned to face the campers and staff. "I can't believe we're all gathered around a campfire," she said with a smile. "I mean, are we slow learners or what?"

Most everyone laughed.

Emily felt she had a lot to say. "I've learned so much this week from all of you. I mean, for the first time since my accident, I haven't felt alone. And, Natasha, I've learned the most from you. I'm nineteen and you're thirteen, and yet you've taught me so much. I love you like a sister. I hope you'll answer my letters, because I am going to write you all through the year.

"We have all had to struggle to win our race, and I guess we have won it, because we're still going on. Whether it's more surgeries or just tackling life, we are all doing it. There are no wimps here, that's for sure."

She couldn't stop without saying what was in her heart. "The greatest thing I've learned from what happened to me is that Jesus Christ is my Savior and that he loves me, and that God is my Father in Heaven. They got me through all this."

She turned to those who worked at the burn unit and said what many of the others had already said: "You guys are so great. I have to tell you, I love you. We all feel the same way too, don't we? Let's give them a big hand."

It was an old Boy Scout gimmick she'd learned from one of the adult counselors. Silently, they all held up a hand.

After all the campers had spoken, the members of the staff each took a turn, explaining why they take time off work every year to be a part of burn camp. Red said it best: "We give away a little part of us when you come to the burn unit. And we can only get it back by seeing you again and realizing how much progress each of you has made. Oh, sure, I could sit around doing nothing on some dumb vacation, but nothing is as great as being with you guys."

On Friday, Emily returned home, grateful beyond expression for the experience. Before she left, she asked Red if she could return next year as an adult counselor.

Red beamed. "Are you kidding? Of course you can."

The next week Emily had another surgery, this one to improve the appearance of the skin on her neck.

It was during the time she was in the hospital that her brother, Jeremy, got home from his mission.

After the sacrament meeting in which Jeremy reported his mission, and following a luncheon at Jeremy's house, after everyone else had gone, Jeremy and Austin ended up where they had spent much of their free time in high school—in the TV room in the basement, sprawled out on the couch.

"It's too bad Emily wasn't able to be here," Austin said. "How's she doing, anyway?" he asked.

"Okay, I guess, considering what she's been through. I saw her in the hospital last night, and she was in pretty good spirits." Jeremy paused. "I don't know how she handles it. It's beeen so tough. But she never complains."

"She was always a cute kid," Austin said. "But I have a hard time thinking of her as all grown up."

"Well, she is. You ought to see the video she made of the broadcasts she did before the accident, when she was in a newscasting class at USU. It blew me away. She was a pro. You want to see it?"

"Do you think she'd mind?"

"I don't think so. She made about a hundred copies of it."

174

"A hundred?"

"Well, maybe a dozen."

They watched the video in silence. Austin was amazed. Remembering how young Emily had always seemed, he couldn't believe how confident and mature she was on the video.

All Jeremy could think about was how sad it was for Emily. He knew her dream was over and how difficult it had been for her to give it up.

When the video ended, Jeremy clicked the VCR off. They didn't say anything for a moment, but just sat there staring at the dark television screen.

"It was hard seeing her for the first time after I got home," Jeremy said. "The fire really messed her up."

"I didn't even know about it for a long time," Austin said. "How bad is it?"

"I've only seen the scars on her face and neck. They're not too bad, but I guess it's worse on her upper body."

"Sorry to hear that."

"She'll be back at USU this fall. I'd appreciate it if you could make sure she's doing okay."

"I will. I promise."

"Thanks, that'd mean a lot to me. Not that she wants any help. She's pretty independent."

"It sounds like it."

"She's going to be the Relief Society president in her campus ward in the fall. I don't know how that's going to work out. I mean, it's hard enough just taking care of herself, so how's she going to be of any help to someone else?"

It was a question neither of them could answer.

The next day, Jeremy visited Emily in the hospital. She knew he was having a hard time dealing with her scars because he would look at her for only a few seconds before turning away.

He said he wished she'd been able to hear him speak in sacrament meeting. She told him she wished she had too. But the truth was that she had scheduled the operation so she wouldn't have to attend his homecoming. Not because she didn't love him or didn't want to hear him speak, but because his friends from high school would all be there, and she didn't want to have to face them and see the looks on their faces when they saw her.

In some ways it was easier to deal with people at USU who had never known her than to face those who had known her before the fire.

"Austin was there to hear me give my talk," Jeremy said.

"Good. I'm glad you two were able to get together. How's he doing?"

"Real good. He's the same old Austin, except there's kind of a depth to him that wasn't there before. He asked about you. He said for me to tell you he's sorry about your accident and that he wishes the best for you."

"If you see him, tell him thanks."

"He'll be at USU this fall too. You'll probably run into him."

"Well, it's a big place. We might never see each other. But no matter. Sit down and let me hear your sacrament meeting talk."

Between Austin going with his parents on a two-week vacation to Hawaii and Emily being in the hospital for skin graft operations, they didn't see each other during what was left of the summer.

The first time Emily saw Austin on campus, she was in the library on the second day of classes. She had a favorite place she liked to sit there, at some study carrels that few people used, on the second floor. She often had the area to herself.

While walking to her desk, she looked down and saw

Austin sitting at a table on the first floor, near the main entrance of the library. He was studying with a girl. Or at least it looked as though Austin wanted to study, but the girl was too preoccupied with him for him to get much work done.

Emily peered over the balcony at them, ready to step back if either one of them should glance up and see her.

Austin looked great. As handsome as ever. He looked a little irritated at the girl's antics as she playfully stole his pencil and put it behind her back, daring him to take it from her. But Emily couldn't tell if he was actually upset or just pretending to be.

She's a real charmer, Emily thought. *Such beautiful hair, too. And a long neck. And a good smile. Austin would be a fool not to fall in love with her. She has everything.*

Emily was surprised to find herself suddenly jealous. She had no claim on Austin. Aside from the few letters they had exchanged, they'd had no contact for over two years. Even so, it was hard seeing him with someone else. *I could have been that girl. I could have been the one he met when he came home from his mission. I could have been the one who went to his homecoming. I could have been the one who rode up with him just before school started. I could have been his friend. And now I could be holding his pencil behind my back, daring him to reach for it, and not being afraid that if his hand brushed my right arm or my neck or the right side of my face that some grafted skin would fall off. They tell me it won't. They tell me it'll be as good as new. But how can grafted skin stay there forever?*

She found herself fighting back tears. Embarrassed to be so out of control, she glanced around to see if anyone was looking at her, then made a dash for her study carrel. Sitting down, she rummaged through her backpack, looking for some tissues.

The girl with Austin has such beautiful skin, she thought.

I'm sure she doesn't even know that. I should go down and tell her. What would I say? You have so much to be thankful for. I bet you take showers, don't you? I used to. Of course, now I don't. Oh, hello, Austin, nice to see you again. You remember me, don't you? Oh, you don't? Well, why should you? Look, I hope you'll be very happy with what's-her-name. She's gorgeous. Why, I'll bet she doesn't even scare little children when she goes to the mall! That's a real plus, isn't it?

Finding a half-empty packet of tissues, she wiped her eyes and nose, then sat in silence, staring vacantly at the desktop.

I know what I'll do. I'll become a masseuse on campus. And people will come, and I, in my pressure garment, will tell each one what good skin they have and how much they have to be thankful for. Maybe some day Austin's girlfriend will come. And I will cry as I work on her and my silent tears will fall on her back, and I will rub them in. I'm sure it will be very good for her.

What ever happened to my life? Someone's taken it away. And all I have left is ashes. What good are ashes anyway? They're not good for anything. Why did I live? It would have been so much easier to die.

She checked her backpack for more tissues but didn't find any. *This is not doing me any good. I can't change what happened. All I can do is move on. I have a test tomorrow and I need to study. That's one thing I can still do, study and get good grades.*

She cautiously entered a rest room on the second floor. She hated people staring at her and was disappointed to see two young women using the mirror. Without looking at them, Emily grabbed a handful of toilet tissue from one of the stalls and quickly left the room to return to her desk. On the way, she glanced down at the first floor. Austin and his friend were gone, and she wondered where they had gone.

Sitting back down to study, she thought, *I don't need a*

relationship. All I need is school. A test is such an equalizer. It doesn't care who you are or what you look like. All a test cares about is the right answers. I need that now. In fact, it's the only thing I've got going for me now.

She paused. *No, that's not true. I'm a Relief Society president. I have a responsibility to help the girls in my ward. Heavenly Father trusted me with this responsibility. I can't let him down. I need to focus my energies on that and forget everything else.*

I don't want to ever run into Austin on campus. It will be better that way. Better for both of us. It's a big campus. He has his world now and I have mine.

She pulled out her notes from class. She felt a sense of relief at only having to deal with a test because, as she thought, *Unlike life, tests are fair.*

The next day when Emily arrived back at her apartment, there was a phone message from Austin for her to call him. She wadded it up and threw it in a wastepaper basket.

Later that night, while at the library studying, the name of one of the girls in her ward popped into her head. Emily and Summer weren't close friends and in fact had never done anything together but greet each other at church, but Summer's name kept going through her mind. The thought gradually came that she ought to go see Summer. At first she thought she'd do it the next day after her test. But before long, the thought came forcefully into her mind, *No, do it now.*

It didn't make any sense. The girl was not one of the ones she was worried about. But the feeling was so strong that she decided to drop by Summer's dorm.

She probably won't even be home, she thought. But she continued on.

Summer was there, but she seemed surprised to find Emily at her door.

"I turned in my visiting teaching report."

"It's not about that."

"What's it about then?"

"Nothing special. I just thought I'd drop by and see you. How's everything going?"

"Fine."

They talked a few minutes about school and then Emily left. *What was that all about?* she thought as she walked to her own apartment.

Austin continued to leave messages for Emily to call, and she continued to ignore them.

A few days later, though, as she was walking across campus on her way to the library, she heard a voice calling after her. "Emily, is that you?"

Her first reaction was dread. She kept walking, pretending she hadn't heard.

Austin was beside her now. "Hey, wait up."

She had to at least acknowledge his presence. She turned to look at him.

"It *is* you," he said.

"Yes, it's me," she said, watching his eyes to see how he would react to what the fire had done to her.

He chose to concentrate on her eyes. They were, at least, still the same.

"Hey, I've been trying to get hold of you. Did you get my messages?"

"Yeah, but I've been so busy, I haven't had time to get back to you."

"That's okay. How are things going?"

"Real good, thanks." She continued walking.

"Did you get my get-well cards?"

"I did. Thanks," she said, thinking, *He wonders why I never wrote back. Isn't it obvious, Austin? What's the point of anything?*

I've got to get out of here, she thought. She didn't want to make it difficult for Austin. When people had taken pity on her, she'd found it was easier on them when she gave them an easy way to escape. "Listen, it's nice seeing you, but I've got to get to class."

"Can I walk you there?" he asked. "I don't have anything better to do right now. In fact, if you don't mind, I could sit through the class with you."

The truth was she didn't really have a class to go to. She'd only said it to give him an out. "It's kind of a boring class."

He smiled. "Hey, if you can stand it, I can."

She began to panic. She didn't want him to find out she'd lied.

"Where's your class?" he asked.

"It's this way."

They walked side by side.

"Where can I touch you?" he asked.

She wasn't much good with sideways glances, so she stopped and turned to face him. "Excuse me?"

He started to blush. "I'm sorry. That didn't come out right, did it? What I meant was, what parts weren't in the fire?"

"My left side is in pretty good shape."

"Your left hand is okay then? Like if I wanted to hold your hand?"

"You don't mean now, do you?"

"Not necessarily now, no. Just in case it ever comes up."

"Look, I'm sure you have better things to do than talk to me."

"Not really. I talk to people all the time."

She was aware that people passing by were staring at them. She imagined them wondering why someone like him was talking to her. She didn't blame them. She wondered the same thing.

She wanted him out of her life. "You can't come to my class."

"Why not?"

"It's a women's health class. We're discussing childbirth today. There's going to be a movie."

Austin gulped. "Some other time then, okay?"

"I'm pretty busy, but nice seeing you." She began to walk away.

"Emily, I'd like to talk to you. Can I call you?"

She pretended she hadn't heard him and headed for the nearest classroom building.

He didn't follow her. She climbed the steps to the second floor landing and watched through the window as he disappeared behind one of the other buildings. *This can't ever happen again,* she thought.

Later that day, in the library, she looked up Austin's class schedule in the computer. She'd need to make sure to avoid those parts of the campus during those times of day.

That night she went over to Don's house to spend time with him. She hadn't been invited, but she'd been told by his parents that she was always welcome. And based on the wonderful way they treated her, she believed it.

She always felt better when she was with Don. She wasn't sure why, except he was always cheerful, and he had a great sense of humor.

She was getting better at understanding him, and when she couldn't, she just asked him to repeat it or to spell it.

"You're my best friend now, Don," she said.

He smiled. "Good for me. You want to play Connect Four?"

"What's that?"

"A game I always win at."

"Pretty confident there, aren't you?"

"For good reason."

"We can't beat him, that's for sure," his dad said.

"That's because he's got a devious streak to him," his mom said with a big smile.

Don laughed. "That's me, all right. Dad, I have a confession to make."

"What's that, son?"

"I stole a book."

"You stole a book from the library?" his dad asked.

Don had a big smile on his face. "Yes."

"What was the book about?"

"Honesty," Don said, laughing out loud.

"He's joking, of course," his mother assured Emily.

"Oh, I knew that," she said.

"Don, do you really want to play against Emily?" his dad asked.

"I do."

"Don't beat her too bad," his mom said.

"Why not?"

"She's a guest."

Don laughed. "This is war."

Don beat her nine out of ten times. "Well, you're too much for me, Don," Emily said.

"Come back. I'll teach you all my secrets."

"That's a better offer than he's ever given us," Don's mother said.

"She's a guest," Don said with a smile.

Don's mother gave Emily a ride to her apartment. "Thank you for coming tonight."

"I always enjoy being in your home. I feel so welcome and safe there."

"Don doesn't get many visitors. Each one is very appreciated."

"Do you ever wonder what he'd be like if he weren't, you know . . ."

"Once in a while. More than that, though, we talk about what it will be like when he's resurrected. Don and his dad have an agreement that they'll have a wrestling match on the day they're both resurrected. I think they both are looking forward to that."

"I'd like to be there to see that," Emily said.

"We'd be delighted to include you."

"It's a date then."

Because she'd had such a great time the night before, Emily woke up the next morning in good spirits, looking forward to another day. She was getting straight A's in all her classes, and she was proud of that. That's one thing that hadn't been taken from her in the fire.

But when she came out of her nine o'clock class, Austin was waiting for her in the hall.

"Good morning," he said.

She scowled. "You're not supposed to be here," she said.

"Excuse me? Isn't this a free country?"

"You have a math class this hour."

"It got canceled. You know my schedule? How come?"

She'd been caught. She didn't want to explain anything, so she walked faster.

"Did you have breakfast?" he asked.

"Yes."

"I didn't."

"Then go get some."

"Will you go with me?"

"No."

"Why not?"

"Because I have a class."

"No, you don't. I have your schedule. Guess what I found out. You don't have a women's health class. You were just trying to get rid of me, weren't you? How come?"

Emily stopped walking and turned to Austin. She sighed. "What do you want from me?"

"I just want to talk, that's all."

In her effort to avoid people, Emily had scouted out

184

many out-of-the-way places on campus—places where she could study or just be alone, without people walking by and staring at her. She took Austin to one of those, down in the basement of one of the buildings, to a small classroom.

"This looks like a great place to study," he said.

"It is."

She didn't want to sit down because she didn't want to encourage him to stick around.

"Is it okay if we sit down?" he said.

"I guess so," she said.

"I hear you're the Relief Society president in your ward."

She nodded. "Big surprise, right?"

"Not at all. I'm sure you're very good at it."

"You should go now," she said.

"Why do you keep trying to get rid of me?"

"I always try to make it easy for people who stop to talk to me. It's usually very awkward for them. I like to give them an easy out."

"I'm not all that uncomfortable. Oh, sure, you look a little weird in that outfit you're wearing, but I pretty much just think of it as a Halloween costume. And you still have pretty eyes."

She wanted to be mad at him, but she wasn't able. She liked it that he faced her situation head-on.

"What can I do to help you?" he asked.

"Nothing, really. I'm doing great now. Thanks, anyway."

She paused, waiting for him to say he needed to go. *Everyone leaves,* she thought. *That's just the way it is.*

"I could carry your books to class."

Austin, look, just say you need to get ready for your next class. You say that, and then I'll nod, and then you can go.

"You want something to eat? I saw a vending machine down the hall. Maybe a candy bar?" he asked.

"I'm fine. Really."

"You don't like candy bars? Well, it doesn't have to be that. They have other things. Just tell me what you want."

She gave a troubled sigh. "A candy bar would be fine."

He stood up and reached into his pocket. "I've only got enough change for one, so we'll have to share."

A minute later he sat down next to her and unwrapped the candy bar. "I'll show you a way to make sure we each get an equal part. I'll break it in two, then you get to choose which part you want."

She took the smallest piece.

"Whoa, talk about being noble," he said.

They each took a bite.

"Good, isn't it? Say, I was wondering if we could see each other once in a while," he said.

"What for?"

"I don't know that many people here. It'd just be for a little while, until I make a few more friends. I know you're busy. I don't want to take up all your time."

"Look, Austin, I know you just got off your mission and you're still trying to save the world, but don't make me your service project, okay? I'm fine. Really, I am."

"Service project? Is that what you think this is?"

"What else could it be?"

"It's not that."

"What is it then?"

After a long pause, Austin said, almost as if it were a confession, "Well, okay, Jeremy did ask me to check in on you and see how you're doing."

It all makes sense now, she thought. *He's doing this because of Jeremy.*

"And you've done it. Tell him I'm doing great. Now go get something else for breakfast other than a candy bar."

He stood up. "Okay, whatever you say. But I might come see you sometime, though. Is that okay?"

"I guess so."

186

She didn't expect he'd come back. It was just what guys said when they wanted to let a girl off easy; sometime never comes.

On Monday morning when she entered her private study room in the basement of a classroom building, Austin was there. He had a plastic grocery sack full of muffins, a couple of cartons of orange juice, and a pile of napkins with Taco Bell imprinted on them. He began laying things out on a table.

"Man, I'm glad you showed up. I was starting to worry some teacher would walk in and catch me here. I hope you're hungry."

He went to the trouble of doing this, she thought. *So try to be nice and then maybe he'll feel like he's done what Jeremy asked him to do and then he'll leave you alone.*

As they ate, they made small talk about school, but when she asked about his mission, Austin opened up.

He kept trying to maintain eye contact, but she kept glancing away.

"In your calling as Relief Society president, when you're talking to a girl in your ward, do you look her in the eye?" he asked.

"Yes."

"You're not doing that with me, though, are you?"

"No."

"Why not?"

"I don't know."

"I like to look into your eyes."

"Why?"

"They say our eyes are the mirror into our souls."

She looked at him, and they gazed into each other's eyes for just a moment, until she looked away.

"Doing the eye thing wasn't so bad, was it?" he said.

She stood up and began stuffing their trash into the plastic bag.

"You want to do this again tomorrow?" he asked.

"No. Look, Jeremy asked you to look in on me. You've done that. In fact, you've done way more than I'm sure he expected you to do. I promise if I ever need help, I'll give you a call. Now please go, so I can study for a quiz."

"Sure, whatever you say," he said, sounding a little hurt by her curtness.

He picked up the plastic sack and moved toward the door. Then he paused and turned back to her and said, "I know you were burned, and that's too bad, but that doesn't mean we can't be friends, does it?"

Before she could react, he was gone.

13

Austin began calling Emily every morning to say hi and to see if she needed him to do anything for her. For the first few days she always said no, but then she thought of something he could do.

"I've got a friend named Don," she told Austin. "He's in a wheelchair, and we're going to see the USU women's basketball team play on Thursday night. It'll probably be okay, but if it snows, like they're saying it might, I may need some help."

"Sure, no problem."

As it turned out, it didn't snow, but Austin came along with them anyway. He walked with Emily to Don's house and met Don and his parents. Before leaving for the game, the five of them sat around and talked for a while.

Emily carefully observed how Austin treated Don. If he had showed any reluctance to be seen with Don, she would have written Austin off. But he didn't.

At first Austin had a hard time understanding Don, but after he got used to Don's way of speaking, Austin seemed to take as much delight as Emily did in being around him.

Just before leaving for the game, while Don's parents were helping him get ready to go, Emily and Austin were alone in the living room.

"The trick with Don," she said, "is not to panic when you can't understand what he says. Just relax. He doesn't mind repeating himself. Oh, and don't try to finish his sentences for him."

"Okay, anything else?"

"Have a good time."

"That's what I plan on doing."

And, in fact, they did have a good time. Emily was impressed by the attention Austin gave Don. And how carefully he removed Don's jacket once they got to the fieldhouse. And how he included Don in every conversation.

The more she saw how he was with Don, the less suspicious she became of Austin's interest in her.

After the game, they walked back to Don's home where his parents invited Emily and Austin in for cookies and hot chocolate. While they were eating, Emily asked, "Don, when it comes to you, what do you wish people did better?"

"People are afraid to be around someone like me."

"I was a little afraid," Austin admitted.

Don smiled his crooked smile and said, "People need to focus on what we can do, not what we can't do."

Don's mother nodded. "Often people assume that because Don has *a* disability, he has *all* disabilities. Even health care professionals often don't know how to respond to him. It's kind of funny, they'll speak too slowly and too loudly or use childlike language, or they'll ask us, instead of Don, how he's doing."

Don laughed when his father said, "One day when Don was trying to get into the library, two people rushed to open the door for him. They opened the two doors, completely ignoring the post in the middle."

"I guess they thought if Don took a run at it, he could knock out the post," Don's mother said with a smile. "People actually mean well," she added. "It's just that they don't know quite how to act."

190

When it was time to go home, Austin walked Emily back to her apartment.

"You want to go out sometime?" he asked. "How about tomorrow night? Maybe we could go to a dance."

"A dance?"

"Yeah. You know, they play music and people sort of . . . dance."

"Look, Austin, I enjoyed tonight very much, but, I mean, let's face it, there's no need for you to waste your time with me."

He threw up his hands in mock despair. "It's because you've heard what a lousy dancer I am, isn't it? Heck, you crush one girl's toe, and suddenly nobody will dance with you."

She started to laugh. "This is insane."

"Why?"

"It just is. You know why."

"No, I don't."

"Look at me," she said softly.

"I am looking at you."

"Why are you doing this?"

"We were friends before my mission, weren't we?"

"You were friends with Jeremy, not with me. I was too young."

"You cooked me breakfast that one time. And we talked. That was nice."

"That was a long time ago."

"So, we're both older now."

She shook her head. "Don't waste your time with me."

"This is not a big deal, Emily. I'm just asking you to go to a dance. We'll go, we'll dance a little, we'll talk. Why not go with me?"

Against her better judgment, she finally agreed to go to the dance with him.

*   *   *   *   *

Why is he doing this? Is this a service project? she thought the next morning when she woke up. She could smell a service project a mile away. People who did service projects came in, made a fuss, and then were gone, never to be heard from again.

But this didn't seem like that. Especially not after she'd seen how he was with Don. Still, though, she was puzzled.

He arranged to pick her up half an hour before the dance was scheduled to start.

"Let's go. We don't have much time," he said on their way out the door.

"Time for what?"

"Time to watch them set up. That's the best part."

They arrived fifteen minutes early. Even before the cashier showed up.

When the taped music began a little after eight, they were the only ones there.

"Would you care to dance?" he asked with a bow.

"I feel self-conscious being the only ones here."

"I know a great, out-of-the-way place we can go."

They climbed a set of stairs to a balcony that overlooked the dance floor. No one was up there, and they were out of the view of anyone from down below.

"Want to dance?" he said.

"This could be a little tricky," she said.

"You just tell me what you want me to do, okay?" he said.

"Okay." She gave a sigh of relief. "And thanks."

"No problem. Now just tell me how we're going to do this."

"I'll come to you, okay?" she said.

"Sure, whatever you say."

She moved close to him. "This seems a little strange."

192

"I know, but it'll be better once we start dancing. Is there some place I can hold you to keep you close to me?"

She thought about it. "I guess maybe you could put your arm around my waist and put your hand on my back. Just above my waist, and more to your right."

"Okay, I'm going to do that now. If I'm in the wrong place, you tell me, okay?"

He positioned his hand. "How's that?"

"Actually, maybe a couple of inches higher would be better."

"Sorry. How's that?"

"That seems fine."

"Can I pull you in a little closer?"

"Well, I don't know. I'd have to think about that."

"Sorry, I don't mean now. What I mean is, if I do, it won't hurt, will it? I mean, my hand is over good skin, right?"

"Yes, it is."

"Okay, good. Well, I guess we could dance some then, right?"

"I think so."

They began dancing. Her face was only an inch from his shirt. She wondered if she looked like someone very nearsighted trying to read a newspaper.

"If you'd like, you can rest your head on my shoulder," he said.

"That's very considerate of you."

She briefly touched her head on his shoulder but then pulled back.

He smiled. "That's okay. It'll probably take some getting used to."

"You're right."

They danced the next five songs. She ended up with her head on his shoulder and her eyes closed as they rocked slowly and gently in time with the music.

He noticed her tears. "Are you all right?"

"I am. I'm having a wonderful time."

"Then why the tears?"

"I don't know. I guess maybe I'm just grateful. I didn't think I'd ever dance with anybody again. It's very nice. Thank you very much."

"You're thanking me? I've got a beautiful girl who's willing to dance close to me. I'm the one who should be saying thanks."

By ten o'clock, she was exhausted. "I guess I'm ready to go now."

"Sure, me too."

"I'm afraid to go down there."

"Why?"

"Because people will stare at me and wonder why someone like you is with me."

"We'll wait for just the right time, and then we'll make a run for it."

When there was a drawing for a door prize and people moved toward the stage, they left.

"Do you want to get something to eat?" he asked.

"No, that's okay."

"Not even some hot chocolate?"

"Going to a restaurant still isn't something I'm comfortable with. People stare at me. I know I shouldn't let it bother me, and most of the time, I don't, but, well, to tell you the truth, it wouldn't be that much fun for me."

"Maybe we could have hot chocolate at my apartment," he suggested.

"Will anyone else be there?"

"Probably not."

"I shouldn't do that then."

"Sure, I understand. How about if we go to your place?"

"Yes, we could go there."

Megan, one of Emily's roommates, came out of the bedroom to see who'd come in. She was wearing a tanktop and jogging shorts and sneakers. "How was the dance?" she asked.

"We had a great time," Emily said enthusiastically. "Well, at least I did."

"I did too. We danced every dance," Austin said.

"But you're home so early," Megan said. "Do you always get your dates home so early?" she teased.

"Well, yeah, I do. In high school, I used to go with a girl who had a paper route."

"If you took me out, I'd keep you busy until at least midnight." The way she said it sounded almost like a dare.

Emily raised her eyebrows. She grabbed two cups. "We came here for hot chocolate." She was hoping that would be enough of a hint for Megan to leave them alone.

"Sounds great. Make me some, too, okay?"

Emily tried not to show her growing anger. "Sure." She got another cup from the cupboard. The way Megan was dressed made Emily very uncomfortable. Her tanktop was barely modest straight-on, but when she leaned forward, it revealed way too much.

Megan sat down at the table across from Austin. "You want to know what I've been doing tonight?" She didn't wait for an answer. "I've been working up my routine. On Monday I'm going to try out for cheerleader. One of the girls got real sick and had to drop out of school, so they have to replace her."

"What did she have?" Emily asked.

Megan shrugged her shoulders. "Beats me. All I know is if I do good on Monday, I'm in. Austin, you want to see my routine? Maybe you'll have some suggestions."

"Sure, why not?"

Austin helped Megan push the table off to the side so she'd have plenty of room. Megan went to her room and brought out her CD player. "Well, here goes."

Emily sat next to Austin as Megan went through her

routine. She was embarrassed for Megan and wondered if she knew how inappropriate her performance was. She felt bad for Austin, who ended up keeping his eyes down as much as possible.

Finally it was over. Breathing hard and perspiring, Megan stood in front of Austin. "So what did you think?" she asked.

"I don't think I'll ever forget it," he said diplomatically.

"Really! It was that good?"

"You had my complete attention."

"Fabulous. That's what I wanted to happen. Emily, what did you think?"

"What will you be wearing when you do this for the judges on Monday?"

"They'll have a cheerleader outfit for me to wear."

"That'll be good," Emily said.

"Well, I'd better go take a shower. If you guys are still around when I get done, maybe we could play some games or something."

"Maybe so," Austin said.

Emily didn't want to stand in anyone's way. "I might turn in as soon as Megan gets back from her shower. But you can stay. Megan is very good at playing games."

Austin laughed. "We've already seen that, haven't we?"

Emily was surprised he'd noticed. "Yes, I believe we have."

He touched her left hand. "What do you want to do now?"

She stood up and carried the empty cups to the sink. "I'm about done for, but, I'm serious, if you want to spend some time with Megan, go ahead."

"Do you really want to get rid of me now?"

She thought about it. "No."

"What *do* you want?"

"To spend some time with you . . . without Megan around."

"Done. Let's go."

"But Megan thinks you're going to be here when she finishes her shower."

"Hey, my date was with you. Let's get out of here."

They parked outside the institute building. Finding it was still open, they went inside and sat on a couch in the hall. Far away they could hear chairs being moved and some guys laughing. The lighting in the hallway was dim.

"You want to tell me what you're thinking?" he asked.

"Megan has great skin. Skin is such a miracle. It prevents infection, you know. Skin does so much for us."

"What's wrong, Emily?"

"Sorry. I guess back there at the apartment I was getting a little possessive. It was sort of like, 'He's mine. Leave him alone.' Jealousy is not very becoming, is it? I mean, it's so selfish."

"I'm not interested in Megan."

"Well, really, it's fine if you are."

"You trying to get rid of me?" he asked.

"No. I'm just saying I'd understand."

"And why do you think I'd drop you for her?"

"Because she wasn't in a fire." She stood up and walked to the window and looked out.

He joined her. Together they looked out at the night.

"See anything interesting out there?" he asked.

She turned and reached up and lightly touched his cheek. "I dream of skin, you know. I really do. I've even thought of becoming a masseuse—to be able to spread lotion on people's backs and feel the sensation of perfect skin. Can't you see me doing that? I can."

Austin was quiet for a moment, then he said, "You've had a great disappointment in your life, Emily, and you're still trying to deal with it."

They returned to the couch. She sat down next to him,

her head down, too embarrassed to face him. Her back was straight, her hands folded in her lap.

"Thank you for listening to me."

"You're welcome. Any time."

"We'd better go."

"Tell me about that outfit you wear. What's it for?"

"To keep the scars from getting thick and inflexible."

"How much longer do you have to wear it?"

"At least another year."

"Is that okay with you?"

"I hate the attention it draws, but it will help the skin look better, so I'm willing to do it. But it sometimes drives me crazy."

"You know what drives me crazy?" he asked.

"What?"

"My mother."

Emily smiled. She could believe that about Austin's mother. "In what way?"

"She's picked out the girl she wants me to marry. Her name is Meredith. Would you like to see a picture of her?"

"Do you have one?"

"Would you prefer the wallet-sized picture or an eight-by-ten glossy? A picture of her on the night she became first runner-up in the Miss Utah Pageant? Or a picture of her as first-chair cellist in the BYU Symphony Orchestra? Or how about a picture of her family? Her father is on a list to fill a vacancy in the Utah Supreme Court. Take your pick. I also have videos taken from her childhood. You can watch her grow up before your very eyes."

"Is she pretty?"

"Yeah, I guess so."

"And you're complaining? My gosh, she sounds perfect for you. Have you been spending time with her?"

"It seems like every waking hour when I'm home since I got back from my mission. Everywhere I turn, my mother has her propped up before me. Not now though. She goes to BYU, so we won't see each other except when we both go home."

He paused. "Do you know what my mom says to me about Meredith?"

"What?"

"'If you don't ask her to marry you, somebody else will snap her up.'"

Emily smiled. "Snap her up? What is she? A special on the Home Shopping Network? How does Meredith feel about you?"

"I guess she likes me. Not that I've tried that hard."

Emily smiled. "It must be tough to be irresistible."

He laughed. "Don't start. I just hate it, the way my mom plans everything out for me."

Emily wasn't comfortable listening to Austin talk about another girl. "I'm sure you'll work something out," she said.

Austin shook his head. "It makes me crazy," he said. "But, anyway, thanks for listening. It's good to have a friend to talk to."

Emily saw it more clearly. *And somebody you have no intention of getting serious with.*

Later that night, as she was getting ready for bed, Emily thought about Austin. *He's going to end up hurting me when he finds someone he can love. He's going to leave me more isolated and lonely than before. We will call this friendship, but it isn't. Not really. Because friendships last forever. And this won't last more than a little while.*

I should tell him no.

But I won't.

I'll be his friend, if that's what he wants.

After church on Sunday, Austin dropped by to talk with Emily. Her roommates were either taking a nap or out with friends.

"You busy?"

"Not really. I've just been going back over this visiting teaching list."

"What for?"

"Trying to make sure everybody's matched up right. I don't know. I've spent so much time on it this week. It's just that . . . well . . . I want everyone to feel a part of the ward."

"They probably do, though."

"No, that's just it, not everybody does. We've got a lot of girls who feel left out. I want each one of them to feel loved and appreciated. Every one of them."

"I know you do."

She smiled. "Sorry for boring you."

"No problem. In fact, I've always wanted to be in a Relief Society."

She laughed. "Really? Why?"

"Mainly for the treats. We never get anything to eat in elders quorum."

At the same time Austin was resisting his mother's efforts to get him together with Meredith, he was also trying to romance Samantha, the girl Emily had seen flirting with him in the library. Samantha was only a freshman, but she was easily the best-looking girl in his ward. She had long blonde hair, a great tan, and was young enough to be impressed just because he'd served a mission.

The first time he'd taken her out, when he walked her to her door, she looked up at him expectantly. It was a gesture that could not be misunderstood—so he kissed her.

"Oh, baby!" she said in a sensuous, breathy voice. Then she winked at him and went inside.

He couldn't sleep that night. *She gave me an "Oh, baby." What exactly does that mean? It must be good, though. And no girl has ever said that to me before. Maybe it means she's falling in love with me. I suppose it could happen. Love at first sight—for her, that is.*

"Oh, baby," he said, trying to say it the way she'd said it. He said it over and over again.

He whispered it a few times in bed, but then he found himself fantasizing about Samantha a little too much, so he got out of bed and went into the front room of the apartment he shared with three other guys.

It was way past midnight, and his roommates were all asleep. He tried watching TV for a while, but there was nothing on he wanted to see, so he went to his room and got the demo videotape Emily had made before her accident. He watched it all the way through—twice. He was amazed by how confident and self-assured Emily came across in the video. She was different now—much more quiet, even self-conscious. It was hard for him to think of the sophisticated news reporter and the Emily he knew as the same person.

He felt sorry for her. The accident had robbed Emily of her dream. It had changed her life. Thinking about the tragedy of what had happened to Emily drove away thoughts of Samantha's amorous "Oh, baby," and not too much later he went to bed and fell asleep.

The next day, after church, he tried to call Samantha, but her roommates said she was out for the day. He left a message for her to call him when she returned.

She didn't call.

At eleven o'clock that night, the phone rang. Austin fully expected it would be Samantha, apologizing for not being there when he called, anxious to see him as soon as possible.

But it was Emily. He was a little disappointed, but tried not to show it.

"What's up?" he asked.

"One of the girls in my ward just called. She's really depressed, so I asked her if she'd like a priesthood blessing.

She said she would, but I haven't been able to get hold of her home teachers. I've called some others in the ward with no luck. Is there any chance you could do it?"

"Sure, no problem."

As soon as he pulled in front of her apartment, Emily hurried out to the car. "Thanks for doing this," she said.

"Thanks for asking."

When they got to the apartment, Emily knocked, and the girl opened the door and let them in.

"Jamie, this is Austin. He's a friend of my brother, Jeremy."

Jamie looked embarrassed. She just nodded in Austin's direction, then turned to Emily. "I'm sorry for bothering you. It's just that I didn't know who to call, and you're always saying to call if anything's wrong. Well, right now, everything's wrong."

"Could you tell us more about it?" Emily asked.

"Everything. My roommates hate me. I'm flunking out of school. I have a part-time job to help get me through school, but I've been sick the past couple of days, so I haven't made it to work. My boss told me today that if I miss one more time, he's going to get someone else who'd be more dependable. And the way I'm feeling now, I won't be able to go tomorrow. And if I don't work, then I can't stay in college." She seemed to be on the verge of tears.

Jamie sat down at the kitchen table and held her face in her hands.

Austin hesitated, then said, "Did you say you wanted a blessing?"

Without raising her head, Jamie gave a muffled, "Yes."

Austin glanced at Emily. "I can't do this without a prayer first," he said. "Jamie, is it okay if Emily says a prayer before I give you a blessing?"

The unhappy young woman only nodded.

"Maybe we should have a kneeling prayer," Emily said.

202

Austin could tell Emily experienced some pain getting into a kneeling position, but she got down with only a small wince.

The three of them knelt next to the kitchen table.

Emily began to pray. Even though Austin felt guilty about doing so, he didn't close his eyes, choosing instead to watch Emily's face as she prayed. She spoke in a quiet voice and paused occasionally in her prayer, waiting it seemed for further inspiration. She spoke of faith in the Savior and hope for the future and asked Heavenly Father to bless Jamie with strength and courage.

After the prayer, as they were getting to their feet, Austin looked at Jamie's face. She hadn't made any sound, but tears were running down her cheeks. He felt he should do something to show his sympathy, but just awkwardly stood there. It was Emily who acted. She guided Jamie to a seat and patted her forearm, the way mothers do to little children when they've hurt themselves.

The thought of giving a priesthood blessing left him feeling weak. *I'm not ready for this,* he thought. *I should have closed my eyes and concentrated on the prayer.* He looked over at Emily. It was the look in her eyes that gave him the courage to go ahead. *Emily has the faith that this can make a difference, so I'll rely on her faith.*

Jamie sat waiting, her head down, her eyes closed, her hands folded on her lap.

Austin asked for her full name, nodded, then placed his hands on her head and gave her a blessing. He felt the Spirit as he reminded her of the Savior's love for her and blessed her with the health and strength to face her problems.

When it was over, she wiped the tears from her face, stood up, and hugged him and thanked him.

"You want to talk?" Emily asked Jamie.

"I would, very much," the girl replied.

"Austin, you'd better go home and get some sleep," Emily said.

"I'll wait for you and give you a ride home when you're through here."

"It's not that far. Besides, this might take a little while."

"It's okay, I can sleep in tomorrow."

"Well, okay, if you don't mind."

Austin went to his car, grabbed a blanket from the trunk, and curled up on the front seat and went to sleep.

An hour later Emily opened the car door. Austin sat up, and she got in.

"Thanks for waiting."

"No problem. How's she doing?"

"Better. I'm glad I stayed."

As he drove toward Emily's apartment, Austin said, "I admire you for the way you were with Jamie tonight. No matter what happens, she'll always know you care about her deeply."

"I hope she knows that. And I appreciate you being someone I can always count on." She reached for his hand and squeezed it. "Thanks for being such a good friend, Austin. That really means a lot to me."

Back at his own apartment, Austin thought about the Emily on the videotape. He didn't feel sorry for her anymore. Remembering her face as she prayed and the confident way she comforted Jamie, he thought, *She's lost a lot, but she's gained a great deal too.*

14

It was not easy for Austin to let go of the pleasant memory of Samantha's *Oh, baby!* He tried several times a day to get in touch with her, but she was never at home and never returned his calls.

Finally, though, after several days of frustration, he caught up with her and she agreed to go out with him on Friday night.

He showed up on time at seven, but when Samantha opened the door, she seemed disappointed to see him. There were seven or eight other young women in the apartment. They were laughing and talking, but they all turned to look at Austin when Samantha opened the door. She didn't invite him in but kept him standing on the porch, with the door open so they could all see what was happening.

"Hi. You ready to go?" he asked.

Wearing a grin and a knowing look, one of them said, "Is he the one you were talking about?"

Trying not to laugh, Samantha turned to her friends and said, "You guys hold it down, okay?"

"It is him though, right?" the girl asked again.

Samantha ignored the question. "Austin, some of my friends from high school came up to see me. So I can't go with you tonight. Some other time, okay?"

Austin felt his face go red. The girls were looking at him with a mixture of pity and cruel humor. He was deflated but not willing to give up. "I don't mind hanging out with you and your friends," he offered.

"No, sorry, that wouldn't work out. My friends and I are very close."

"Oh, let him stay," one of the girls said. "He's kinda cute."

"No, like I said, it wouldn't work out," Samantha said, then turned back to Austin. "You'd better go now."

He started to say, "I'll call you," but the door closed before he could get it out.

A few minutes later he was complaining to Emily about being stood up.

"She won't return my calls, she gives me one excuse after another, and now this."

"So? Give up on her then and try someone else."

"It's not that simple."

"Why isn't it?"

Austin got up and paced the room, trying to decide if he should completely open up to Emily or not. Finally, because she was a Relief Society president and so understanding of other people's problems, he decided to risk it.

"The first time I went out with Samantha, I gave her a goodnight kiss."

Emily stared at him in disbelief. "You kissed her on the first date?"

"It wasn't my idea. She gave me *the look.*"

"What look?"

"You know . . . *the look.*" In an attempt to demonstrate, he wet his lips, partially opened his mouth, and looked up expectantly. "That's *the look.* It's an invitation to be kissed."

"Maybe her contacts were bothering her."

"No, there's no mistaking *the look.* But that's not all. After I kissed her, she said, 'Oh, baby!'"

Emily burst out laughing.

"What?"

"Sometimes it's hard to believe you're two years older than me."

"When a guy kisses a girl, and she says, 'Oh, baby!' what does that mean?"

"I have no idea."

"Emily, c'mon, you're Relief Society president, for crying out loud. You're supposed to know things like that."

"If it ever comes up in a stake leadership meeting, I promise, you'll be the first one I tell."

"It must mean something."

"How old is this Samantha, anyway?"

Austin cleared his throat. "Well, she's a freshman."

"Are you serious? She's a year younger than me?"

He felt threatened. "Well, yeah, I guess so, but she's very mature for her age."

Emily laughed again. "Not with 'Oh, baby!' she isn't."

"I can't believe you're making fun of me. I didn't expect that from you. You're a Relief Society president. I thought you'd give me some advice."

"You want some advice? I'll give you advice. Grow up, Austin."

It wasn't what he wanted to hear, but, by the time Austin left Emily, he had decided to give up on Samantha for good.

I'll find someone else, he thought. *Someone older and more mature.*

Austin's mother was not happy about Austin staying in Logan every weekend, instead of coming home to spend time with Meredith. How was he going to fall in love with her if he never saw her?

She kept coming up with plans to get him home more often. Every time she called him, there was always a family gathering or some important event he needed to be to. This time it was to celebrate his father's birthday. There was going to be a surprise party for him on Saturday night, and nothing would do but that Austin be there. He dreaded having to endure another of his mother's fully orchestrated, big deal parties, but he left Logan on Friday afternoon, after his last class. He took a big bag of dirty laundry with him. *At least I can get my wash done,* he thought.

Before Austin went to bed that night, his mother casually mentioned that she had invited Meredith to have lunch with them on Saturday.

On Saturday morning, his mother gave him a haircut. She'd been cutting his hair since he was a little boy. They did haircuts in the kitchen, with Austin sitting on a stool, with a beach towel draped around him. Like everything else his mother did, she was good with the scissors and clippers.

"Too bad Meredith wasn't able to come home last night. She's in a string quartet and had a performance in Provo. When I talked to her mother yesterday, she said Meredith will probably be home in two weeks. It would be wonderful if you two could get together again. She's such a marvelous girl."

"I'll be busy that weekend."

His mother raised her eyebrows. "Really? Doing what?"

"I don't know . . . maybe spending time with Emily."

"Emily?"

"You know, Jeremy's sister."

"Oh? She seems so young for you."

"She's the same age as Meredith."

"She doesn't seem that old." There was a long pause. "Turn your head to the left, please. I'm not surprised you're spending time with her. You feel sorry for her."

"It's not that. We're friends. We get along real well. For one thing, we talk about things and help each other out."

"Does she ever talk about the extent of her injuries from the fire?"

"Not much."

"I don't blame her. I wouldn't either. Poor thing. I feel so sorry for her. Can you look down, please? Thank you."

Austin waited for the other shoe to drop.

"I understand the damage to her stomach and chest was extensive. I'm not sure she'll even be able to nurse her babies. Poor girl."

Austin jumped up. "Why are you telling me this?" He yanked the towel off his shoulders, threw it on the stool, and walked out.

He hurried to his room and began packing.

His mother appeared in his doorway. "What are you doing?"

"I'm leaving," he muttered.

"You can't leave now."

"Why not?"

"Meredith is driving all the way up from Provo just to have lunch with you."

He grabbed some socks from a drawer then slammed it shut. "You asked her—*you* have lunch with her."

"I really don't appreciate your attitude. If I offended you by what I said, I apologize. I'm not against Emily. Not at all. I think she's a wonderful girl. I just think you ought to understand how badly she was hurt in the fire and that she is going to require medical attention for years to come."

"Why did you tell me about the damage to her chest? Did you think I'd lose interest in her because of that? Do you have that low of an opinion of me? Sometimes I just don't understand you, Mother. I really have to get out of here now before you poison my mind any more."

"You can leave now if you want, even though I'm sure Meredith would like to see you at least for a few minutes. But if you insist on going, at least let me finish cutting your hair. You look ridiculous with only half a haircut."

Though he was still steaming, Austin decided his mother

was right. It didn't make sense to leave before she finished cutting his hair.

He resented her control over him. He'd experienced the same feeling his whole life. When he was growing up, he'd had no interest in becoming an Eagle Scout, but his mother just kept coming at him with little projects that would only take a few minutes, and before long, he'd done enough to earn the rank. He used to think, *They should have given the badge to my mom. She's the one who earned it.*

Taking his place back on the stool, he asked, "Are you afraid your precious Meredith might see me this way?"

"I don't know why you're so against me all of a sudden. All I've ever wanted is for you to be happy."

"Yes, but it's always happiness according to your terms, isn't it?"

She gave him one of her *I'm so misunderstood* sighs. "I don't know what you're talking about."

"How come you never wrote and told me about Emily being badly injured?"

"I'm sure I did."

"You didn't. If it hadn't been for Jeremy writing me, I'd have never known about it."

"I didn't want to distract you from your work."

"You had plenty to say about Meredith, though, didn't you?"

"I'm only trying to look out for your best interests."

While finishing his haircut, his mother brought up the subject of Emily again. "I apologize for saying what I did. I'm sure it sounded quite heartless. Ordinarily it's not something I would have ever said to you, but I thought you should at least know how much damage was done. It was quite extensive. And the operations just keep coming. Oh, in time, I'm sure she'll be fine, but when you consider the cost, the hospital time, the recuperation after each operation, it's all quite overwhelming. And who knows how much longer her insurance will continue to pay those costs? These are practical matters one has to consider. Can you move your head to the right?"

During the haircut, Austin did as he was told, moving his head up or down, or from side to side, to give his mother the best light—so she could make of him what she wanted.

The haircut seemed to take longer than usual. And by the time she finished, it was eleven-fifteen.

"Meredith will be here in a few minutes. If you could just say hello to her before you go, it would mean so much to her."

Austin had nothing against Meredith. She was a nice enough girl. "I'll only stay for a few minutes and then I'll go."

"You will stay for lunch though, won't you?"

It seemed ridiculous to go without lunch. "All right, I'll stay for lunch."

"That's my good boy," his mother said. He hated when she talked to him like that. It set his teeth on edge, to be called her "good boy," but he said nothing.

He decided that if he was going to spend time with Meredith, it couldn't be in the same room with his mother. And so when she showed up, he asked if she'd like to play Ping-Pong downstairs in the family room.

"You won't pout if you lose, will you?" Meredith teased.

Austin was still struggling to control his resentment of his mother. "I never lose," he growled.

"Really? Let's see what you got then, Kid."

Sometime during the first game, he looked across the table at Meredith and thought, *She's always been the chosen one, the best-looking girl in her school and the smartest and most talented. What would it be like to grow up like that?*

She had dark brown hair and dark eyebrows and eyelashes that enhanced her green eyes, which he had to admit were fascinating. He could see why she'd done so well in the Miss Utah Pageant, and he wondered what the girl looked like who'd beat her out. And yet she seemed unaware of her beauty, or at least she didn't flaunt it.

He played a civilized game and let her get ahead of him. Then, just before losing, he unleashed his specialty, a wicked spin on the ball that made it take a sideways bounce when it hit the table.

"Oh, my gosh! Where'd that come from?" she asked.

"Just lucky, I guess."

She laughed. "You've been toying with me, haven't you?"

He couldn't help but smile. "Something like that."

"Well, I guess it's time I got out my monster serve, but first help me find the ball."

By the time he joined her, she was on her knees, peering under the couch, looking for the ball. There were three soft pillows on the couch. It was too good an opportunity to pass up. He grabbed a pillow and threw it at her. It hit her on her shoulder and bounced off.

She turned to him with a big smile. "You know what? I think this is war." She grabbed the pillow and tossed it back at him.

They went from pillow fighting inside the house to chasing each other around the yard with glasses of water.

She tossed some water in his direction, and when he tried to take the glass away from her, she turned and ran through a door into the back of the garage.

He followed her into the garage and closed the door. "There's no way out of here except through me."

She shrugged her shoulders. "No problem."

They stood there, both trying to catch their breath from all their running.

This is so much fun, he thought. *Chasing and being chased. And I don't have to worry about hurting her like I would with Emily.*

"How about a truce?" he asked.

"For real, or is this just another one of your cheap tricks?"

212

"For real."

She nodded. "Okay."

"Let's go back and look for the Ping-Pong ball."

A few minutes later they were both sitting cross-legged on the floor, about five feet apart, lobbing a pillow back and forth to each other.

"Can I ask you a question?" he said.

"Sure."

"Why did you come here today?"

"For lunch."

"You drove up here from Provo just for lunch?"

"I drove up last night after the concert."

"Oh."

She laughed. "Don't worry. It's not just because of you. I needed to get my mom to do my laundry."

He gave a sigh of relief. "Good. Me too."

"Although, I must say, my mom is very enthusiastic about you," Meredith said.

"So it doesn't bother your mom that I'm a serial killer?"

She laughed. "Hey, nobody's perfect."

Just then, his mother called out from the top of the stairs. "Can you two pry yourselves away for lunch?"

Even though it was just sandwiches and tomato soup, having his mother preside over the meal created a certain formality and, for Austin, constant tension.

His mother was doing her best to impress Meredith about him. After reading Meredith the letter President Merrill had sent just prior to his release, she said, "We think Austin is going places in the Church."

Austin cringed. He hated it when people talked as if the Church were a business and that the goal was to go from one leadership position to another until finally becoming a General Authority.

"I'm sure he is," Meredith said.

Austin could not let his mother's statement stand

uncorrected. "Yes, someday I hope to be a really good home teacher, or maybe, if I work hard at it, someone who 'mourns with those that mourn, and gives comfort to those that stand in need of comfort.'"

"Mosiah, chapter 18," Meredith said.

He was impressed that she knew.

"It's hard enough to try to be a disciple of Christ without worrying about things that don't really matter," he said.

"I agree," Meredith said.

I wish you didn't, he thought. *It would make it so much easier not to like you. And it would be so much easier to like you if it weren't for my mother trying to force us together.*

When they were finished eating, his mother reminded them that the new Disney movie had just opened. "Have either of you seen it?" she asked.

"I'm usually too busy for that," Meredith said.

His mother looked at Austin, who did the right thing. "You want to go now?" he asked Meredith.

"Sure, that'd be great. Just let me phone home and tell my mom."

While Meredith was on the phone, Austin's mother said, "She's very thoughtful of her parents. That's so nice to see."

The movie theater was a madhouse. By the time Austin and Meredith entered the theater, it was dark and full of kids. They found two seats on the second row from the front, right up against the wall.

In order to watch the movie, they had to lean their heads back and look almost straight up. The picture on the screen was distorted from that angle, and the floor beneath their feet was sticky from someone's spilled drink.

They were showing previews from upcoming movies, mostly action-adventure, where nothing was said, but one explosion after another lit up the screen and assaulted their ears.

Austin felt moisture seeping into the seat of his pants. He

214

felt with his hand and discovered that someone had previously spilled their drink on his seat.

"We'll have to move," he said, cupping his mouth with his hand and speaking directly into Meredith's ear.

"What?"

"We have to move. Somebody spilled their drink on my seat, and now it's all wet."

She turned around and looked at the packed theater. "Where can we go?"

"I'll go talk to someone," he said.

He worked his way out of their row into the aisle and went into the lobby. Everyone who worked there was at the snack bar, trying to service the long line of kids waiting to get something to eat. He tried to get a girl's attention. "Excuse me, my seat is wet."

She either didn't hear him or didn't care. "I'm sorry. You'll have to get in line."

It wasn't actually a line. It was more a mob of little people trying to be served, and as new ones came they wriggled their way ahead of Austin.

Austin felt as though he were living a nightmare. His head began to throb from the noise. He looked outside. It seemed so inviting. And so he walked out to his car. Feeling the wetness on his pants, he took the blanket out of his trunk and spread it on the seat before getting in.

He felt a deep sense of loss, that life after his mission was going to be the same as before he left, that all the lessons he had learned would leave him, and that his life would stand for nothing, that he'd spend his life in meaningless activities.

I'll marry Meredith because that's what my mother wants me to do, and I'll go to law school because that's what my father wants me to do, and I'll spend the rest of my life marking time, having children I'm not close to, going off to work or to meetings, and the one thing that I've found to be worthwhile will be lost in the shuffle, and my life will end up like spending time in a packed theater showing movies that have no meaning. What is the point of any of this?

I promised myself I'd always be a disciple of Jesus Christ, but I'm not sure I'm strong enough to sort through all the things that don't matter in order to concentrate on what does.

What am I going to do? At least Emily is still my friend. She's a good example. She's been through so much. She can take whatever comes her way.

I've never seen where she was burned. What will I do if it's so bad that when she doesn't have to wear the pressure garment anymore I won't even be able to look at her?

I need to face the fact that when Meredith and I were having a water fight and I was chasing her with a glass of water, I was physically attracted to her. If I spend much more time with her, I'm sure I'll end up kissing her. She's so much fun. So what would be so wrong with being married to her?

Am I going to end up with a trophy wife like Meredith? It's what my mother wants. And I always do what my mother wants.

I need to talk to someone, someone I trust. Not my mother. I know what she'd tell me. Not my dad. He has in mind for me to run for governor of Utah someday. And he himself has a trophy wife. So what good will it do to ask him? I know what he'll say: "All things being equal, marry the girl who can help you get ahead." That's just the problem. I don't know what it means to get ahead.

There's only one person I really trust. And that's Emily.

If I marry Meredith, what will happen if we hit hard times? I'm not sure she could take it. Would she fold if one of our kids had serious medical problems? Or if she got sick herself? Or if I lost my job? Or if one of our kids got on drugs? Maybe she's the storybook princess who can only get by if she gets to live happily ever after.

216

He looked at his watch. He couldn't stay there. He had a responsibility to Meredith.

He returned to the lobby. It was empty, except for the girls at the counter.

"Your ticket?" a girl working there asked.

"I got a ticket twenty minutes ago, but my seat was wet."

"But you just walked in."

"I know. I tried to get somebody's attention, but there were too many kids at the snack bar."

"Where's your ticket stub?"

Austin searched his pockets. "I guess I threw it away."

"So you just want me to take your word for it, is that it?"

"I can prove that what I'm saying is true."

"How?"

"My date is in there waiting for me. She'll vouch for me."

"You left your date there all this time?" the girl asked.

"Yes."

"Where'd you go?"

"To my car. I had some things I had to work out."

"What kinds of things?"

"Things in my head."

"Things in your head? What are you, some kind of a psycho? Sir, tell me the truth—did you just imagine you paid for a ticket?"

He turned around and pointed to the seat of his pants. "Look, you can see where my seat was wet."

"I don't see anything."

He touched the back of his pants. "It feels wet."

She panicked, thinking he was about to suggest she touch the seat of his pants to prove it was wet. She backed away. "Mr. Hoffman," she called out, "can you come over here, please?"

The manager approached them. "Is something wrong?"

"This guy walks in here saying he bought a ticket but left because the seat he was sitting on was wet."

"If the seat was wet, you should have told us right away."

"He says he had some mental things he had to work on, so he went out to his car."

"Sir, if you left the theater without telling anyone, then you'll have to pay to get back in, unless you have your ticket stub."

"Look, I can prove that what I'm saying is true. If we go to where I was sitting, you can feel the seat, and then you'll know that I'm telling the truth."

"The movie's showing now. I don't want to cause any kind of disturbance for my customers."

"What about me?" Austin complained. "Aren't I a customer?"

"You would be if you bought a ticket," the girl shot back.

He knew that no matter how much he complained, they weren't going to budge. So he paid for another ticket, and then, thinking he needed an excuse to give Meredith about why he had been gone so long, he bought a huge box of popcorn with extra butter and two drinks. He also asked for two empty popcorn boxes he could lay on the seat to keep himself from getting more wet.

"So you're still sticking with that story, are you?" the girl asked cynically as she gave him the empty boxes.

Once in the theater, Austin had to wait for his eyes to adjust to the dark. Then he slowly made his way down to the second row, precariously shuffled through the kids in the same row, and handed Meredith the cardboard containers he was carrying.

"Where have you been?" Meredith whispered.

"Long line at the snack bar."

"What about your seat?"

"I brought some empty boxes to sit on."

In arranging the boxes, Austin knocked one of the drinks on the floor.

His head was throbbing from the noise and from the tension from his argument with the manager and the girl in the lobby.

"You want some popcorn?" he asked.

"No, thanks."

"How about a drink? It's grape." He took a taste. "It tastes just like cheap cough syrup."

"No thanks. I'm fine."

"More for me then, right?"

"I guess so."

A woman in a seat behind them leaned forward. "Could you two be quiet so we can watch the movie?"

Austin leaned back and looked up at the distorted images. He turned around to face the woman behind him. "Excuse me, but how can you stand to sit this close? It's like staring into a giant's nose."

She was not amused. "Am I going to have to get the manager to get you to quiet down?"

He turned around, rested his head on the backrest, and grabbed a big handful of popcorn. It was soaked in butter. By the time he finished one handful his hand and mouth were covered with grease.

He leaned over to talk to Meredith. "My hands are so greasy, if I tried to hold your hand, it'd keep slipping off."

He finished about a third of the huge box, and then, feeling that he might get sick if he ate any more, he leaned over and scattered the rest on the floor to soak up the drink he'd spilled.

He put his arm around Meredith and said, "So, you want to make out?"

She started laughing. "In a Disney movie?"

"Why not? It's like they say . . ." He began singing the words to "It's a Small World after All."

Unfortunately this was the saddest part of the movie.

Everyone else was holding back their tears. But Austin and Meredith began laughing hysterically.

"That does it," the woman behind them said. "I'm getting the manager." The woman took off up the aisle.

"Oh, man, we've been busted," Austin said. "Let's get out of here."

They made a dash for the exit next to the screen, ran to the car, and drove away.

"If my mom asks how the movie was, tell her it was real good," Austin said.

"Why not just tell her the truth?" Meredith replied.

"No. That'd be a big mistake."

"How come? It's a very funny story."

"She'd spend an hour telling me what I should have done. I can't take that now. I've got a headache."

"This is very complicated, isn't it?"

"What?"

"Your relationship with your mother."

He nodded. "You have no idea."

"Austin, if you end up liking me, will there be a part of you that will resent the fact that your mother got us together?"

He shook his head. "I don't know." He sighed. "It's a good question though."

"Yes, I think it is. Can you take me to my car now?"

"Sure, no problem."

As she got into her car, Meredith said, "Next time you want to see me, come to Provo. And leave your mother at home. In your mind, too."

On Sunday after church, Austin went over to see Emily to tell her about being with Meredith.

"She sounds like a winner to me," Emily said.

"I suppose."

"You don't sound all that convinced."

"Of all the rotten luck—she's everything my mother said she was."

"And that's a problem for you, isn't it?" Emily asked. "You like her but you're afraid to give your mom the satisfaction of admitting she knows what's best for you."

"You are so far off the mark on this, Emily," he said defensively.

"I don't think so. You're just too proud to admit it. Look, Austin, just because your mom is for something doesn't mean it's a bad idea. I think you need to go see Meredith in Provo, on her turf, like Meredith suggested."

"You really think that might make a difference?"

"There's only one way to find out, isn't there?"

"Well, okay, I'll give it a try. Thanks."

"You know what? My life will be so much simpler once you're married off," she said with a smile, which faded much too quickly.

It was a new thought to him. "I just thought of something. Once I get married, we won't be spending as much time together, will we?"

"Are you serious? We won't be spending *any* time together. You know that."

"I'll miss that. You're the one I always run to when I need someone to talk to."

"I've noticed that. Oh, there's one thing I need to tell you."

"What's that?"

"If you share an *Oh, baby!* moment with Meredith, spare me the details, okay? I don't really want to know about it."

When Austin phoned Meredith in Provo, she seemed surprised but pleased to hear from him.

"I'll be down in Provo next weekend, so I was wondering if I could see you," he said.

"Only if you'll play me another game of table tennis. I don't lose easily."

"This will be good practice for you then," he teased.

"Good practice playing, or good practice losing?"

"Losing, of course."

"We'll see about that." She paused. "Let's see—things will be a little complicated for me, but I think we can work it out. I have a symphony concert Friday and Saturday nights, and a practice Saturday morning, but I'm sure we can work around that."

"I would even be willing to go to your concert."

"Oh, my gosh! Really? You must really like me then, to actually be willing to attend a symphony concert."

"Actually I've been to several concerts in my lifetime."

"Is that right?"

"Oh, sure. In fact, I don't really mind concerts where they play stuffy classical music. I mean, where else can you get together with five hundred people to take a nap?"

She had an easy, infectious laugh. "Actually, that's true."

"I'm glad you're such a good sport about this."

"And I'm glad you're coming to my concert," she said.

"It's all part of the package. If you were a nurse, I'd give blood."

"Really? What if I were a mortician?"

On Friday night Austin took Meredith to dinner before the concert, then got through the performance by eating candy. Whenever he felt sleepy, he'd pop another jelly bean into his mouth.

They went for dessert after the concert. After they'd spent some time talking at the restaurant, he began to feel as though he'd spent the concert applauding the orchestra, and then afterwards, applauding her.

"This summer I might have a chance to play with the Cleveland Symphony in their Young Artists Series. At least I'm one of the finalists."

"That's really good," he said.

"The only trouble will be if it conflicts with me compet-
ing again for Miss Utah."

Austin knew he should say, *Wow, Meredith, it must be
great to be so talented!* The only trouble was by that time of
night he was tired of telling her how wonderful she was.
Isn't there anyone in your ward who needs your help? he
thought.

He stayed at Jeremy's apartment that night. Spending
time with him was the best part of the weekend. He filled
Jeremy in on what a good job Emily was doing as Relief
Society president.

"Also, she's one of my best friends at USU," he told
Jeremy.

Jeremy smiled. "Thanks, bud, for looking after her."

"Actually, she's doing more for me than I'll ever do for
her."

The next morning Austin met Meredith at her symphony
orchestra practice. Afterwards, she had some errands to run,
and since she knew the area better than he did, she offered
to drive her car.

With Austin standing around looking bored, she spent
over an hour shopping for a dress to wear in her next beauty
pageant, but she didn't find anything she wanted. By then
she was running behind schedule, and she still needed to
drop by the mall to pick up some things her hairstylist had
ordered for her.

Since it was a Saturday, the mall was crowded. After
cruising the parking lot for a minute, Meredith pulled into a
handicapped parking space and shut off the engine.

"We can't park here," Austin said.

"Why not?"

"This is a handicapped parking space."

"I won't be more than a couple of minutes."

"We still can't park here."

"Why not?"

"It's illegal. Besides, I have a friend who's in a wheel-chair. He has cerebral palsy, and it's very hard for his parents to get him around. They need to be able to park close to where they're going."

"Where does your friend live?"

"Logan."

Meredith took the keys out of the ignition and opened her door. "No problem. I promise I'll never do this in Logan. Let's go." She stepped out of the car.

Austin got out of the car. "I'm serious, Meredith. You can't leave your car here."

"Why not? We've already taken longer arguing about this than it will take me to run in and get what I need."

"That's not the point, and you know it."

"What is the point, Austin? That you have a few gimpy friends?"

Austin threw up his hands. "I can't believe you said that."

"Oh, I'm sorry—that isn't the politically correct term, is it? How insensitive of me. How about *mobility-challenged*? There, does that make it all better, Austin? Now let's go. I'm in a hurry."

"Meredith, look, we can work this out. Just give me the keys to your car. I'll drive around until you're done."

"That doesn't make sense. We're almost there."

"But what if someone who's handicapped wants to park while we're in here?"

"Don't feel sorry for the ones around here. They're all just faking it to get easy parking."

"That's not true."

"It is, though. Believe me. I see it all the time."

He caught up with her and stood in her way. "Answer me this—do you ever think of anyone but yourself?"

"I really don't need this now, Austin. I've got a concert tonight, and a pageant to prepare for. On top of all that, I've got homework and a paper due on Monday. I just wish you'd be a little more understanding of the pressure I'm under today."

"What pressure? What's the absolute worst thing that could happen to you today? That you might flub a note in your precious concert? Who really cares? What if you'd lost twenty percent of your skin in a fire? What if you couldn't do something as simple as turn a page or brush your teeth? You try living your life in a wheelchair for even one day and then you'll know how easy you've got it."

"All right, Austin, that really is enough. You've made your point, okay? I'll never do this again. There, are you satisfied now?" She gestured to a store coming up on their right. "Here's where we're going. Like I said, it'll only take a minute."

A few minutes later they were out of the mall and headed back to Meredith's car. There was a policeman standing next to it, writing out a ticket.

"I told you not to park there," Austin said.

"It's no problem. Do you want to be the one with a limp, or shall I do it?" Meredith said.

"Just pay the ticket," he grumbled.

"Why should I? Watch this. It works every time. I'll just tell him I lost my handicapped sticker."

She started limping toward her car. He wanted no part of any plan she might come up with to get out of paying the ticket, so Austin hung back.

He watched as she used her charm and outright lies to talk her way out of getting a ticket.

Austin approached them.

"Thank you so much for being so understanding," Meredith said, smiling warmly at the police officer.

"Don't let her off," Austin said. "Give her the ticket. She's lying about having a handicapped sticker. She faked the limp, too."

Meredith whirled around and glared at him.

The ticket was for seventy-five dollars. Without another word, Meredith drove him to Jeremy's apartment, dropped him off, and sped away.

* * * * *

On Friday, while passing through Ogden on his way to BYU, Austin had dropped off his laundry at home for his mother to wash. And so, on Saturday afternoon, on his way back to Logan, he stopped by to pick up his clean clothes.

When he stepped inside the house, all he wanted was to gather his things and leave, but he knew that wasn't going to happen. The only question in his mind was how big an argument was he going to get into with his mother. It depended on how much he dared to tell her.

"Well, how did it go with Meredith?" she asked.

"Not too good, actually. We probably won't be seeing each other again."

"What happened?"

He didn't want to explain. He just wanted to go back to Logan. "It just didn't work out, that's all."

"But there must be a reason."

"Mother, please, don't start. I've got a killer headache, and I feel a little sick to my stomach. Just let me pick up my things and leave and then I'll e-mail you a complete explanation tomorrow." He hurried to his room and started to pack up.

His mother intercepted him before he made it out the door.

"At least give me some kind of explanation."

Don't talk. You'll only make it worse, he thought.

"I will later, but I can't now." He stepped past her and went out to the car and shoved everything in the trunk.

226

"You should hang the shirts up and not just throw them in the trunk," she said.

"Why can't you leave me alone!" he shouted, slamming the trunk of the car shut.

Her mouth dropped open.

"You're always after me to do something, just like you were in high school. Well, I'm not in high school anymore! I'm different than I used to be! I'm different now than before my mission! I know you can't see that, but it's the truth, and you've got to recognize it because I can't stand to have you always managing me!"

He jumped in his car and backed it hard out of the driveway.

Halfway back to school, racked with conscience, he stopped and opened the trunk of the car and hung his ironed shirts carefully on the hooks in the backseat of his car.

That night, he knelt to say a prayer but nothing would come. *What a hypocrite I am. I keep saying I'm a disciple of Jesus Christ, but I don't act that way. I yell at my mother and, out of spite, betray Meredith's friendship. There must have been a better way to teach Meredith to be more considerate of the handicapped than to end up costing her seventy-five dollars.*

It's so hard being off my mission and having to deal with so many things all at once. It's like being on a slippery slope. Every time I try to go up, I end up sliding further down.

Disgusted at the direction his life was taking, he shook his head. *I'm just like everyone else now.*

15

On Sunday after church, Austin took a walk with Emily. He told her about his weekend with Meredith.

"I'm sorry it didn't work out," she said.

"Yeah, me too. Well, it's okay. When you're fishing a river, and you don't catch anything in one place, you just move upstream and try a different place."

She smiled. "Why is it, that, to a guy, everything in life is like some sport? My gosh, it must be nice to be able to think in such simplistic terms."

He wasn't about to let her get away with that. "And I'm sure it's great to think that every church lesson requires a tablecloth, a centerpiece, and some artsy doodad handout. I mean, what has that got to do with anything?"

She couldn't help but laugh. "Okay, you made your point. Truce?"

"Truce." He paused. "So, the thing is, right now I'm out of prospects. You're a Relief Society president; you know a lot of girls. How about picking out a few for me?"

"I'm not running a dating service here, Austin."

"I realize that, but you know me, and you know the girls in your ward. There must be at least one you can come up with."

"I'll think about it and let you know, okay?"

They ended up in her apartment, sitting at the kitchen table, eating Oreo cookies.

"Do you know what people in your ward say about you?" he asked.

"Not really."

"They say that when you look into someone's eyes, you can see all the way into their heart." He paused. "By the way, do you see anything in my eyes?"

"No, I'm sure I don't."

"Well, maybe if you tried . . ."

They gazed into each other's eyes. "So, what do you see?" he asked.

She looked into his dark brown eyes. "I see a guy who's willing to do whatever he can for a friend."

He smiled. "Anything else?"

"If you want to hear nice things about yourself, buy a box of fortune cookies."

He laughed. "Maybe I'll do that."

"I'm sorry. That wasn't very nice of me to say, was it?"

"Emily, it's me, remember?" He got a knife and split open the two halves of a cookie and scraped the frosting off, then ate the cookie.

"Can I have your frosting?" she asked.

"Sure, help yourself. Oh, by the way, you sure eat a lot."

She might have been offended by him saying so, but they had become good enough friends that she didn't mind.

"Well, thanks for noticing," she said.

He realized he'd made a mistake. "I'm sorry. It's not that you're fat, or anything. I just couldn't help noticing that—"

She laughed. "Don't worry about it. It's from when I was in the hospital. Burn victims have to really stuff it in because the body needs so much energy to rebuild itself."

"You can have my frosting anytime then."

"Thanks. It's a deal."

He formed an assembly line, scraping the frosting off his

Oreos and stockpiling the white paste on a plate for her to eat later on.

"Guess what?" she said. "I've found a way to be more accessible to the girls in my ward."

"How?"

"The secret is not to look busy. If I look busy, girls with problems won't come to talk to me. So I've turned a lot of the details of conducting our meetings over to my counselors. And I just go around looking like I've got all the time in the world."

"Does it work?"

"Yeah, it does. You know what I've found out? Everyone has problems. And you know what else? If I can talk with a girl about her problems and, you know, just let her share them with me, then things don't seem so bleak to her."

"That's really good, Emily."

"I'm boring you, aren't I?"

"No, not at all. You should see the way your eyes light up when you talk about Relief Society."

"What would you rather talk about?" she asked.

"Do you have a ward list with pictures? Maybe you could fill me in on each girl as we go through it."

"You pretty much have a one-track mind, don't you?"

He smiled. "Yep, that's me, all right."

She got her ward directory and began paging through it.

"Wow, what about her?" Austin asked.

"I don't think so."

"How come? She's kind of cute."

"She's not your type."

"How do you know?"

"Just trust me, okay?"

"Okay."

He turned the page and scanned the pictures. "How about this one?"

Emily shook her head. "She just got engaged."

"I can see why. She's really beautiful."

Emily nodded. "That's important to you, isn't it?"

"Yeah, sure, why wouldn't it be?"

"No reason. How about her?"

Austin studied the girl's picture. "So, how come she wears glasses?"

"Well, this is just a guess, but I'd say to improve her vision."

"What I mean is, why isn't she wearing contacts? I'm not sure I trust a girl who wears glasses."

Emily shook her head. "Please tell me you're not serious."

"Let me go through this for you: The thing is, a girl who wears glasses when she could just as easily wear contacts is making a statement about herself."

Emily looked totally confused. "And that statement would be what?"

"It's . . . *I don't care what you think, I'm not going to wear contacts just because they'd make me look better.*"

"And that's bad?"

"Not necessarily. I just worry that, if I married someone like that, she wouldn't be willing to change."

"Oh, I see, you expect the woman you marry to do all the changing? Austin, that is so egotistical."

"I suppose." Austin turned the page. "Whoa! What about her?"

"She's a freshman."

"So?"

"I know you don't want to date freshman girls."

"Well, okay, I did have one bad experience, but I'd be willing to try it again. I mean, she's really not too bad. Oh, one thing, is she taller than you?"

"I think so."

"That's good. I like 'em tall."

"If you want someone who's tall, we've got a girl who's six-foot-three."

He shook his head. "Not *that* tall. Tell me about the freshman. My gosh, what a face. She's spectacular."

"She's younger than most freshmen. In fact, I think she skipped a grade. So she's probably, what, seventeen?"

"Well, that's pretty young, but, hey, at least she's in college, so that counts for something, right?"

Emily shook her head. "I can't believe you'd be willing to date a girl that young."

"It's kind of like the draft in the NBA. When they open the bidding for the nation's best college players, the better they are, the sooner they get taken."

"I see," she said quietly, closing the ward directory. "Physical beauty's really important to you, I guess."

Austin nodded. "Well, yeah. Why not? But I'd want her to be spiritual too."

"Really? And what do you suppose will have made the girl of your dreams become spiritual? Always being the favored one in every social setting? Being happy every day? Never having to endure a difficult experience? Is that what you think fosters spirituality?"

"I see your point. Okay, what I mean by spiritual is that she graduated from seminary and that she's living Church standards."

"Well, that should be easy to find." Emily wasn't smiling as she tucked the ward directory under the phone-book in the kitchen.

"We're not all the way through the directory yet."

Emily turned away. "Austin, I've got a headache, so if you'll excuse me, I need to take it easy for a while."

"Tomorrow then?" Austin asked.

"Whatever. Can you let yourself out? Good night, Austin."

Emily, who loved every girl in the ward, and who had even gone with some of them to meet with the bishop for

232

the help that only he could give them, now also needed her bishop.

It was easy to get an appointment to meet with him. She thought he would think it was about one of the other girls in the ward. But it wasn't. This time, it was about her.

She told him about her friendship with Austin, and then said, "He wants me to pick out a girl from the ward for him to date."

"Is that a problem?"

"It wasn't at first, but now it is."

"How come?"

She didn't want to say it. "I care about him in a different way now."

"More than just friends?"

"I'm afraid so."

"Does he know that?"

"No, it would scare him off if I told him."

"Why's that?"

"He likes pretty girls. I don't blame him. The fact is, I have nothing to offer Austin."

"You're good friends though, so how can you say you have nothing to offer him?"

She couldn't look the bishop in the eye, and she wasn't sure she could tell him how she felt. "I'd better go now, Bishop. I know how busy you are."

"I have all the time in the world for you."

Several long moments passed as she struggled to decide how much to say. She'd seen this before, with the girls she'd talked to, reluctant to admit they weren't perfect, embarrassed to open up their inner world to outsiders. *Well,* she thought, *now it's my turn.*

"Emily, please, I want to help, but you have to tell me what's bothering you."

She wanted to be strong, to act out the role she had created for herself, of always giving and never needing anything. But the dam was full, and she couldn't hold it in any longer. She began to cry.

Bishop Cameron came around the desk and sat next to her and, gently, because he didn't want to hurt her, patted her on the back.

It took a long time before she could confess the one thing she had never told anyone before. "I have nothing to offer."

"That's not true. You have a great deal to offer."

"I mean, to a man."

The bishop cleared his throat. "You mean if that man were your husband?"

"Yes, that's what I mean," she said softly, her hands covering her face.

"I don't know how to respond to that, Emily. I'm not a doctor."

"It's not medical."

"What is it then?"

"I'm so ugly now."

"Emily, that's not true. You're beautiful to me and to all the girls in the ward. My gosh, Emily, you've done such a tremendous job, reaching out to the girls who would otherwise feel left out. You have such a gift."

"That's not what I'm talking about. I want Austin to desire me physically, too. Is that so wrong?" She began to cry even harder.

Bishop Cameron didn't have an immediate answer. He sat quietly, praying to know what to say. Emily went on.

"Austin wants me to help him find a wife. That's not easy to do when you love someone. I think you should release me as Relief Society president."

"What for?"

"Because at first I could concentrate all my efforts to helping the girls, but now it's different."

"Why is it different now?" he asked.

234

"Because I like Austin too much."

"Is that the only reason?"

"I guess so."

"Emily, let's be realistic. You've done so much in your calling. But the truth is you don't have to be a miracle worker. Okay? Try being just average for a little while. That'll be plenty good enough."

"You're not going to release me?"

"No, I'm not. You're the one Heavenly Father wants to watch out for the girls in our ward. You're doing a fantastic job."

"All right," she said softly. "What about Austin?"

"For now, all you can do is to continue to be his friend."

On Friday night, Austin cringed as he got out of the car to pick up his date. He knew this wasn't going to work out. "I definitely don't want to date a returned missionary," he'd told Emily when she'd first suggested he take out Helen.

She'd cut him in two with her answer: "You can't keep dating freshman girls all the time, Austin. You don't want a relationship between equals. You just want to be idolized. Well, that's not right. It's time to face reality. Besides, I've run out of freshman girls."

"That's not true—I'm pretty sure you're hiding some of them from me," he complained.

"That's because they're not right for you. It's either Helen or nothing."

And so he was now about to enter a new dimension—dating someone a little older than he was.

Helen was a returned missionary who had discovered on her mission that all elders are not equally valiant. It had made her skeptical of guys, and she wasn't easily impressed. Emily had known that but thought it would be good for Austin to have to earn her respect.

Physically, Helen met all of Austin's requirements,

although at just an inch shorter than he, she was perilously close to being too tall. He would have preferred her to be slightly shorter. She wore her long, blonde hair natural. When she came to the door, Austin couldn't help thinking she looked like an ancient Nordic warrior. He could imagine her standing in the bow of a ship, her sword raised, as she and her comrades were about to board an enemy vessel.

"So what have you got in mind for tonight?" she asked as they drove off.

"I thought we might go to a movie."

"What for?"

Austin was stumped. He shrugged his shoulders. "That's what people do on dates."

He drove past the theater looking for a place to park.

"That movie is R-rated," she said, glancing at the marquee of the movie theater.

Austin shook his head. "It can't be."

"It is. I don't go to R-rated movies."

"And you think I do?" he asked.

"You're the one who drove us here."

Austin backed up and looked at the rating on the sign over the box office window. Sure enough, it was R-rated.

"I didn't know it was R-rated," he said.

"Maybe that's true, and maybe it isn't."

"I'm telling you, I didn't know. They must have just changed the movie."

"You can look things like that up in a newspaper, you know," she said.

"I am fully aware of the value of newspapers, okay?"

"So now what are we going to do?" she asked.

Austin desperately wanted to get her into a movie, so they wouldn't have to talk. "We'll find another movie."

"I see. Well, I can hardly wait to see what you come up with next."

The pressure was too much for Austin, and he cracked.

"Oh, sure, it's all up to me, right? And all you have to do is shoot me down every time I come up with a new idea? Is that the way it is with you?"

"You're just mad at me because I wouldn't go to some stupid R-rated movie with you."

"I told you that I didn't know the movie here was R-rated."

"Actually, I don't even want to go to a movie."

"What do you want to do?"

"I want to have a talk with you," she said, sounding like his third-grade teacher.

"Man to man?" he asked sarcastically.

"Sure, if that's what it takes. See that restaurant? Let's go there and get something to drink. Oh, one thing, I only drink diet."

"Yes, dear," he muttered. *This is the last time I'm ever going to have Emily line me up with a returned missionary!* he thought. *Man, what I'd give for a freshman girl right now. I'd speak a little Vietnamese; maybe talk about serving in the mission office. And she'd tell me just how wonderful I am. That's what a date should be. Not this. Not Helga the Nordic warrior.*

Because Austin wanted the fastest possible service, they sat at the counter.

After the waitress left with their order, Helen began: "Girls in the ward talk. We know you've got Emily looking for a girl for you. We just don't understand why you aren't dating her when you're such good friends. Is it just because she was in a fire? Are you really that insensitive and shallow?"

Austin flagged down their waitress. "Ma'am, could you make those drinks to go?"

He turned to Helen. "I'd better get you home. You probably have things to do. I mean, the night's still young—there must be other guys you can shoot down before the evening's over."

"You do realize that Emily's in love with you, don't you?"

"You're crazy. We're just friends."

"She'd do anything for you—even help you find a girl to marry, just because you asked her to. That's how much she loves you." Helen shook her head. "Personally, I don't know what she sees in you, but we'd probably better not get into that."

"She's not in love with me, okay? We're just friends."

"Everyone in the ward knows it. Why don't you?"

The waitress brought their drinks to the counter. Austin paid for them, then escorted Helen to the car. He just wanted to get rid of her.

As soon as the car stopped by her apartment, Helen opened the door by herself and got out.

He followed her to her door. "I like Emily as a friend, but nothing more serious than that."

She turned around. "Fine, I can understand that. But, you know, that's why people agree to see each other exclusively, to see what will come of their being together," she said. "I need to go now. Thanks for the drink." She looked down at the plastic cup. "Like I said, though, I would've preferred diet."

"I got you diet," he complained.

She took another sip. "This is not diet."

"You can't tell the difference just by tasting. Nobody can."

"I can. And I'm telling you, this is not diet. Let me taste yours. Maybe it's diet. Maybe the waitress switched the cups by mistake." She reached for his cup.

He put out his hand. "No, get away."

"What?"

He scowled. "I don't want you getting your germs all over my drink."

238

"Well, answer me this then, does yours taste like diet?"

"Look, could we just change the subject?"

"Sure, anything you say." She gave him a superior smile. "How many baptisms did you have on your mission?"

"Well," he stammered, "if you count the ones who got baptized right after I was transferred—"

She scoffed. "They don't count—everybody knows that."

"How many did you have?" he asked.

"Thirty-three. What about you?"

A long pause. "Less than that."

She snorted. "Why doesn't that surprise me? Hey, think about what I said, okay?"

Surprisingly, even though his worst nightmare was being on an endless date with Helen, Austin couldn't stop thinking about what she had said about Emily.

On Saturday he went to the Logan Temple. After the endowment session, he lingered in the celestial room. Being in the temple had made him think about the direction his life was going. He wasn't entirely happy with his focus and the things that had become important to him. *Everything was so clear to me at the end of my mission. I thought about the Savior all the time.*

What have I learned from all this? Or have I learned anything? And what would be worse, to go through my life taking the Savior for granted, or to know how important he is but never let that knowledge make a difference in how I live my life?

I need to decide what I want. Would I rather be rich and powerful and struggling to find meaning in my life, or poor, yet having my life centered in the Savior?

He stepped into the hall and paused in front of a painting of the Savior that was hanging on the wall. *Emily and I are a lot alike. We've both grown because of what we've gone through. Of course the disappointments I had in the mission field are nothing compared to what she has had to endure. But our experiences led both of us to the Savior.*

I feel good when I'm with Emily. She's a good friend, not only to me, but to Don. I'm glad she introduced me to him. He's an amazing guy.

It's funny, but I didn't pay any attention to Emily until just before I left on my mission. And then, all of a sudden, there she was. It's like she grew up overnight. She was always a cute kid, but by the time I left on my mission, she was really starting to look good.

That was a long time ago though. Things are different now.

Too bad about her accident. I wonder how badly her face and body were burned. Probably pretty bad. She says the operations are making her look better all the time. So maybe it won't be too bad by the time they're through with her.

She's good for me. She helps me stay focused on what's really important.

I suppose I could marry her. I respect her a lot, but do I love her? I'm not sure. She'd be good for me though, that's for sure.

Maybe Emily and I should see each other exclusively. Just to see how it goes. With the idea that we might end up getting married. Of course she might not want me. I wouldn't blame her. At least her flaws are on the surface. Mine are deep within me and rock-hard solid.

One thing's for sure—if I were married to Emily, she'd inspire me to be a better person.

It's something to think about.

On Monday night, after Emily and her roommates had finished having family home evening, Austin came over to see her. There were still five or six people in the apartment.

He asked her to step outside with him. She put on her coat, and they walked out to his car and got in.

"I have something I'd like to ask you," he said.

"What?"

"I'd like us to start seeing each other exclusively."

Emily stared at him. After a few moments, she said, "I don't think that's such a good idea."

"Why not?"

She decided to be blunt. "Because when I finally get this compression garment off, and you see the way I really am, and you decide you can't stand to be around me anymore, it will be that much harder for me, because I'll know the reason you walked away."

"I won't walk away, no matter what. We're friends, aren't we?"

"For both of our sakes, look some place else. Okay, look, I admit I've still got a few freshmen you can try." She got out of the car and walked quickly back to her apartment, went in her room, and shut the door.

A minute later, he knocked on the door to her room. "Emily?"

"Go away please," she called out. "I'm not feeling well."

"We need to talk."

"No, please just go away."

He opened the door, walked in her room, and closed the door.

She was very much aware of the girls in her apartment and some guys from another apartment who'd seen Austin go into her room. "You can't be in here."

"You're worrying about me making a move on you? My gosh, Emily, what could happen? It would take three technicians and a crane to pry you out of that outfit of yours."

She suppressed a smile. "That may be true, but, still, it isn't right for you to be in my room. I am the Relief Society president, you know."

"All right, I'll go, but there's something I have to say. I know you're worried about what will happen when I can see where you were burned. I worry about that too. I realize that some parts of your skin might not be perfect, but there's something about you that keeps bringing me back. I can't define it, but it's there."

"What?"

"I'm not sure. You tell me. Why do I feel so much peace when I'm with you?"

"Is that what you feel?"

"It is. The question is, why?"

"I don't know."

"You know, Emily, but you won't open up to me. I think you should. You owe me at least that much."

"What do you want to know?"

"I want to know what it was like for you when you were burned, and what it's like for you now."

"Why should I tell you?"

"Because that's what friends do."

They could hear laughter and the sounds of a game going on in the living room. She was embarrassed that she, a Relief Society president, had a guy in her room, against every rule she'd ever given to the girls in her ward.

Maybe if I tell him what he wants to know, he'll leave me alone.

"All right," she said, standing up, "I'll tell you, but not here."

They ended up in the institute building again. He moved the couch next to the window so they could look out and talk. She asked him to turn off the lights in a nearby empty classroom so it would be dimly lit in the hall.

When he sat down, she said, "All right. I'll tell you about the fire and what it did to me."

It took her over an hour. At first she was the only one dabbing at her eyes with one tissue after the other, but after a while they were both in tears.

"That's what I am," she said when she finished.

242

"No, that isn't what you are. It's what happened to you."

"It's the same thing."

"I don't think so. What you are came from that experience, but what you are is one of the most wonderful girls I've ever known. I care about you, Emily."

"You feel sorry for me. It's not the same thing."

"I don't feel sorry for you."

"Austin, look, don't use me to get back at your mom."

"This isn't about that."

"Of course it is. What else could it be?"

"Why do you find it so impossible to believe I want to see if we can be more than just good friends?"

"Because I can't understand what you see in me."

"I see beauty and kindness and consideration for others. Don't you know how beautiful you are?"

"I'm not beautiful, Austin. There are parts of me that are ugly."

"When you get the compression suit off, do you think I will only value the parts of you that weren't burned?"

"I don't know."

"I would still cherish every part of you."

She shook her head. "Not even I can do that."

"The marks on your body from the fire helped make you the person that you are now. So if I appreciate what you are, then I must value what made you that way."

She stood up. "I don't think we should see each other anymore."

"Why not?"

"Because it will only end up hurting us both."

"I thought you were the expert at pain."

"Not this kind of pain."

"What pain is there in my telling you that I want us to see if we can grow closer?"

"I won't be able to take it when you walk out on me after you see the way I am now."

"That won't happen," he said emphatically.

"You have no idea what a fire can do to a person. No idea at all."

"What if I go through the burn center with you?"

"Why do you insist on this? Why not just walk away now?"

"I'm not prepared to do that. When can we tour the burn center?"

"Don't, Austin, just leave it be."

"Saturday morning?"

After an agonizing pause, she slowly nodded her head.

They drove to Salt Lake City Saturday morning. Emily had called ahead and received permission to take Austin through the burn unit. Word had gotten around that they were coming, so when they arrived, Red, Brooke, and Doug were waiting.

"This is Austin," she said.

"Oh, very nice," Brooke said, beaming at Emily.

"Yeah, I like him better than all the others you've brought around for us to see," Red teased.

"There haven't been any others."

"He doesn't have to know that, does he?" Doug piped in.

"We're here for a tour, not for your blessings," Emily, red-faced, said.

"Well, then, let the tour begin!" Red chanted.

At the time there were only two patients in the unit. To protect their privacy, the group stayed away from them.

They ended up in the tank room.

"This is where we tortured Emily," Red said.

"You'd better explain what you do here," Emily suggested.

Austin found himself wincing as they talked about removing the dead skin and harvesting the donor sites for skin grafts. And about the daily baths. And about changing the dressings twice a day. And about physical therapy.

"I had no idea there was so much involved," Austin said.

"Not many people do," Red said.

Emily touched the stainless steel gurney where she had lain during washing. "I remember screaming my head off here."

"Me too," Red teased. "My hearing is still shot."

"But at least you cooperated with us," Brooke added.

Red placed his hand on Austin's back, then leaned over to look directly into his eyes. "She was one of the best patients we've ever had here. It wasn't easy for her. The way I look at it she can take anything life can dish out. That must be of some value, right?"

"I completely agree."

Red continued. "The skin we took from donor sites is in good shape. I mean it's not going to fall off someday, even though she might be afraid it will. Well, it's not. It's on there for keeps."

"It might have a slightly different texture than the skin around it, but it's still good skin," Doug added.

"Absolutely," Red said with pride.

Looking at her watch, Emily said, "Thanks for the tour, but we really need to go now."

As he shook Austin's hand, Red said, "Emily's a rare gal. She's gonna make somebody a great wife."

"Red!" Emily warned.

He feigned innocence. "What did I say?"

"I'm glad we did that," Austin said on their way back to Logan. "I think I understand things much better now."

"You haven't seen me yet," she said, then turned away because she didn't want to talk about it.

Austin wanted to believe it wouldn't make any difference to him when Emily no longer needed to wear the pressure garment and he could see the effect of the burns on her face and neck. But, in all honesty, he wasn't sure either.

He turned on some music. It gave them both an excuse not to talk.

16

Emily stood looking at herself in the bathroom mirror. In a few days she would no longer need to wear the compression garment that had covered her neck and head and face for so long.

She was not out of the business entirely, though. She would continue to wear a pressure garment that looked like a short-sleeve turtleneck, and, because they'd harvested so much skin from her thighs and backside, she would, for months, still be wearing compression shorts that went down to her knees.

But at least her face and neck would be freed.

She was trying to see how she'd look in public. Her hair was still much shorter than she would have liked it, and she'd thought about getting a wig to wear until hers was grown out long enough to hide part of her face and neck. But she'd decided against it. She was tired of covering up the truth about herself.

Sorry, world, but what you see is what you get, she thought.

I'll be glad when Austin decides it's not going to work out with us. It will make my life so much simpler. No waiting around for him to call. No wondering when we'll see each

*other that day. I'll get so much more done when I'm rid of
him.*

She washed herself and then struggled to get back into
her pressure garment.

That night Austin went over to Don's house. He found
Don working at the computer with his mother in a small
home office just inside the front door of the house.

"If it's convenient, I need to ask you for some advice,
Don," Austin said.

"I'll go worry about the dishes," his mother said.

"Don't just worry about them," Don quipped.

She smiled. "He's such a perfectionist." And then she left.

"What's up?" Don asked.

"Well, it's about Emily and me. I really like her a lot,
Don. Has she ever said how she feels about me?"

It was never easy to read Don's face; he smiled most of
the time. But he wasn't smiling now. It suddenly occurred to
Austin that asking Don for advice about Emily maybe wasn't
the best thing to do. Austin had never stopped to think how
Don might feel about her. But it was suddenly clear.

"I hope you're not mad at me for moving into your terri-
tory," Austin offered.

"It's okay," he said. "It would never work for me."

Austin didn't catch the last part. "I'm sorry, Don. What
did you say?"

"It would never work for me," Don said. After a moment,
he added, "She likes you a lot."

Austin was feeling very uncomfortable. The last thing he
had wanted to do was hurt Don, yet he had obviously done
so.

"Don, I'm sorry. I didn't take your feelings into account.
It never occurred to me that . . ."

Don shook his head slightly. "Don't worry about it."

Austin said, "I guess you know that she adores you. She's

248

always talking about you. We both admire you a lot." Somehow that didn't seem like much to say.

It was Don who got Austin off the hook. "So I get two friends for the price of one," he said, smiling again. Austin had to have Don repeat himself twice before he finally understood, and then Austin smiled.

"I just want you to know that, no matter what happens, Emily and I will always be your friends, either separately, if things don't work out, or else together."

Don smiled. "I'd like that very much."

The next Saturday, in the morning, Austin asked Emily if she wanted to go for a drive, knowing full well that he intended to end up with her at the Logan Temple grounds.

It was a sunny day, warm enough to stand being outside for a while. When they got to the temple, he asked Emily if she would take a walk with him.

They got out of the car, and he held her left hand as they walked around the temple grounds. "We need to talk," he said.

"Really? About what?"

"I've never told you much about my mission. I think I'd better. It might help you understand me better."

"Okay."

"You remember that morning before my mission when you cooked breakfast for Jeremy and me?"

"I'll never forget," she said, smiling. "I did more cooking than I'd ever done before . . . or since."

"You remember me saying I wanted to become a zone leader or mission assistant? Well, it didn't happen."

"It doesn't matter that much, does it?"

"Not only that. I didn't have very many baptisms, either."

"As long as you did your best, that's all that counts."

He nodded. "Yeah, I know." He reached down and picked up a pebble that had strayed onto the sidewalk and tossed it back in the flower bed. "I don't talk about my mission much."

"How come?"

"I guess because I had so few successes. Oh, one thing, I was very good at helping out in the kitchen, preparing lunches after zone conferences."

"Good for you."

"For a while I had a companion who was sick a lot. From that I learned to be patient. On the days he felt good enough to work, we prayed hard for help because we had so little time. And our prayers were answered. We started teaching some really good people." He sighed. "But I was transferred before they were baptized."

"But they were baptized, and you had a part in that."

"I know, but it didn't count as far as statistics go."

"I don't think that matters a great deal to Father in Heaven, do you?"

"Probably not." He cleared his throat. "The fact is, Emily, a lot of times on my mission I felt like a failure."

"But you weren't, though, as long as you did your best."

"I know, but, sometimes, when other missionaries are baptizing all the time, when they're having the success you thought you'd have, well, you start wondering what's wrong with you."

She squeezed his hand. "I will never believe there's anything wrong with you."

"Thanks, but let me finish. The next thing that happened was I was transferred to work with Vietnamese families. Since I couldn't speak the language, all I did was smile and shake hands. I remember thinking, *This isn't at all how I thought my mission would be.*"

"You never wrote me about any of this," she said.

"I thought it'd be better to be cheerful and positive."

"I wish you'd have let me know."

"Yeah, I should have. But it worked out eventually. When

I was at my lowest, I talked to my mission president. He taught me that the most important thing is to try to live a Christ-centered life, not just on my mission but for the rest of my life."

"What a great lesson to learn."

He nodded. "One more thing. For a time I served in the mission office, in charge of the commissary. I know it doesn't sound like much, but the thing is, I tried my best to do a good job. And this one time I asked Father in Heaven if he approved of what I was doing."

Austin paused and his hand went to his eyes, ready to wipe away the tears he felt coming.

"It's okay, Austin," she said.

He lowered his hand from around his eyes and looked straight ahead. "He answered my prayer," he said softly. "I felt the Spirit so strong. And I knew that He accepted me and the service I was giving. So, after that, it didn't matter where I served, only that I did it with all my heart, as a demonstration of my love for him."

They stopped walking and faced each other. He looked deeply into her eyes. "Basically, that's what my mission taught me," he said. "Some would say that's not much for two years."

"I think it's the most important thing you could have learned."

"That's true. It is."

He paused. "So now maybe you know why I'm the way I am."

"Thank you for telling me."

They walked around the temple grounds for another few minutes, enjoying the beauty of the snow-covered landscape and being close to the tall, rock building. While they walked, Emily debated in her mind if she should open herself up to him.

Finally she decided to risk it. "I have something I need to tell you."

"Okay."

"When I was in the burn center, the pain was so bad that sometimes I didn't think I could stand it another minute. I prayed for Heavenly Father to help me." Barely able to talk, she whispered, "And he did."

She wiped her eyes. "I found that Jesus Christ was able to help me get through the hurt. I found out that he loves me."

"That's an important lesson," Austin said, "but what a hard way to learn it."

"It was, but, you know what, lately I've been thinking— if I could go back in time to the morning of the day I was burned, and if I were given a choice, to continue on the way I was going, or else experience what I've gone through, what would I choose?"

"What did you decide?"

"I would never want to give up what I've learned about the Savior. So I guess that answers the question."

They had come to a bench where they sat down, holding hands and looking out over Logan and the bright sun reflecting off the snow-covered farmland of Cache Valley. They sat for a time without speaking.

Then Austin smiled and said, "Isn't it interesting? Things didn't work out for either of us the way we'd planned, yet it's okay. You got burned, but ended up learning something you might not have discovered any other way. I wanted to be a mission leader, but now I can see it was better for me that I wasn't."

"Why do you say that?"

"It's not good to think of yourself as the hope of the world when there's only One Hope of the World."

He was looking at her. "You have the most beautiful eyes."

"It's a good thing, isn't it? It's about all I've got going for me now."

"No, that's not true. You've got a lot going for you. You know what? I always feel better when I'm with you."

"I love being with you, too."

"I don't even notice the pressure garment either. It's like it's not even there."

"I won't have to wear it much longer. And then you'll see how my face and neck were burned."

"What do those areas look like?" he asked.

She turned away.

"I'm sorry," he said quickly. "I shouldn't have even asked."

"No, it's a fair question."

She bowed her head and closed her eyes, almost as if she were about to pray. And then she spoke softly. "The right side of my face has a different coloration than my left side. The fire completely took my right earlobe. They made one for me at the burn center. My neck has some scars and discoloration on it."

Tears started to slide down her cheek. "I've had reconstructive surgery on my right breast, but it still needs some more work. The skin on my stomach looks a little bit like a wrinkled shirt. I have patches of scars on my thighs and backside. Not from the fire but because they used those areas as donor sites for skin transplants."

Her head remained bowed, her eyes closed.

"It's okay," he whispered.

"I'm sorry. You probably didn't want that much detail, did you?"

"It was my fault. I had no right to ask a question like that."

"It's okay. We're friends. I trust you. Austin, I just want you to know . . . that . . . if I could, there's nothing I'd rather do than be more beautiful . . . for you."

He stepped back.

Her head was still down. He touched her chin with his finger and raised her gaze until she was looking into his eyes. "You're magnificent just the way you are now."

"That's very kind of you, but—"

"You know what? I doubt there's anybody who's totally happy with their body. Some want to be taller, some want to be shorter, or weigh more, or weigh less. And even if somebody is perfect, it's not going to last. We just take the body we were given and do the best we can with it. So, when you think about it that way, you're not that much different from anyone else."

"You're so good to me."

"Oh, no, I'm the lucky one. You know what? Before I left on my mission, I began to see you in a different light. All of a sudden, you weren't just Jeremy's little sister anymore. I remember thinking how good-looking you were. It was like I had never noticed before."

"I had some interesting feelings about you too," she said, suppressing a smile.

"But there's no comparison to the way I see you now. You were plenty good-looking then, but now . . . do you have any idea what you are now?"

"Not really."

"You are a woman of grace, dignity, and great beauty."

"That's it," she said, wiping her face with her hand as more tears welled up in her eyes. "From now on," she said, smiling through her tears, "I'm not going anywhere with you without a box of tissues. Please tell me you have some in your pocket."

"No, but there are some in my car. But I call firsties."

"Not if I beat you there," she said, racing him to the car.

* * * * *

Late that night, Emily sat alone, watching the demotape of her presenting the news. It was the video she had once made to send to TV stations—the video that was going to bring her fame and fortune.

254

It was the first time she'd watched the video since the accident. *I still love Emily–2,* she thought. *What smooth skin. Not a blemish, not a mark, not even a freckle. What a catch for some guy. I'd have made such a good wife. I remember the good old days when I could touch my face or my neck or my stomach without recoiling at the patchwork of skin from assorted places. I remember when I could touch my neck without counting the number of surgeries I've had on each section of skin.*

This isn't right. I'm torturing myself, she thought, turning it off.

She went to her room and closed the door and removed the part of the compression garment that covered her face and neck.

This is what the world will see of me from now on, she thought. She grabbed a study light and set it on a dresser and shone it on her face, then studied herself in a mirror.

She could hide much of the damage by wearing her hair longer. And, of course, only the man she married would see the damage to her stomach and chest. And there were still more operations scheduled to repair that.

What's going to happen next week when I don't need to wear the pressure garment covering my face and neck? What will happen when Austin sees me the way I really am? What will the girls in my ward think? Will they shun me? Will they quit coming to Relief Society? Will the bishop have no choice but to release me?

What will happen next week?
I wish I knew.

* * * * *

The next Saturday, Emily stood in front of the mirror and got teary-eyed again as Jamie fussed over her, helping her

255

get ready to go out with Austin. It would be the first time he would see her without the compression suit.

It was three o'clock in the afternoon, and Austin wouldn't be there for another four hours, but word had gotten out. Girls from her ward had been drifting in and out of the apartment since noon. They had come with dresses, jewelry, shoes, and some wigs for Emily to try on.

They were all so willing to help, to give her whatever of theirs she might be able to use. They were her sisters from Relief Society, and they'd all come. And as they fussed over her, tears flooded her eyes because of their kindness and concern.

They used every makeup trick they knew to help mask the discoloration on her face and neck. And when they at least partially succeeded, she cried.

And they tried one wig after another on her, and she cried.

And they put dress after dress in front of her so she could see the effect, and she cried.

And they told her she shouldn't cry because it would show; but she couldn't help it.

When each one left, she gave them a hug. They knew enough to let her decide how tight the hug would be.

At six-thirty, when most of them had gone, she was wearing a blonde wig furnished by one girl, a peach colored dress from another, a tiny necklace from yet another, and makeup applied ever so skillfully by still another girl.

Just before seven o'clock, Austin showed up. She couldn't face greeting him at the door, so she had one of her roommates answer his knock while she retreated to her room.

"It's going to be okay," Megan said.

"I hope so."

"It will be. You'll see."

"Please go dim the lights."

256

"It's too late for that. Besides, you look terrific."

She felt exposed, walking out to see Austin without the pressure garment.

"Hi," she said shyly.

"Hi, yourself," he replied.

She stood there, not daring to look him in the eye, aware of his eyes looking at her, seeing the whole of her face and neck for the first time since before she was burned.

He smiled. "You've done something different, haven't you? Don't tell me. I'll get it." He appeared to be studying her with even greater scrutiny. "I've got it now. You used to wear glasses, right? What'd you do, get contacts?"

She gave a slight smile, and then suddenly the tension was gone.

They danced for an hour and then they decided to rest. Austin went to get them some refreshments while she sat waiting at a table.

When he returned, he sat down next to her. "Can I ask you a question?"

"Sure, I guess so."

"If I wanted to kiss you tonight, how would that work?"

"You're thinking of kissing me?"

"Not now, of course."

"Then why ask?"

He laughed. "It's something I learned from my mission . . . plan my work, then work my plan."

"Well, I guess it'd work pretty much the same as with any girl."

"What would be best for you, standing or sitting?"

She thought about it for a moment. "I'd say standing."

"Could we go off a ways and talk it through?"

"Whatever you'd like," she said, standing up.

"You're blushing," he said.

"Am I?"

"Yes, pretty much evenly on both sides. So it's all working the way it's supposed to."

"Red will be happy to find that out."

He took her hand, and they went off to a dimly lit corner of the ballroom.

"Okay, let's suppose I've just walked you to your door after the dance. Then I say something like, 'Thank you for a wonderful evening.'"

"Oh, thank *you*. I had a great time."

"Now what?" he asked.

"Well, in a way, I guess it's like dancing."

"Okay, so I put my hand around your waist like this." He completed the move. "Okay, I've got my hand on your left side. Is this a good place for my hand to be?"

"Just a little bit higher."

He moved his hand up. "How's that?"

"Good."

"All right. Now let me pull you in toward me, like this." They were now looking into each other's eyes. "Okay, how is that for you?"

"I'm not feeling any pain," she said.

He chuckled. "Your roommates are going to ask if I kissed you tonight. And you'll say yes, so they'll go, 'How was it?' And you'll say, 'About the same as a bad toothache.' Good grief, Emily, what a romantic you are."

She laughed. "Sorry."

"Okay, here we are, in position. And we're looking into each other's eyes."

"Yes, we are," she whispered.

Seconds passed.

"I've always liked to look in your eyes," he said softly.

They stood there gazing at each other.

"This is just a run-through, right?" she asked.

He cleared his throat. "Yes, of course. Now I guess I would move in for the . . ."

"Kill?" she said with a smile.

"Kiss."

"Yes, that seems reasonable."

Their lips slowly began to converge. But then someone working the dance rolled a food cart filled with cookies past them.

The magic was gone. "Not that it will necessarily ever happen, of course," she said, moving away.

"Of course not, but just in case it does."

She was watching the band as it started to play again when he softly touched the side of her face that had been burned. "Your face looks good, Emily."

"That's very kind of you to say."

"I mean it."

"Austin, I will always be a burn survivor. That's not going to go away. You know that, don't you?"

"Yeah, I do. But it's fine. Really."

"I hoped it would be all right. Not so much for me as for you. I wanted it to be okay for you."

"It is. It's fine. They did a wonderful job."

"You're right. They did. I'll forever be indebted to them."

"I don't even notice anything wrong."

"You would though if you saw me in a better light."

"The light of your goodness is plenty bright."

She fought back her tears. "You're not helping me with my makeup here, you know. I can't believe how much I've cried today."

He started laughing. "You were dreading our date that much?"

"It wasn't because of you. The girls in my ward helped me so much today in getting ready for this. I love them so much, Austin. I really do."

They were holding each other, swaying back and forth slowly to the music. "Emily, I have a confession to make," he whispered in her ear.

"What?"

"I wanted to see what your face and neck looked like before I decided what I wanted to do."

"That's perfectly understandable."

"I'm not proud of it."

"Why's that?" she asked.

"It shouldn't have made a difference."

"But you knew it would."

"Yeah, I guess I did."

"I understand."

"Thanks. In all the ways that count, you're better than you were before the accident."

"I hope that's true."

"You are the kindest person I've ever known in my life. I've seen the way you are with the girls in your ward, the way you talk to them, the love you show especially to those who need a friend. I wish I were more like that. Things like that don't come easy to me, but they do with you. If I'm ever going to amount to anything in this life, I'll need a good example, like you. I can see that now. Emily, will you marry me?"

Her mouth dropped open. "What?"

"I'm asking you to marry me."

"Why?"

"Because I'm in love with you."

"Really?"

"Really."

They were standing close together, holding hands, their eyes closed, rocking back and forth to the music.

She wet her lips. "So, are you going to kiss me now?"

"You haven't answered my question yet about us getting married."

"We need some time, but, if you want, we can consider the idea."

"Okay, we'll do that. We'll consider the idea."

260

They continued to rock in time to the music, which would have been fine, but Emily was ready for some action. "What does a person have to do around here to get kissed?" she asked.

"I'll get right on it."

"Good. You know what? Just before you left on your mission, I dreamed about you kissing me."

"What was it like?"

"In my dream, when it happened, I remember thinking, 'Wow! This is the kiss of the century.'"

He smiled. "Really? It was that good? Looks like I've got a lot to live up to then, doesn't it?"

"We both do, actually."

And then they kissed for the first time.

"Oh, baby," she whispered in his ear, followed by a lusty chuckle.

"Don't start with me," he said.

"I'm not. It was a very sincere, 'Oh, baby.'"

He smiled. "Really? On our first kiss?"

Actually though, it was their second kiss, if you count her kissing him just before he left on his mission.

Or their third kiss, if you count her dream.

But it was their first kiss after they both realized they were deeply in love.

And that nothing else mattered.

TEN SUGGESTIONS FOR APPROACHING SOMEONE WHO IS DISABLED

BY DON CROASMUN

1. Speak to the person who is disabled, not to his or her companion.

2. Don't shout or speak unnaturally slowly. Allow time for the person to respond. Don't be uncomfortable and jump in, even if it takes a while.

3. Be yourself—be a friend.

4. Stand in front of a person in a wheelchair. While conversing, look the person in the eyes and listen.

5. Take time to really talk and listen, not just exchange pleasantries.

6. It's okay to ask the person to repeat himself if you don't understand. (That's better than pretending to understand and faking it.)

7. Do things together. Spending even a short amount of time together helps.

8. Think: If I had an accident and were disabled tomorrow, I would be the same "me" inside and have the same needs.

9. Recognize that the disabled person's needs are greater than your fears. Face your fears.

10. Even people in a coma are responding inside. Overt response is not a reflection of what that person may be thinking and feeling.

In this book, Don is patterned after Don Croasmun, 458 Yale, Rexburg, ID 83440. Don's e-mail address is doncrow@srv.net

REMINDERS FROM THE INTERMOUNTAIN BURN CENTER AT THE UNIVERSITY OF UTAH

1. Gasoline is dangerous. Remember, it is not safe to use it as a lighter fluid or a cleaning solvent. Misuse of gasoline commonly causes serious burns or death. Don't be "fuelish."

2. Treat campfires with respect. Coals can remain hot for hours or even days. Children can easily "fall" victim to an unattended campfire.

3. Do **NOT** prime carburetors with gasoline. We skin graft dozens of "experts" each year.

4. Sunburns are not only painful, they can also have long-range detrimental effects on your skin and health. Protect yourself from the sun by wearing Factor 20 or greater sunscreen. Wear a hat and protective clothing. Take advantage of shade.

REMEMBER! GETTING BURNED IS NO PICNIC!